SHIFTERS

Edward Lee
&
John Pelan

NECRO PUBLICATIONS
—2011—

«««« — »»»»

SHIFTERS
Trade Paperback Edition

This edition © 2011 Necro Publications

Cover design, book design & typesetting:
David G. Barnett
Fat Cat Design
www.fatcatgraphicdesign.com

Copy Editors:
Amanda Baird, John Everson, Jeff Funk, C. Dennis Moore

ISBN: 978-1889186559

a Necro Publication
5139 Maxon Terrace
Sanford, FL 32771
www.necropublications.com

«««« — »»»»

Though the authors are in debt to many, they would like to particularly thank the following:

The bald guy who drinks behind the 7-Eleven on 40th and Stone, The Brotherhood (they know who they are), Dave Barnett, Bob Brown, Doug, Wayne, P.G., Ryan, Brian and Dolly, Craig Jenkins (wherever the hell you are), Matt Johnson, Alex Johnston, R.K., Paul Legerski, Dallas, C.M., Tim McGinnis, Wilfred Owens (rest in peace), Mike Paduana, Michael Pearce, Kathy, Mary Pelan, Larry Roberts, Sergeant E-5 Sanders, Sarah and Dawn at Verotik (don't know your last names), Eunice Seymour, Scott Siebert, Brian and Jan, Russ Snyder (for the cool nautical passages), Susan, Lucy, Terry Tidwell, Steven Wardlaw, t. Winter-Damon (for initial interest), Mark and Cindy, and lastly a heartfelt thanks to the respective staffs of Murphy's Pub, The Ram's Head Tavern, and the Mecca Café where much of this book was conceived and the staff of the Knarr Tavern, where all the signature pages were done.

When, by a decree of a greater power,
The poet makes his appearance in a bored world...
Who calls on a pitying God at whom these curses
Are hurled.

—BAUDELAIRE

PROLOGUE

Evil is relative. But so is blood.

Have you ever tasted blood—I mean really tasted it? No, not like when you bite your lip, or suck at a thistle scratch. I mean, have you ever cupped it in your hands and let it pour into your mouth? Have you ever gulped it down your throat like wine from a goblet? Have you?

Have you ever killed anyone?

Questions—yes! I can't help it, I'm curious. Curiosity is a challenge, and challenges excite me. Have you ever slit open someone's throat and watched the blood squirt out? Have you ever eaten human brains from a freshly cracked skull, or sucked out an eyeball? Hmm? Have you?

Have you ever bitten into a man's heart while it's still beating?

I have.

I've done lots of things.

Yes.

Blood. Flesh.

It's all relative, like good, like evil, love and hate, and like anything born of humanity.

So where does that leave me?

«« — »»

I can see the moon from here. It's huge and bright. It's beautiful. It seems to be following my eye along the water like a luminous spirit, a companion.

Or like a lover.

Love is all I've ever wanted. It's also the only thing I've never really had. Love. Real love.

Is that so much to ask?

I've been on the water for days now, or perhaps weeks. Time, too, is rel-

ative. It scarcely matters. I feel like I've been standing on a ledge for a thousand years. I feel like I'm falling off a mountain. I don't even know where I'm going.

Love sings to me; it beckons me like a siren, like something only half-real melting in my fingers. Love is all that leads me on, that fuels my pursuit. It's all that gives me life. One day I will find it, but until then...

My days are dreams. My nights are black/red scraps of memory. The memories are hot, erotic. They taste like salt, like spicy metal on my lips. They're as beautiful and as relative as the moon.

Their blood bursts hot from my mouth, runs quickly down my breasts and my belly. In the moonlight it looks gorgeous black on my white skin. Sometimes I stand naked beneath the moon, and I rub their evil blood like hot oil all over my body. Sometimes...

...it makes me come.

Right now I'm lying between wooden crates marked GLASS, USE NO HOOKS, ONITA BREWERIES, MUTO, HENNIG, & ANDERSON IMPORTERS, INC., SAN FRANCISCO, CA. *I'm in the cargo hold of some ship. When I get bored, I touch myself. I just think back, and I go to sleep in the memories. I'm the beautiful tousled stowaway hiding in darkness from the rugged men above. If they only knew they were shipping more than beer! Some cargo.*

The ship rocks back and forth, on and on and forever, like the time I first died.

When you made me. Then I loved you, now I just don't know...

«« — »»

You've brought me a long ways, do you ever wonder if there's more? If there's something more to feel, to touch, to maybe love? Do you?

When you close your eyes, do you see angels or devils? Do you see love or hate? That's what it all burns down to in the end, if there really is an end. Blood and flesh. Time. Good and bad. It's about what we really are in our hearts.

I'm a killer, a murderer. I've eaten men's flesh and drunk their blood. I've rived them open with my pretty, bare hands and drawn their innards out of their bellies like strings of yarn. I've watched the life go out of their eyes as I've grinned down, drooling in their mouths, and I've felt them twitch between my legs as they've died.

Oh, yes—a murderer. Me.

But when I close my eyes, I still see love.

««—»»

It's a curse sometimes. It's like lust.

I can smell the men above me on deck. Some stand watch, others idly run engines and boilers, or study charts. Many lay asleep in the bowels of the old ship. I can smell their dreams. Oh, what I could do to them! I could take them apart like dolls of clay, twist off their arms, their legs, their heads. I could bite open their skulls and suck their brains. I could burst their bellies and dress myself in their warm, steaming guts. I could gulp down their blood and swallow their hearts. I could, but I won't.

Not yet…

ONE

DISSOLUTION

(i)

"I don't love you anymore."

The words, *her* words, suffused beyond the wall of his sleep. They seemed like ghosts. Richard Locke shuddered in the darkness of his closed eyes. The bedsheets had somehow become entwined about his body and legs—they weren't sheets as much as pale serpents come to feed on his dreams. *Dreams,* he thought. What had happened to his? He opened his eyes and stared.

"I don't love you anymore," she'd said on the last day of August. But that had been months ago. Months, yet he felt no closer to being over it today than he did then.

Locke moaned, staring at the ceiling. Somewhere, a clock was ticking. *Months...*

The drear of autumn daylight which lay across his face seemed used, secondhand. He got out of bed as if rising from a coffin. Yes, he felt dead. Pale, gaunt, tacky. Sweat plastered his hair to his scalp. His joints ticked as he walked sullen across the room and looked blankly down at his desk. A piece of paper hung out of his typewriter platen.

CENOTAPH by Richard Locke

My love is now a cenotaph,
an extant, keening door
slammed shut on my heart
by her five little words:
I don't love you anymore.

"What a bunch of shit," he muttered. He ripped the sheet out of the machine and tore it up. Suddenly, he felt maniacal; he tremored in place, eyes frozen open. He must look ludicrous: a pallid, skinny 33-year-old man standing in the middle of a disheveled room in baggy underpants with his hair sticking up. He rushed to the window, heaved it open, and leaned out. Several pedestrians looked up and laughed. Locke didn't care. He let the torn-up poem slip from his fingers. He watched the pieces separate, then float dreamlike from the second-story window to the street.

                                      (ii)

Locke was a poet. He may even have been an acclaimed poet in some vast local sense. The interest from the money his parents had left him was slightly less than enough to get by. He worked one day a week at the bookstore on Greenwood Avenue, and occasionally he filled in as a substitute teacher at Lincoln High, but that was all. He knew there were far more functional ways to live; instead of writing poetry six to ten hours a day, he could've pursued a more conventional career. That, however, seemed false to him. He felt obsessed with being true, whatever that meant. He was put on earth to write, and write he would. Poets made little or nothing from their work—when an editor did offer money, Locke turned it down—but he didn't care. He wasn't a materialist, he didn't even own a television. To be real, all he needed was a roof, a typewriter, and his muse.

He'd been writing for ten years. By now, he'd had hundreds of poems published—he'd lost count years ago. His work appeared regularly in any number of college literary journals, small press magazines, newspapers, and poetry anthologies. He'd also gotten some into national magazines: *The New Yorker, Esquire, Atlantic Monthly,* even *Cosmopolitan*, but he had yet to establish himself on a national level. He didn't really care if that ever happened; he didn't need recognition to feel real about what he did. Perpetuation was all that mattered to him creatively—it need not be widespread. Locke figured that if only one other person read any given poem, then that poem, and the corms of its creation, was given truth.

Truth, he thought now.

He stared past his Smith-Corona, feeling like the displaced soothsayer of Shakespeare's play. *How can one define truth?*

The question bid any poet's quest. Locke had spent a decade pondering that, writing about it, even reveling in its premise. He wanted each of his poems, if only minutely, to touch the flesh of that question.

Locke wasn't sure what truth was, but he was sure what it wasn't. Truth was not any physical reality, it was not something you could see or hear. It was not solid. It was not tangible. Locke knew that truth existed somewhere *between* the lines of life, and exploring those spaces was what gave his muse power.

Or at least it had.

Until now.

His work desk was a big old black metal eyesore. Bookshelves surrounded him like ramparts. Pictures lined the wall facing him, the great poets: Keats, Shelley, Jarrell, Seymour, and a sullen kerchiefed Edgar Allan Poe. Locke liked the idea of being looked upon by these great men as he worked. The pictures enlivened him.

But there was one more picture, not on the wall, but right up close on the desk. A small photograph in a flat gold frame.

It seemed to radiate at him now, more than a photograph but a providence of some sort, a piece of his past and a piece of his future.

I don't love you anymore, the picture seemed to say.

It was Clare.

The picture had been taken at Concannon's, on her birthday. She smiled brokenly into the lens after having just downed one of the barkeep's notorious "Birthday Shooters." And sitting right next to her, with his arm around her, was Locke.

She was beautiful—she was *resplendent.* She was the only woman Locke had ever loved in his life.

And now she was gone.

(iii)

Who knew what love was? How could it be defined? Locke didn't know. He'd been infatuated in the past, many times. He'd even been *involved* a couple of times. But he'd never felt strongly enough about a girl to voice the cryptic words *I love you.*

Until he'd met Clare. It was a strange rapport, an instantaneous one. He'd walked into Concannon's one night last October to have a beer and shoot the shit with Carl, the barkeep. The night felt funny: mild, warm, when it should be chilly. 45th Street was desolate when traffic should have been backed up to the freeway. And Concannon's, when ordinarily it would be packed at this time of night, was empty. Except for her.

She sat up at the bar chatting with Carl and drinking a shandy. A little lemon wedge floated in her glass. Her pose stunned Locke in the entrance. Who was this beautiful, beautifully dressed woman all by herself in the bar? She looked opulent, regal: a long dark-jade organdy dress, Ferraganno high heels, big bright gold earrings. She had short tapered blonde hair with perfect bangs, which gently sifted each time she tossed her head to laugh at one of Carl's notorious jokes.

"What's the difference between a rooster and a lawyer? A rooster clucks defiance."

Of course she laughed; she worked for a law firm.

But what was it about her, outwardly? Locke remained seized in the vision of her. She looked classy without looking overdone. Where most beauty in this town was fake, she looked *real*. Had providence put her there, just for him? Locke considered this—he *believed* in providence.

He walked up. "Hi," he said, rather stupidly. "My name's Locke."

Her head turned. Huge blue eyes beamed. Locke nearly swooned at the scent of her perfume.

"My name's Clare," she said, and smiled at him. "It's very nice to meet you."

(iv)

Good conversation commenced instantaneously. Locke, of course, told her that he was a poet. Her response had surprised him. "What are your themes?" she'd asked. Usually girls in bars replied, *Oh, really?* or *I wrote poetry in high school.* "Societal naturalism," Locke answered. "I try to do with words what Munch and Ryder did with paint." That's when things really got going; Clare had minored in art, she even did a little painting herself. Through their discourse he discovered that they shared many of the same views, tastes, and ideals. He was also happy to learn that she was here to meet some friends, (girls who hung out in bars by themselves were usually bad news in the long run). She was a paralegal for one of the firms in Queene Ann, one of the big ones.

They'd talked for a solid hour; Locke's enthusiasm never lapsed. She fascinated him, not topically, but in some more oblique, deeper way. She was far more than just some attractive girl he'd met in a tavern. She was scintillating, diverse, abstract and intelligent. She was *cool*. Eventually her friends arrived, they were cool too, and even though the initial introductions had been quick, Locke could tell that her friends liked him, which made him feel even better. Later, Clare and her friends had left; Locke didn't want to push anything. "Do you hang out here much?" she asked before departing.

"Most nights I stop in for a few."

"I'd really like to see some of your poetry. Why don't you bring some in? I could meet you tomorrow night after work."

"Sounds good. I'll be here."

Her friends waved. Clare smiled again, donned her coat, and bid, "Goodnight, Locke."

"Goodnight. See you tomorrow."

She left the bar. Locke stared after her. Her perfume lingered about him like an aura. His beer got warm as he sat, thinking. His thoughts seemed to carry him away.

Carl snapped his fingers in front of Locke's face. "Locke, Locke. You check out to the Twilight Zone, or what?"

Locke roused, looked around. "Clare," he muttered.

Carl poured him a cold McEwans. "I didn't think you had it in you, buddy."

"What?"

"Clare," Carl said. He flipped a Marlboro Light in the air and caught it perfectly in his mouth. "She likes you."

"Oh, yeah? How do you know?"

"She's in here three or four nights a week after work. Guys hit on her right and left, but she always gives them the brush-off. Every time, Locke. You're the first guy I've seen her talk to for more than two minutes."

"Is that a fact?" Locke pondered this. "You say she's in here three or four nights a week? I've been hanging out in this john of yours for five years, and I've never seen her."

"That's because you're a denizen," Carl informed him. "You come in too late. She's here a lot. She's a nice girl."

You're telling me. "And she's never with a guy?"

"Nope. Never. I'm a barkeep, I know everything. If she was dating anyone, I'd have heard about it."

"But guys hit on her a lot?"

Carl laughed. "As good-looking as she is, what do you think? She's got guys trying to pick her up all the time, but she shoots 'em down like Sopwith Camels. Until tonight, that is. Until she meets Concannon's renowned resident poet."

"I wasn't trying to pick her up," Locke pointed out. Suddenly he craved a cigarette, and regretted that he'd quit years ago. "I was just being the charming, level-headed, and deeply intelligent guy I always am."

"Right, and my name's Dick. Take my word for it, Locke. When you work this side of the bar long enough, you start to get a knack for seeing things that other people don't see."

Locke nodded, frowning. He had a knack himself, for being cynical in the light of the positivity of others. "Okay, Carl. So tell me, what did you see?"

"That girl's nuts about you."

Locke paused in the middle of a sip of McEwan's. Carl's observation seemed to remain alight behind his eyes, like details of a nice dream. Locke didn't know how to interpret Carl's mystic analysis, but that didn't matter. Locke *felt* something, and whatever it was, he knew it felt awesomely real.

That's all he wanted. That's all any poet wanted. To find something in the chaos of society that was *real*.

And what he said next he didn't so much say to Carl, or even to himself. He said it to the world. He said it to fate, or to oblivion, or perhaps even to God.

He said: "I could fall in love with her in the wink of an eye."

TWO

SHORN HEART

(i)

Locke fell in love with Clare Black in the wink of an eye.

It was almost too easy, it was almost *too* real—the spontaneity through which their relationship commenced, and through which they'd not only become lovers and best friends but also each other's confessors. Locke was a poet, and poets were almost always obscured from the conventions of life. Though he'd accepted his reclusion for a decade, he was never happy with it. It was Clare that had brought him back; her outgoingness, her sociability, and her vast circle of friends had welcomed Locke back into a world that he thought had abandoned him forever. No more of the brooding, recluse poet. No more sitting alone in Concannon's, speculating his creative visions on bar napkins and wondering why he felt so different. He wasn't different, he was just misguided. The vibrancy of Clare's love had built him back up again. With her, he'd never felt more real in his life.

And he thought the same went for her. She was in the legal profession, which was hectic, highly pressured, and relentless. All of her closest friends were in the same business too, and this left her without advice and conjectures that were unbiased. Now, though, whenever she had a bad day, she could relate to Locke in a scope of feeling that she didn't have elsewhere. He was the only aspect of her life that did not have a deep root in the same occupational realm. Locke became the diversity that she needed, and had never had until now.

They had lots in common, but not *too much*. Locke knew too many couples who had too much in common; staleness set in eventually, and the relationship went to hell every time. But he and Clare were different enough yet the same enough that, regardless of where they went or what they did, the harmony between the two of them never faltered. *Love can't be this easy,* he'd wonder to himself a million times. But apparently it was. *Verity,* he thought. That must be the difference. Most relationships existed through compromises, but Locke and Clare's differences only augmented each other. Their love evolved as a machine whose most intricate parts never failed.

It was impossible to describe. Clare's love for him erased his sins, his errors, his inadequacies. He felt reborn in it: she was the ray of light that his darkened life had been yearning for, for longer than he cared to remember. The more involved he became with her, the more complete he felt, the more perceptive, the more real. He seemed to fit into every aspect of her life without a hitch—soon they became a fixture of the city's social heart. With every week that passed, their love only became more sure of itself, more convinced of the very same truth that had joined them in the first place. In the spring they'd driven down to Portland to visit her family. It was more of the same: full acceptance. Her parents had thrown a big party; Locke met all of Clare's relatives, who, like all of her friends, proved to be among the most congenial people he'd ever met. Her parents, who were even more congenial, thought Locke was great. At the party, Clare's mother had taken him aside and said: "You've really done a lot for her, and we love you for that." Locke wasn't sure what she meant, but then she went on: "You're the only boy she's ever dated who's been good for her." Locke couldn't hope for a better mark of approval. And then, later, Clare's father had taken him aside. "You're a great guy, Locke," he'd informed him. "And that's what Clare needs—a great guy. I really hope things work out for the two of you." Locke was flabbergasted. He was *brimming* in elation.

That was the word. Elation. Locke was elated with his love. They never even argued. The few times they had problems, their love for each other refused to let them fight. Instead, they'd make deliberations, they'd reason, and then they'd resolve the problem. Soon they were talking of living together, of marriage, of *their future* together. They'd catch themselves going on out-of-the-way drives, looking at houses, looking at yards. They talked about children...

Months went by. Seasons changed, but their love didn't. It only steepened, it only evolved a little more each day into something more real for them. Clare's love laid Locke's whole life out for him—a wonderful, meaningful *life*...

And on the last day of August, the day he would officially propose to her, Clare Black opened her door, let him in, and said: "I don't love you anymore."

Locke's world fell apart.

THREE

WOMAN OVERBOARD

(i)

Ramsey's vision plummeted—into blood. He tried to scream but his voice froze, his mouth locked wide open in the deafening silence. Shadows merged—what? Figures? People? Ramsey didn't think so.

He was running through a chasm, underground. He was running *away* from something. Pits and rabbets pocked the chasm's walls, oozing ichor. Every so often he'd step on something and slip. Some hot, wicked panting seemed to follow him, and rapid footfalls. At a bend in the grotto's channel, Ramsey turned, paused, looked...

It was a wolf.

Ramsey gulped. Yes, an immense, gray timber wolf darted down the channel. But it wasn't coming for Ramsey. Instead it pounced upon another figure—a man with a knife. Ramsey didn't know how he knew—yet he was certain that the man was a murderer. His aura seemed to throb in frantic waves, greenly evil.

The wolf's great maw spread like a bear trap. The man wailed, lashed out with the knife. Then the wolf's jaws snapped shut, and the man's hand, still gripping the blade, dropped to the stone floor.

Jesus... Christ..., Ramsey slowly thought.

It was not *what* happened next as much as what he somehow sensed behind all this. The dank air felt charged with energy. *Evil for evil,* he thought, though it seemed like someone else's thought. And what was he doing here? What *was* this awful place?

The killer's screams didn't even sound human now. The wolf had cleverly snapped off each of the man's feet just above the ankles. He lay spread-legged before the beast, twitching. The wolf glared at him. Was it smiling? Could an animal *smile?*

Regardless, Ramsey wasn't smiling. No way. Yet he continued to watch, hand and cheek pressed against the wall of warm, pitted rock. He didn't *want* to watch this, he was *forced* to.

But by what?

The wolf, he thought.

Somehow he knew it was the wolf.

It waited. It stood solidly on all fours. When it looked at Ramsey, its red eyes twitched.

Ramsey wet his pants.

Footless now, the killer could only shift in retreat, pushing away from the gray beast on his clipped stumps. The wolf returned its gaze to its prey.

Watch, the word bloomed in Ramsey's brain.

The wolf lunged. It bit directly into the killer's crotch—one quick snap!—and tore the genitals out of the groin. The man's screams cessated—too much pain often paralyzed the larynx, not that it would've mattered a moment later. For next the wolf's jaws tore that out too, along with the rest of the throat.

Evil for evil?

But whose words were they? Not Ramsey's.

The wages of sin?

Ramsey gaped.

The wages of evil?

Then rose the laugh: black, cynical, a fluttering chord in his head. Who was whispering these awful things to him?

The laugh replayed—a siren now, a fever-pitched insanity. Then, again: *Watch.*

Again Ramsey thought of a high-torque bear trap. The wolf's jaws snapped opened and closed, on and on, bursting into the killer's gut. Blood exploded. Flesh and muscle parted easily as new lard. Each jerk of the wolf's huge head shot wet innards this way and that. Ramsey watched now in the lowest disgust. This was no natural predation, this was not simply a beast feeding upon unfortunate prey. This was a jubal: the complete systematic destruction of a human being, purely for sport.

For fun, Ramsey realized. *It's doing this for fun.*

The great snout delved, swallowing organs whole as it emptied the abdominal vault. The fur of the wolf's angular face up to the forehead shone spiky red. Blood dripped off the tip of its lower jaw. Ropy segments of intestines lay about the dead killer like pink snakes, the bowel hung limp from the rive of flesh. It was then that Ramsey noticed the entirety of the chasm floor lay thick with offal, unwanted scraps of human meat and fat, and masticated bones. Black cavern flies buzzed in shifting sheets, oblivious in their feast. Maggots churned in jellied blood, marrow, and spoiled flesh.

Welcome, Ramsey, the unseen voice fluttered.

A crackling-crunching sound split the fetid air. Now the wolf's jaws closed steadily down upon the killer's head, like a high-pressure vise. The cranium split to large pieces which fell away, leaving the brain exposed and raw in dark light. The beast, almost daintily now, picked the shiny convoluted orb out of the base of the skull. It looked up at Ramsey, like someone's pet dog with a ball in its mouth. The wolf wagged its tail.

Then its jaw crunched down on the brain and ate it.

Welcome to my home.

The voice, if it even was a voice, sounded forlorn. Did Ramsey hear weeping beyond? It was the sound of sadness, or regret.

Ramsey's basest instincts kicked in. The killer lay dead, the wolf was finished with him. But what would the wolf want next?

Me, Ramsey thought.

He darted right, sprinted into the grotto's veer. A rock wall faced him. *Dead end.* Then left, and the same.

I'm trapped.

Ramsey turned in the cragged juncture, refaced the beast. *I'm dead,* he realized. But the wolf seemed disinterested in him. It calmly bowed its head, lapping at the vast puddle of blood.

Sated, full-bellied, its red eyes glanced a final time at Ramsey. His knees were shaking. The front of his pants were drenched, and the back of his pants, he grimly noticed now, felt warm and heavy.

The wolf stared at him—

Oh, please, God, please…

Then it turned and walked away.

Welcome to my home, the soft sad voice wept away in the darkness. *Welcome to my domain.*

(ii)

"Ram! Ram, get the lead out!"

Ramsey felt submerged in swamp muck. His body shook, he felt hands on him. It felt as though his soul were being dragged up from a bottomless, black pit.

"Come on, Ram! Shag ass!"

Ramsey awoke, enslimed. Cabin light fumed in his eyes. He lay in his bunk as if in a casket.

"Rise and shine, pal."

Yeah, right. It was fifteen till midnight. Ramsey leaned groggily up in his bunk, and bumped his head. Peering down at him, and none too pleased, was Winslow, one of the engine techs, dressed in jeans, boots, and a heavy deck coat.

"We got watch, buddy," Winslow said. "Fifteen minutes. I'm aftpoint, you're on the portquarter. Captain's worried; we're in a bad chop."

Shit. Ramsey could feel it, low in his gut—the slow, steady churn of the ship on the sea. When he tried to rub the sleep out of his eyes, he saw blood.

The dream, he remembered.

What a dream. He shook his head, as if to dislodge something. But the images only lurched closer. The wolf. The destruction. And the blood. *All the blood,* he thought.

"Ramsey!" Winslow fairly bellowed. He'd been drinking; Ramsey could smell it. But Ramsey could use a drink himself. After a nightmare like that, who wouldn't want a drink?

"Sometime tonight, huh, man?" Winslow was getting ticked. "Captain wants us up and out *now*. You all right?"

Ramsey squinted. He felt sopped in gelid sweat. "I just had the worst nightmare."

The wolf... He could still hear the screams, the manic jaws snapping, the bones as they crunched.

"I gotta drag you outta that bunk?"

"Sorry, man," Ramsey apologized. *Get your shit together! It was just a dream.* "Portquarter watch. I'm rolling, I'll be up in five."

"Good boy." Winslow headed to the hatch. "And wear something. It's colder than a nun's cunny tonight. And it's weird."

"What?" Ramsey asked.

Winslow turned at the end of the bunk aisle. Suddenly he seemed remote. "I don't know, it's just kind of weird out. Really high chop but no storm brewing. No clouds. You know what I'm talking about. Just...weird."

Winslow went topside. Ramsey crawled out of the narrow bunk compartment. *Weird night,* he thought. He dragged on long johns, jeans, three shirts, his wool coat, and a watchcap. Gloves, too, and his best insulated boots. It was still only autumn, but when you were on watch, on the sea at night, the world could get very cold.

It was not this certain anticipation, however, that touched Ramsey into a fit of shivers. It was the shards of the nightmare that remained imbued, like lesions, in his mind.

The wolf. The screams.

The blood.

Death.

(iii)

Their ship was called *The Angus Scrimm*, a 200-foot, 20-year-old bulk carrier known as a "pallet tramp." Year round it traveled unscheduled routes up and down the coast on private and independent delivery contracts. A tub, a typical rustbucket. Ramsey had been hired last spring as a prop and shaft technician—decent pay for decent work. He liked the job and all its aspects, save for one.

Nightwatch.

Standing alone at the catline, at night, made him feel like the last man on earth. Ramsey didn't mind solitude, but desolation was something else. The awesome vision often scared him: they were a gray speck bobbing on the universe. Both night and sea stretched on forever, a turbulent and cruel infinity.

Ramsey rose from the steel climb, stepped onto the port deck. *Weird night,* he reflected. Winslow was right. His face seemed to shrink at once against the cold abovedecks. It was bitter, icy, yet there was no wind. The ship pitched on the water; it was a bad chop, all right, real bad. The sea seemed to roil in infinite darkness, it seemed to *play* with the ship. Ramsey's guts sunk against the heavy motion.

He walked past amidships, his hand trailing along on the tight stanchion cable. The ship continued to toss; he nearly lost his footing several times. Heading to the portquarter, he stalled.

What was it?

He squeezed his eyes shut against the still cold. A scent seemed to flirt with him; he looked down.

#4 HOLD, read black stenciled letters. Ramsey lifted the manway hatch, peering into blackness. Yes, a strange scent wafted from the freightway, something musky, like a warm animal. Sometimes they freighted exotic animals from Japan; to Seattle or San Diego, but not this trip. Just pallets of Japanese beer and auto parts from Osaka bound for Puget Sound. Ramsey's face lingered at the opened hatch. The scent seemed seductive somehow, pleasant, heady. He stuck his face in and breathed.

Get on watch.

He closed the hatch and took his post. *Captain'll probably keep me out here till daybreak,* he pondered, gazing out. From here, the world extended as a hostile, black, freezing scape. Stars blurred whitely overhead, and below, the sea churned within itself, throwing foam around the great plumes from the props. Low on the edge of the world, a full moon glowed.

Yeah...weird night. He closed his eyes, the moonlight swelled.

He tried to blank his mind. Suddenly he felt invaded. Images assaulted him: the dream, the nightmare. Blood dripping from the huge wolf's maw...

Then: *Snap!*

Ramsey whirled. He was sure he'd heard a sound, something metallic, like—

Like a hatch closing, he realized.

The bridge loomed above him as he faced the bow. It looked like some great stone deity, a horned god. *What was that noise?* he asked himself. He walked back toward amidships. The vessel's old metal groaned through a rise of sea.

Ramsey froze in his tracks.

A figure stood by the manway of the fourth hold. Was it Winslow? *No, no,* Ramsey could see. It was a woman.

But there were no women on board.

"Hey! You, there!"

The figure didn't flinch. Cold air blasted Ramsey's face. The figure, impossibly, seemed to be removing its clothing.

What the hell is this?

Then it occurred to him. A stowaway. It happened sometimes. Abused kids and runaways would sneak on board for a free ride up the coast. But...but...

"What are you doing?" Ramsey commanded. "Put your fucking clothes back on, are you crazy! It's freezing out here!"

The woman ignored him. Piece by piece, she stripped off her tattered garments and dropped them into the sea.

Then she turned.

Ramsey faced her, speechless, stunned in the silent midnight clarity of what he was looking at. The world seemed to stop as he stared. His heart nearly stopped.

She was beautiful.

Fully naked now, she stood stock-still by the port stanchion. Ramsey, as the ship continued to pitch, could not even conceive of a physical beauty this absolute. Moonlight bathed the flawless white skin and hourglass figure. She seemed to have no body fat at all, yet she wasn't skinny. Instead she reminded him of a lithe beast—full-formed, muscular, tight. A tumult of dark russet hair hung well past her shoulders, and a plush patch of hair the same hue showed between the sleek, full legs. Big conical dark nipples pointed at him, stiffening in the ice cold.

Then Ramsey looked at her face...

A vertigo stole into him. His vision seemed to shift. Somehow the reality of her face became enlaced with memory: the nightmare. Like flitting a deck of cards. In stark flashes he saw her face, then the wolf, her face, then the wolf—

"Did you dream?" she asked. Her voice dripped with every imaginable desire: hot, dark, penetrating. Her breasts glowed in the still moonlight, her tight abdomen, her firm, creamy hips.

"What?" Ramsey muttered.

He felt adrift like the ship, something tiny in the clutches of something so vast as to be immeasurable. He felt helpless, inconsequential, *meaningless* before the image of her. She was an icon of flesh. She was a testament to an ideal of beauty that ruptured the limits of mere humanity.

Ramsey fell to his knees.

"Are you a sinner?" she asked him. She looked down in a coy, tiny smile.

"Yes," Ramsey moaned in response.

"We all are."

He was not himself now. Whatever she was at her heart radiated a power that crushed him. The ice-cold air dried the surface of his eyeballs as he stared at her perfect flesh.

"I could kill you," she whispered.

"Kill me," Ramsey said. He was lost. He was inferior before her: total flaw dwarfed by flawlessness. She wasn't human. He knew that now. She was something more than human.

Something terrifyingly more.

"Did you dream?" she asked again.

He was freezing, his teeth chattered. His face felt like brittle porcelain in the dead night air.

"Yes," he said.

"It wasn't your dream." The woman turned, stepped toward the stanchion cable. "It was mine."

She looked over the side. The sea misted on her face and breasts. "You never saw me," she said. "I was never here."

Ramsey nodded, open-mouthed, numb.

When she looked at him again, the vertigo returned. Her face. The wolf. Her face. The wolf.

The wolf, he thought.

Ramsey blinked.

The woman's eyes, only for a moment, were blood red.

She placed one bare foot on the stanchion cable. Ramsey's gaze followed up the long, sleek leg, her rump, her sleek beautiful back. The muscles in her leg tensed. Next she was standing on the cable with both feet.

"Goodbye," she said.

She dove off the cable, into the water.

(iv)

"What the bloody hell?"

Winslow ran to the stern. He knew he wasn't imagining things: he'd heard a splash. Goddamn Ramsey must've fallen over the side on that last pitch.

His feet pounded the steel deck. He tore past the main cargo holds, the cold burning his face. He was about to shout "Man overboard!" when he saw Ramsey on the portquarter, looking over the side.

"Goddamn!" Winslow yelled. "What happened? Is someone overboard?"

Ramsey blinked at him. "What?"

Winslow leaned over the cable, scanning the sea at the waterline. "I heard a splash! Is someone overboard?"

"No, it was just a porpoise or something," Ramsey said.

Winslow relaxed. *Thank God,* he thought. The sea churned below him, relentless, terrible. *Thank God.*

A person wouldn't last a minute in that chop.

(v)

I think I was actually afraid for a moment. The water is black, endless, frigid. It's like death. I felt consumed, I felt swallowed up and digested by its depths. Yes, I think I was actually afraid for a moment. But that's silly, right? What do I have to be afraid of?

I'm purged. I'm free!

At least for a little while, anyway.

The ocean excites me now. Its deadly cold gives me life! It seems to shape my body in its great formless hands, remaking me in purity, in absolution. The awful cold makes me hot inside. It makes me feel passionate, loving, sincere, even crudely horny. It makes me feel a lot of things. Oh, how I love to just feel.

I'm dead.

It's so nice to be able to feel when you're dead.

I'm swimming now. I'm changing. I'm gliding through the black awful water—sleek, fast, nimble. I'm a shark. I'm a portent. I'm a destroyer.

I'm fine. I don't know where I am or where I'm going, and that's the only way I can feel safe. Because if I don't know where I'm going, then maybe he won't either.

FOUR

MALEFACTOR

(i)

Locke awoke with tears in his eyes. When he couldn't write, he slept. He'd been sleeping a lot lately. It was dusk now. The sun looked like blood in the window.

He got up, coughed, and went to the desk.

REFRACTION by Richard Locke

I always got less than
the least from you.
Now I hope that the rats come
and feast on you.

Was that how he felt? Bitter? Vengeful? These were useless emotions. They were false. He knew why he'd written it: because he thought that was how a man was *supposed* to feel when summarily rejected by a woman. *Asshole. You're supposed to write about how you feel, not about how you're supposed to feel.* The senselessness of the observation seemed to make perfect sense. What else could poetry be except for the re-creation of an emotion into an image, via black and white words?

To be a true poet, he must reflect truth in his poems. The truth of how he saw things. The truth of how he felt.

How did he feel? How did he feel really?

I still love her, he answered.

He cranked the four-line poem out of the typewriter and tore it to shreds. It was phony, a lie. Bitterness and spite often eased the edges of sorrow—Locke wished he could feel bitter. But he didn't. He purely and simply *didn't.* In all the time that had passed since she'd broken up with him, he still loved her. He still wanted her.

He still wanted to spend the rest of his life with her. It would be so much easier to hate her for the inexplicable and expeditious manner in which she'd ended their relationship. But that would be false too. He didn't hate her, he couldn't. Even now, after over two months, Locke loved her as much as he ever did.

The emotion was a lie. Hence, so was the poem. He dropped the shreds of paper into the wastebasket, which sat full with many, many more shreds. The garbage can of his muse.

He stood in the middle of the room. He felt desolate. He wiped the crust of his tears from his eyes, and felt ashamed. *Grown man,* he thought. *Bawling like a baby.* He'd even cried in front of her once, on that last night. He'd begged her, he'd pleaded with her, he'd cried at her feet. What must she have thought about that? Had she been disgusted? Repelled? Locke had no idea. He had no idea about anything anymore. When Clare had told him that she no longer loved him and that the relationship was over, he'd begged her to give it one more chance. He'd assumed complete responsibility for her sudden unhappiness even though he was certain he'd done nothing to make her unhappy. He'd felt last-ditched. He would do anything to save the relationship that she'd already decided was over. It was useless.

And today? Just now? He'd been asleep, he'd been dreaming of Clare. Of course he had—he always did now. It didn't seem fair, that his own mind should conjure memories of their past, back when her eyes were bright with love for him. Locke felt betrayed by *himself.* Each dream unreeled as slow torture: their first kiss, their first date, the first time they'd made love, and the first time she'd said *I love you.* It was terrible.

Locke sat down to write. It was his only escape, or at least he thought it was. Before, he'd written of social themes, relevancies re-formed in art for the reflection of the reader. Now, though, he could only write of her. He'd written nothing good in months.

Writer's block? No, there was no such thing. Writer's block was an excuse for writers who didn't want to write. Locke *always* wanted to write. *Mode,* he thought.

Selfishness. I'm being selfish. Poetry was emotion—a personal one. But real poetry must always be relatable. Locke must change the mode of his vision. He must turn his indulgence *into* art, or at least try. God knew, nothing else was working.

He must transcribe how he felt in a way that was relative for the work. But how?

Be honest.

Even now, he would do anything to have her back. But she didn't want him back. He knew that—she scarcely spoke to him anymore. Where once he'd seen the brightest love in her eyes, he now saw only discomfort or dressed-up annoyance. Locke was a blight to her—that was how *she* felt.

But how do I feel? he asked himself again.

I still love her. I love her more than anything in the world, and I'd do anything to get her back. I'd do anything. I'd even wait forever.

Really? Forever?

Yes! he thought.

He began to type.

FOREVER by Richard Locke

I ascend in light, then I fall
In the ashes of this last curtain call.
There's nothing else but love, you see,
And this beckoning siren that carries me
Into heaven or the saddest realm of nether.
And even though you've cut the tether
My love for you goes on forever.

Yes. That was it. That was how he felt.

He stared at the piece of paper. He saw black ink on white pulp transcended into an image of his truth.

Then he tapped out another, a gust of spontaneity:

What sad phantoms stalk the warrens of your spirit?
What pale shapes rise on angel's wings?
Have you traded the chasm for resplendence?
Or have you stopped believing in all of those things?

The window darkened. His eyes flicked down at the picture of her: beautiful, resplendent, in love.

My love for you goes on forever.

A single tear crawled down his cheek.

Forever, he thought.

(ii)

Forever, the malefactor thought.

"I am forever," he whispered.

"What?" the girl inquired. "Did you say something?"

He smiled and faintly shook his head. She giggled, quite childlike. She'd unbuttoned her bright vermilion blouse several notches. He could smell the sweet youth of her flesh. He could smell her heart.

I am oblivion, he thought.

He wore black, all silk; he shimmered in his own darkness. The heater kicked on and fluttered the dark-green drapes. He peeked out, frowning. *San Francisco,* he thought. *An abyss. A canyon. Seamy light, crime, lust. What wonderful blood for a city. I'll miss this city, but it's time to move on, she'll be northward, and we'll find each other, and she will be mine again... forever...* The lights looked like stardust in ebon streaks, through which tiny dots travailed—tiny dots that were human beings. *How insignificant,* the malefactor considered. He hadn't been here in ages.

He'd only loved one woman in his ancient life. The girl, here, in the vermilion blouse and short black-leather skirt, was something less. No, he didn't love her, but he rejoiced in her. She was warm. She was alive. She was food. How old could she be? Twenty? Twenty-five? Her vitality whispered to him. The malefactor sensed a deep and wonderful dichotomy: the absolute contrast of her youth and the sheer age of what she was. *Strompet,* he thought. *Whore.* The consideration impressed him. Her profession was perhaps the only human thing on the earth that was close to his own age.

He'd paid her a thousand dollars cash, five times what she'd asked.

She looked wholesome somehow, cherubic—another contradiction of self and effect. She wore no stockings, her young legs looked smooth and sleek in the lamplight. Nor did she wear any panties, he noted, when she wriggled out of the tight leather miniskirt. The malefactor watched from across the room. Fake, pretty blonde hair, long and straight. Chocolate-brown eyes. A trimmed and nearly black pubic patch. Each of these images assembled into a complete contemplation. The *freshness* of her being. The *surge* of her youth. Her blouse slid off her shoulders to reveal smallish, pert breasts and pointed nipples.

"What's your name, by the way?" she asked.

My name is oblivion, he thought. *My name is forever.* What would her reaction be if he actually said that? *I don't really even have a name. What worth are names?* He smiled at her again.

"I know." She laughed. "It's John Smith, right? I get lots of John Smiths."

"My name is Lethe," the malefactor said.

"Well then why don't you come over here and join the party, Mr. Lethe? You've got me for the whole night."

No, I've got you forever. "Just..." he began. His eyes grew wide on her, the vision blooming. It was an erotic vision, a fleshy and sensual one: the young girl sitting naked at the edge of the big hotel bed, coyly smiling. All she had on were black high heels.

"I know," she postulated. She leaned back, splaying her pose. "Lotta guys like to watch a little first. They like to look."

"Yes," the malefactor said.

She lay back on the bed and parted her legs. She closed her eyes and sighed, and began to caress herself. The malefactor felt enraptured; this was beautiful, watching the beautiful young girl delight in the pleasures of her own body. Her hands roved her breasts, distending the nipples. In moments she was touching her sex, fervidly plying it with her fingers. She writhed on the sheets. Her heels kicked out of the black shoes. And in just moments more, she'd climaxed.

Yes, the malefactor thought.

She seemed exhausted, astonished. After lying back to catch her breath for a minute, she leaned up. "God," she whispered. "I don't know what happened."

"What do you mean?"

"I…" She faltered, squinting at herself. "I never come that fast. Usually I don't come at all, when…" Her finish dissolved.

"When you're with a…client," the malefactor finished for her. "You don't generally find pleasure in the province of your profession."

She looked at him. Sweat dried on her chest. "Something like that," she said, at once seeming sad.

"But why shouldn't you? Why shouldn't you find pleasure in yourself? Why shouldn't you *rejoice* in yourself?"

Now her smile was a crux. Of course, she didn't understand him. She would, though, in a little while.

She didn't scream at all—they never did. She wrapped her legs around him as he thrust. With each thrust he could feel the frantic contractions of her sex, her repeated climaxes. "I love you," she breathed each time she came.

The protracted incisors sunk into the beautiful white flesh of her throat. *Sleight of mouth,* he thought. She continued to climax as his teeth dug out the sternomastoid and scalenus muscle groups, exposing the jugular and the common carotid. They pulsed side by side amid the shorn muscle. The malefactor bit into them both.

She writhed beneath him, still convulsing her own silent, hot ecstasy. *Lovely,* he thought. It was lovely, to consume her so ardently. He swallowed all that she was in essence, not just simply her blood but her beauty and her vitality, her youth, her whole life.

The malefactor sucked her dry.

I am forever. I am oblivion.

He felt warm deep in his guts as he dressed. She didn't look beautiful anymore, she looked vitiated, wizened. But that was all right. Her beauty was in him now. *She* was in him.

Faith was power. *Belief* was power. He'd known that for eons.

Everything was either an insouciant lie or an unassailable truth. In all his years, in all his centuries of gleaning, that was perhaps the only real thing he'd ever become convinced of. It often depressed him—the fait accompli that the true quintessence of meaning was meaninglessness.

But I still have my love, he accounted. He adjusted the knot in his tie, aware of himself in the mirror. More superstition. He saw a thousand different things. Were they facsimiles? Were they falsehoods? He saw himself red as blood, covered in the blood of ages.

He stuffed the girl's poor shriveled mouth with clumps of garlic. There was no potential here, no reason to bring her along as he had others, she was, regrettably, just food. He opened her eyes with his fingers. *Love like blood,* he thought. From the small bag he'd brought along, he removed a common red-bladed hacksaw.

Then he sawed off the girl's head.

Words drifted across his sentience. They weren't his words. Whose could they be? *Into heaven or the saddest realm of nether...my love for you goes on forever.* A poem, an edict. Someone's love unloosed unto the night. The malefactor felt sad now, not for the girl whose head he'd just sawed off but for himself. It was a cruel trust. *I still have my love,* he repeated. Even that sounded like a lie.

The malefactor left. He did not leave through the door. He did not leave as a bat. He left instead as a desire, an...edict. He left as a longing, or as the passion behind the saddest tear.

I am forever. I am oblivion.

He fell adrift, into the sea of night. Drifting.

I...am...Sciftan...

FIVE

THE ARRIVAL
OF THE DEAD

(i)

Locke walked down Sunnyside Avenue. An odd ambiance struck him—
it always did. It was night, obviously there was, at present, no sunny
side...as with the neighboring Meridian Avenue, which certainly wasn't the
nexus of anything that Locke could determine. It seemed to show him something. Poets were weird.

Am I weird? he pondered. He knew he saw things differently, but he felt
that, as a poet, he was supposed to. Walking at night was more than that to
him. It was walking through imagery, through a panorama of visual abstraction which solicited creative assessment.

The night's chill air enfolded him. Down the street to his left, bright
light hung in a still explosion about the Open Book: "A Poem Emporium,"
enshrouded by crisp darkness. It had been a few months since Locke had
done a reading there; he liked the place, they sold nothing but volumes of
poetry and little literary journals, and thus were always on the verge of bank-
ruptcy, but the little shop was true, no contradictions in its Quixotic purpose.
He passed the church, the small office buildings where up-and-coming law
firms shared floors with down-and-out telephone boiler rooms, some small
shops. Renovated rowhouses which all seemed to tilt at odd angles
descended down dark streets. Old streetlamps cast umbrae of spoiled light at
each corner. Yes, Locke liked walking at night. There was a time, in his positivity, that he regarded walking as a symbolic act: each step forward became
an acknowledgment, or—yes!—a *celebration.* Every single step he took
through life felt like a celebration of his love.

Clare appeared in his mind. *Not anymore,* he realized. Now, walking
seemed little more than a celebration of ambulatory capability. His positivity
turned black.

Still, he liked to walk. Locke didn't own a car, he didn't need one. His
world was *here*; he needn't own a car to reach his muse. The bookstore and

the high school were walking distance. When he'd been dating Clare, his friend Lehrling often loaned him his second car, an old gold Dodge Colt with a dent in the side. Lehrling's first car was an Austin Martin Volante, which got a nice eight miles per gallon and cost a hundred grand. Lehrling was Locke's best friend; he was a good guy. He was also a heinously materialistic, pompous schmuck. At least he picked up Locke's bar tabs, so he couldn't be all that bad. Poets needed someone to pay for their alcohol. It seemed proper that the rich support the creative poor.

Oh, where is she now, and what are her dreams, he recited a part of the poem that was to be his marriage proposal. *But he remembers how the moonlight gleams, a resplendent angel in fine light dressed, and the poet thinks: Yes, I am blessed.*

Blessed, he thought. He couldn't get the darkness out of his heart. *Cheer up!* He tried to make a joke out of it. *In all that we were meant to be, thanks a lot for dumping me.* But it never worked. Never. *Some joke.*

The street felt as dark as his soul. Suddenly red and white throbs appeared around the silent corner. It was an ambulance—lights flashing, but no siren. It seemed to rove, driving slowly. Locke understood that when they did that, it meant that the victim had died on the way, so why hurry? The throbbing vehicle passed in a wake of eerie, lit silence; Locke watched it turn down 45th heading to the Swedish/Ballard Hospital some miles south. It seemed like an arrival of some kind. *Or a message?* he considered. But why should he think that? Why must he apply symbols to everything? It often aggravated him. *Carrying the dead,* he thought nonetheless. *The arrival of the dead.*

The moon peeked at him over rooftops, like a face trying to hide. Was someone shouting? He heard no other bar commotion. Clare drove a blue Sentra; Locke, as always, scanned the lot for it. *Not here.* But what would he do if it *was* here? Would he go in? Would he run away? He frequently asked himself this. He hadn't seen her now for over two months. What would happen when their paths crossed again?

Where does she go now? What does she do?

The questions were a tumult, an avalanche.

Who sleeps with her now?

That was the killer, the dread of any jilted lover. An unbidden image lit in his head: Clare in bed with someone else, whispering her passion into another man's ear, wrapping her legs around another man's back...

Locke stopped, dizzy. Did he hear arguing? He had to lean against a fence post to steady himself. His love seemed like a cheap trick, an intricacy through which he'd become abandoned by truth.

He let the moment pass and moved on.

Locke generally entered Concannon's by the back way—more symbology. The thief in the night. The fugitive. He pushed through the back gate, remembering all the times he'd come here with Clare, arm in arm, in love. His throat felt thick as warm pitch.

Locke was right; he *had* heard arguing. Two figures bickered by the back door—a nondescript guy in a white shirt, and a tall beautiful brunette who looked like a model. Locke froze in gridded shadow. Neither figure noticed him.

"What are you doing now that's so much better than me?" the guy in the white shirt hotly inquired. "You're more fulfilled *now?* You're happier *now?*"

"Well... yeah," the girl replied.

"Bullshit! You've never had a better relationship in your life!"

The girl seemed wearied. "When will you understand? I don't *want* a relationship."

"What do you want then? You want to spend the rest of your life shaking your ass on some dance floor? Giving your fucking phone number to every guy who wears the right clothes, has the right *haircut?* Getting laid by a bunch of anonymous cockhounds and dance club scumbags? Jesus Christ!"

The girl just shook her head, keeping her cool. "You don't know what you're talking about. Why can't you just accept it that things didn't work out for us?"

"Things?" White Shirt laughed. "Work out? You used to love me, remember? There's a lot more to love than 'things,' for Christ's sake!"

The girl's eyes looked huge in the moonlight. They looked flat, disimpassioned. "But I don't love you anymore," she said.

Locke watched with his mouth hanging open. *Familiar words.* Clare had said those exact same words to him, in the exact same way. The same blank expression. The same flat, disimpassioned eyes.

White Shirt seemed to stand in his own ire, minutely shaking.

"I have to go," the girl said.

"But I still love you," White Shirt croaked.

"So what's that supposed to mean?" she objected. Yes, she was beautiful—tall, elegant, even in faded jeans. It was her beauty that gave her the calm, cruel power. "Just because you love me doesn't mean I have to love you. I don't. Why can't you get that through your thick skull? I'm with someone else now, and, yes, I *am* happier, I *am* more fulfilled—"

"You only think you are," White Shirt denied.

But again the girl only shook her head. She began to walk away.

White Shirt's face looked corrugated. He pointed his finger like a gun. "Let me tell you something, baby! One day somebody's gonna do to you what you did to me, and you're not gonna like it! One day you're gonna give your heart to someone, and they're gonna spit it right back in your face! It's gonna happen! My God, I *hope* it happens, I can't wait! Then you're gonna know how it feels!"

The girl shrugged and moved on. She passed Locke in the shadows without noticing him. The back gate slammed closed.

Familiar story, Locke thought. White Shirt went back into the bar. Locke mulled over the bitter scene, abstractly as always. Strange ideas drifted up. He remembered the ambulance, lights on but no siren. He thought of Clare. He thought of walking in the night, each step a celebration of his broken dreams.

The words meshed, not just Clare's, not just the pretty brunette's, but the same words spoken in the voices of a thousand ghosts:

I don't love you anymore.

Locke gritted his teeth.

The night was something more than a night. The moon was a stoic overseer. The cold air was the last kiss of every shattered love affair in the world. The night was an arrival.

Locke went down the steps into the bar.

(ii)

Lehrling glanced up from a bottle of EKU Edelbock; he smiled, waved Locke over to the next stool. Carl the barkeep was making time with three girls at the other end of the bar who giggled, fawning over him.

"The poet extraordinaire!" Lehrling greeted. "Have a seat, let me buy you a beer."

"Why don't you buy me *ten* beers?" Locke returned the greeting.

"Uh-oh. The self-reflection of the stalwart artist. Hey, Carl! Get this man *ten beers!*"

Locke sat down. His thoughts winded him. Lehrling slapped him on the back, a bit hard for Locke's liking. "So what's up, buddy? How are things in the poet's domain?"

Locke sighed. He looked around. Not much of a crowd, it was still early. But at the midbar pillar, he noticed White Shirt slamming back a pint glass of Red Hook, a cigarette lit.

"I need to talk to you, Lehrling," Locke bid. Best friends, yes, but they addressed each other by their last names, since their first names were the same.

"No, no, no, *please*. Don't tell me you're still in the pits because of Clare. Please don't tell me that."

All right, I won't.

"Ten beers?" Carl came over and asked. Carl was good-looking enough to disgust most men. "Oh, no wonder—Locke's here. Should I bring the whole keg over?" He put a pint down in front of Locke, which he drank from at once. In several gulps, it was gone. Lehrling and Carl raised brows at one another.

"So how's the writing?" Lehrling asked, serious now.

"Sucks gorilla peckers," Locke eloquented. "I haven't been able to write anything good in months. I'm in a block and I can't get out."

Lehrling frowned over his stout. "That's an excuse. You're either a writer, or you're not. You either get the job done, or you don't. 'Writer's block' is the refuge of the candy-assed dilettante. You write or you don't, it's just that simple."

The job, Locke thought. That was the difference between them. Lehrling was a novelist; to him, writing *was* a job. It was something he did for money. Locke's view, though, was that writing for money was a perversion of creativity. To be real, it must *never* be a job. It must be a *passion.* Money subverted the passion to lust. It seemed evil in some psychical way. Locke hadn't read a novel since college; he'd never even read any of Lehrling's books. Theirs was a strange relationship: they were best friends yet they constantly condemned each other's creative motivations. Lehrling's "speculative" novels had earned him close to a million dollars; he wasn't famous, really, he was just rich. But to Locke, fiction was a lie. The only truth in the written word as an art form came through verse, not prose.

"You're a schmuck, Locke," Lehrling offered. "And I'm saying that as your friend."

"Some friend."

"Look, you want the truth, right? Isn't that what all poets think they want? The truth?"

"Sure."

"The truth is, a real writer uses every emotion in his life to make himself a *better* writer. You're not doing that. You're letting this Clare thing make you a *worse* writer."

Locke gave this some thought. Had Lehrling hit it on the head? And if so, so what? What could Locke do?

"But that's not really what you want to talk about, is it?"

No, Locke thought.

"How long's it been since the two of you broke up? Month and a half, two months?"

"Almost three."

"And you're still not over it," Lehrling observed. It was no question. "You want my advice?"

"No, I came here to look at your pretty face," Locke said.

"You're not gonna like it."

"What's the advice?" Locke nearly moaned and rubbed his temples.

"Cut bait."

Locke winced. "What?"

"Cut bait. You don't need the headache."

"I can't *cut bait,* Lehrling!" Locke shouted. "I still love her!"

Silence.

Locke glanced to and fro, head down. *I just shouted in the bar,* he realized to himself. Lehrling was looking at him. Carl was looking at him. The three girls at the end, and even White Shirt, were looking at him.

"You need to get a grip on yourself," Lehrling suggested after giving the outburst some time to pass. "You need to calm down."

"I know."

Lehrling ordered them two more. "So what happened? You never seemed to want to talk about it before."

But what *had* happened? Even Locke didn't know that. "It wasn't anything ugly. One day she just looked at me and told me she didn't love me anymore."

Lehrling nodded. He poured more of the amber bock slowly into the pilsner glass. "But who knows what love is, really? Are you sure she ever loved you at all?"

Yes! he wanted to scream. He *knew* she had. He was certain of it. That's what love was, perhaps—not something you could define but something you simply *knew.* "I know she loved me," Locke said, very quietly now. "Same way I know the sun comes up in the morning. I *know.*"

Lehrling, a cynic, left it at that. "Then you gotta ride it out."

"Ride *what* out?"

"The despair." Lehrling's eyes sought Locke out. "I know all about despair."

"Yeah?"

"Yeah. Shit, Locke, you're not the first chump in the world to have a relationship go bust. If you let it mess up your life—in your case, your poetry—then you fail as a human being. So you ride it out. You tighten up the bootstraps and you move on."

Lehrling didn't understand anything. It was male pride, Locke knew, that induced these ideas. Locke felt above that, he felt superior to such a falsehood. But if he felt above it, why did he feel so low now? He finished his second draft and let the buzz kick in.

"But you're lucky," Lehrling continued. "You're one up on the average guy in the same situation."

"How's that?"

"You're a writer."

"I know. Catharsis. Aesthetic reversion. It's all a load of shit."

"No it's not. It's true. And believe me, it's the only thing that's going to save you. Everybody deals with life in different ways. Writers deal with life by writing. We're the most fucked up people in the world—that's why we're writers. If we didn't have our writing, we'd all be in psych wards. Writing is the way we're able to exist normally in society. I write speculative novels—"

"You write *pulp* novels," Locke corrected.

"And you write candyass poetry, but that's beside the point. My novels exist in a duality. On the outside they're just novels, invented characters within an invented plot. But on the inside, somewhere in between the lines, they're my displacement. In between the lines, Locke, my novels are *me*. All my perceptions, all my feelings, all my joys, sorrows, hopes, and dreams. It's more than catharsis, Locke. Writing is exorcism."

Locke signaled Carl for another beer. *Exorcism,* he thought. *Displacement.* Maybe Lehrling was smarter than he thought. *Or maybe he's just full of crap.* Because Locke still didn't know how to use what Lehrling had just said.

The novelist went on. "I've been shit on by women more times than pigeons have shit on the White House. I've *never* had a relationship that's worked. I've loved girls, sure. Lots of girls. And when it falls apart, it hurts, it seems like the worst thing in the world. But I get out of it every time. I save myself—every time—with my work."

Locke was looking down, running his finger through water rings on the bar. His beer seemed to taste like regret. All of his visions, then, reverted to a whorl of memory, plummeting. He felt ruined, even after three months. And now here was Lehrling, the know-it-all rich novelist, claiming to have all the answers. Locke didn't even know what the questions were.

"You take it out of your heart," Lehrling continued to postulate, "and you put it somewhere else. You put it on that piece of paper that sticks out of your typewriter. There's no other way to get away from it, Locke. You're a visionary, a dreamer—all poets are. Everything you feel, you've got to write about it. That's the only way you'll ever get over Clare. That's the only way you'll ever be free."

Free... But Locke didn't want to be free, he didn't want to *get over it,* not if freedom meant that his love abandon him forever. He wanted Clare back—the way it was—that's what he wanted...

White Shirt inexplicably pounded his fist on the bar. "Never," he exclaimed. He was drunk and then some. "Never, never..."

Carl plunged beer mugs two at a time into the triple sinks. "Never *what?*" he asked.

"Never fall in love with a girl you meet in a bar." White Shirt's bloodshot eyes drifted up. "Never—" Again he pounded his fist. "—and I mean never ever ever!"

I hear that, Locke thought. Never fall in love with a girl you meet in a bar. He'd met Clare in a bar, in *this* bar. He'd never forget that first moment he'd seen her...

"Never, never... ," White Shirt stammered on.

...the impact, the *power,* in that first single glimpse of her beauty...

"—never, never, ever, ever fall in love—"

...yes, the sheer resplendence of her...

"Like this asshole over here," Lehrling whispered to him. "Look at him. He's wasted, ruined, because of a girl. He's got nowhere to put his feelings, so his feelings are turning him inside out. You want to end up like that?"

Locke glanced down the bar. White Shirt was staring up into the rafters now, his eyes pasted open, mouthing *Never, never, never...*

Love was supposed to be a wonderful thing, but look what it had done to this guy. No, Locke didn't want to end up like White Shirt. That was scary. But what scared him more was not knowing exactly *how* he would end up.

Locke quickly grabbed a bar napkin. Lehrling said he must write about his feelings, he must take his feelings from his heart and put them some- where else. *So be it,* he resigned, and took up his pen.

He quickly scribbled:

POEM ON A BAR NAPKIN by Richard Locke

This is how I feel, my love...
in the muse of the poet, or the destitute hack.
You would love me again in the wink of an eye
if you knew how bad I want you back.

Lehrling looked on, afrown. "You're shitting me, right? That's not a poem. It's frivolity. I'm talking about real work, Locke, a real communica- tion of your psyche, not some little ditty you doodle down on a bar napkin. That's shit."

"I know," Locke muttered. *Everything I write is shit.* But it wasn't a self-condemnation. That was how any real poet should feel: that nothing could ever be good enough to be art. Lehrling was a novelist—naturally he didn't understand. Locke wadded up the napkin and with a sigh tossed it into the can behind the bar. More of his heart crumpled and tossed away as so much garbage.

"Hey, keep," White Shirt drunkenly demanded. "Another beer."

Carl put a mug of coffee down.

"That's not beer," White Shirt observed.

"It's the closest thing to beer you're gonna get tonight," Carl came back. "In case you haven't noticed, you're drunk."

White Shirt shrugged. "I guess you're right." Carl's eyes widened as White Shirt gulped down the entire steaming mug at once, scalding his misery.

"What do I do?" Locke pleaded.

"Write off the loss," Lehrling said. "I told you. Forget it."

I can't forget it.

"Look at the facts. You fell in love with a girl. The girl dumped you. It happens every day. The only way you can preserve what you are is to forget it. And the only way to forget it is—"

"Yeah, right. Catharsis."

"Catharsis," Lehrling concurred. "Exorcism. Turn your feelings into art. Write the best poem you've ever written. Then you'll be free. Take my word for it."

But Locke could only frown at this emphasis of advice. The moment merged then into a hectic chaos. The three girls at the end of the bar jabbered meaninglessly, like parrots. Music beat bleakly from the stereo; it sounded far away. White Shirt resumed the forlorn pounding of his fist: "Never fall in love with a girl you meet in a bar! Never! Never!" But all Locke could see was his love. All he could see was Clare.

He felt supplanted. He felt unreal.

"Get drunk," Lehrling suggested. "That'll help."

It did not help. Locke's beer tasted like loss, like every loss in the world. He finished his second pint, then his third, then his fourth.

"That's the spirit."

Spirit? Do I even have one anymore?

Locke's eyes lifted to the window. Murky light throbbed, moving— light the color of blood. Another ambulance roved slowly down the street.

Its lights were flashing, but its siren was off.

(iii)

Arrivals?

That's what I thought, I guess, as I stepped naked up onto the cold splintery wooden dock. I thought of arrivals. Plural. Not merely my arrival to wherever this place was, but something more complex. Many arrivals, in many different meanings.

Rebirth!

The water gives me up now, from its depths like the calm monotony of death. Am I trite to say I feel reborn? Before me the sea stretches on forever, and behind me looms the city, like an intricate, carved mesa in black, flecked in tiny lights. I feel cleansed, vibrant. I feel alive in heat against the wet, dragging, deathlike cold. In my death, I'm alive. In my age, I've emerged like the first second of life from the sanctuary of the womb.

Am I here by chance?

I'm standing on a pier, looking out. I cannot distinguish where the sea ends and the night begins. Ice cold salt water drips off my hot skin. Boats bob in their slips, in total silence.

I like the silence. It makes me feel blessedly alone and so aware in this vast and awesome night. The big bright moon is looking at me. I can feel its vibrant light on my face, my breasts. I'm caressing myself in the light. I feel like the gleam on the edge of a razor.

I feel so beautiful now!

But I sense something else—I can feel it like a joyous promise in my heart. I know it's something good, even though bad things follow me wherever I go. I know now, my face staring up into the moon, my breasts cupped in my hands, that I'm not here by chance.

I'm never anywhere by chance.

Then comes a third sensation.

Hunger.

SIX

SUSTENANCE

(i)

Fisherman's Terminal, the gaudily lit ornament of Puget Sound, made Jason think of palm trees, hurricane lamps, large thick drinks and Anna wearing nothing but red ribbons. Silly thought those ribbons, but so were palm trees in November. For that matter so was the possibility of seeing Anna in the buff. He had his chance and took it, just before they turned in that evening. Say, "good night," a gentle kiss dragged out, maybe run your tongue past her lips. He thought the chance was good, but she pulled away before he got a taste of her lips. Anna kept Jason at arm's length for a moment, then retreated to her cabin.

All shipping ground to a halt as police boats and helicopters circled the area north of the marine terminal. The area was secured, and no one was offering explanations. Yachts circled the barges that floated idly and waited. Tugmasters kept their vessels at idle throttle to keep their charges stationary. The bitter cold morning pulled sea smoke from the factories on Harbor Island to shroud the tugs in a mist that gave them the majesty of distant mountains.

A ghostly moon was sinking behind Seattle. The Sea of Tranquility was still visible to the naked eye as the sun cleared the Cascade Mountains. Jason braced the morning chill in a knit sweater and Levis jeans. As a rule he hated early mornings. He also hated paying taxes and waking up for the 2 a.m. watch change during deliveries. Jason took all this in great stride. Most of it was, after all, part of the job. The concept of being a professional marine captain seemed luxurious to most people. On paper it looked good: $100/day plus expenses. Reality was often a different creature. Leaking hatches, contaminated water, faulty electrical, and twelve hours a day worth of watches could make it a tough way to earn a buck. In truth, he was always glad to finally reach port with someone else's vessel.

Coffee would be nice, he thought. The newly varnished teak wood door, to the main cabin, nudged him in the back.

"Coffee," Anna announced or possibly asked as she handed him a mug. Things like that were hard to distinguish through her German accent. She had a warm, inviting smile. Though after last night, Jason was pretty sure that the invitation ended with coffee.

Jason nodded at the gangway, "Heavy bastard."

They both were watching the crews reassemble the passageways. "Ja was es das?"

The question knocked Jason for a loop. Lethe had hired Anna to be Jason's crew, which suited Jason fine. After all, it was one less detail to work out. Jason assumed that she was to become a permanent crew on the boat after he departed. "You don't know either?"

"Nien."

He was starting to get aggravated by it all. Lethe openly offered Jason a two-hundred-dollar-a-day fee for the delivery—along with provisioning cash and transportation to the Emerald City, both of which were standard. Two-hundred-a-day plus expenses made him wonder what he was in for. The doubled fee sent alarms off in his head, but…well, he needed money.

And then there was the guy himself, this… Lethe.

"Weird trip, and a weirder client," Jason muttered aloud to the fog. "Not to mention a mystery cargo, and a frigid crew that can't speak English."

"Swine." Anna retorted and stalked off to the galley. His eyes followed her. She filled her jeans well, not lacking in the sweater either.

Jason, next, caught the eyes of the laborer, who was resetting the teak doors to the aft salon. The man had been watching them, or possibly only her. He smiled a toothy grin and went back to work. Below deck, other locals of the boat yard were reassembling hand rails and more doors which led aft. An hour and a half before they had to disassemble everything to accommodate the passage of one 7 X 3 metal box through the *Betruger's* companionway.

Yeah, that's some mystery cargo, all right, Jason thought.

With four double staterooms with baths, this yacht, the *Betruger,* could double as a small hotel. The main salon and dining room were all art deco. Salmon-colored wall-to-wall carpeting, which ran to the ceiling, was trimmed out in black and gold tiffany molding. The word "exquisite" kept popping into Jason's mind. He asked himself if this guy was a swish or something. The *Betruger's* galley rivaled most restaurant kitchens in his home town. Even the engine room was carpeted. Her heart was driven by twin 343TA Cat diesels which could propel her at a speed of 10 knots for about 3,000 miles. To help make life comfortable aboard the 97-foot yacht, there were three generators on line which powered everything from the reading light in the head to the windless, which raised both 150-pound anchors. The bridge was fully enclosed with all the essentials; fore and aft thrusters, three VHF and a pair of single side band radios, two Furuno radars, a Furuno sonar unit, LORAN and SAT-NAV. Her lines were the pride of the Burger design team. For a million-five-plus, before amenities, she could be anyone's pride.

In Jason's case the *Betruger* happened to be the pride of a man named Lethe, and like the yacht, Lethe was full of amenities; elegant, stylish, respectable, and on a first-name basis with the word money. Jason met the owner of the vessel at one of the posh restaurants which overlooked Fisherman's Wharf (Their money was paid upfront. Again another alarm.) Lethe drew the attention of the waitress just by sitting down.

Lethe was tall, about a head larger than Jason, slim and graceful. He wore his clothes in the way a king might wear a crown, an accentuation of his own power but not its source. His face was wan yet healthily so somehow, and his hair was a wave of salt and pepper. It made it impossible to calculate the man's real age; late forties, early fifties, Jason could only guess. He could even be in his sixties.

"Did the *Betruger* pass your personal inspection, Captain?" asked Lethe. His eyes gleamed like polished onyx and his voice betrayed a proper English accent. It was properly spoken, like one would hear from someone who was taught the language.

"It's quite a yacht, Mr...."

"Just Lethe. It is the only name I go by."

"Is the *Betruger* a corporate vessel?" asked Jason.

"Why do you ask?" he replied, but those eyes burned their way past all Jason's thoughts to the secret recesses of his mind.

"It's just that some marinas apply discounts to corporate vessels. Also some have kitchens that'll provide catering."

"No, the *Betruger* is my private yacht."

"Most of the vessels that size usually have some big money to back them unless they're doing charters," Jason fished a little more.

Lethe smiled, a long finger unconsciously tapping the table by his napkin. "Ah, let me speculate, if you will. I've offered you the job of transporting my yacht up the coast, and entrusted you with making arrangements for transporting its cargo to my estate in North Bend, and you're curious as to why I won't be on the yacht myself, why I choose, instead, to meet you at the destination-point, hmm? Curious? And about the fact that I'm paying twice your fee, plus abundant expenses?"

"Well," Jason began. "I, uh—"

"And more curious still are you, about the 'strange cargo,' yes?"

"Well, Mr., er—excuse me, Lethe," Jason fumbled. "You have to admit, the cargo is kind of strange. I mean, sure, lots of owners prefer to pay someone more experienced to transport their yachts long distances, and sometimes they prefer not to go along for the ride—fine. But this cargo of yours, this crate— it's so big that you're actually having contractors take apart the companionway just to get the thing on board. Why not just truck it up to Seattle?"

Lethe sipped from his glass of Montrachet. Jason had peeked at the wine list—$270 a bottle! "Let's just say that it suits me far more to transport the crate by water. Hiring a truck seems... mundane." Then Lethe smiled. "But, seriously, Jason. Do I look like a drug smuggler?"

"Hey, sir, really," Jason jabbered too quickly. "I wasn't for a minute suspecting—"

"Please, Jason." Lethe seemed utterly amused, pausing to sniff at his wine every so often. "It's your job to be suspicious, and it is that level of thoroughness that I expect. If you want to know what's in the crate, why don't you ask?"

"Okay, uh," Jason said. "What's, uh, what's in the crate?"

"A twelfth century footstand."

"A *what?*"

"An entablatured footstand. Think of it as a medieval coffee table; it's solid oak, weighs close to three hundred pounds."

"What, some kind of antique?"

"Perforce. This footstand was the actual gold carrier in which a ransom of 150,000 marks was paid to Emperor Henry VI of France, for the safe return of England's King, Richard I, in the year 1192. It's quite dull to look at, I'm afraid, but of course the entails of its history make it very valuable."

A...footstand, Jason thought dumbly. "So you're an antique collector, is that it?"

Lethe made an odd smile. "A collector, yes."

"And I guess this footstand is worth a lot of money."

"Oh, yes. Actually, it's worth about as much as the yacht."

Jason nearly spat out his Killian's Red. *A million-five for a fuckin'* footstand! *You gotta be out of your mind!*

"Because," Lethe continued, sipping more wine, "the footstand also happens to contain the original ransom agreement, which is signed by both kings. It happens to be the only surviving document, in fact, that bears Richard's signature."

I guess that'll do it, Jason thought. Collectors, what a weird bunch. If Jason had a million-five to blow, he'd pass on the footstand.

"Ah," Lethe announced as a sultry waitress wended to the table. "Here come the snails. Have some, Jason."

Jason took one glance at the things on the plate, and that was all she wrote. "No thanks. I'm trying to cut down."

"Anna?"

Jason's silent accomplice made a face and shook her head, but she didn't hesitate to let Lethe pour her more wine. It was then that Jason noticed that most of the women in the restaurant kept stealing glances in their direction. Their waitress seemed to appear at Lethe's shoulder about every five minutes, as if she seemed eager to serve on bent knee for him. When he commanded her it was by her name. Her face glowed every time he spoke. Lethe was getting her hot and bothered. Jason expected her to pull off her panties at any minute, and beg Lethe to take her on the table.

Jason leaned close. With a conspirator's tone he commented, "I think she likes you."

Lethe dismissed the attention as something that he was used to. "It is, after all, her job."

Jason gravitated to the man. He also noticed that Anna seemed more reticent than before. It was clear that she was not comfortable around her new employer. Jason didn't really care—money was money. And this was *good* money.

At any rate, the deal was done. Jason and Anna would take the *Betruger* up the coast in the morning, and meet Lethe in Seattle. "That reminds me," Jason spoke up. "I'll need the number of your hotel so I can call you once we've arrived."

"No need," Lethe replied and rose. "I'll find you."

"You're leaving now?"

"Yes, I must go. So I'll see you both in a couple of days."

"Guten nacht," Anna bid.

"Goodnight," Lethe said, and then he walked away, leaving five one-hundred-dollar bills on the table to cover the tab.

«« — »»

"Eh man, all done here," said the lanky black man, who headed the marina crew, as he handed Jason an invoice for the work. The man in the army issue jacket that said EMMERSOM was all teeth under his mustache.

Jason signed it and handed it back. "Heavy son a bitch."

"Damn straight. Weighed more than my Uncle Albert."

"What's that?"

"Took twelve of us pall bearers, and he was in a pine box. The old bastard ate fried clams three times a day at Benny's when he was workin' the dock. You ever had a plate of fried clams at Benny's, man?"

"Uh, no," Jason replied.

"Pile of clams bigger than your head. No wonder Uncle Albert weighted four-fifty when he kicked."

Jason didn't give a hoot about Emmersom's uncle, but he knew what he was getting at. He felt the flush in his cheeks and a cold razor's edge work up his spine. He had to admit, the crate looked like it could hold a coffin. "Tell me, you saying you think that's a coffin?"

"I think nothin', but whatever is in that thing ain't secured, like machinery would be, you dig?"

Hmm. The crate was meticulously packed, a steel box on the outside, which stood to reason considering what Lethe claimed to be in it. But—

Jason shuddered. A hazy chill of old childhood dreams came back....*ashes to ashes, dust to*...

"Man, you all right? You look pale."

"Just a long night."

"With that bouncy little German thing? Shee-it, I'd probably look pale too," Emmersom barked. Jason just smiled and let it go. But the chill hung on as they stood a moment more to look at the huge crate now secured in the master stateroom.

"And it was a perfect bitch gettin' down here, hadda practically take the whole companionway apart and put it back together."

"Hey, better you than me," Jason laughed.

Emmersom displayed his middle finger. "And just what kind of a fuckin' nut'd wanna do that anyway?"

Lethe, Jason thought. *A nut?* "I wouldn't necessarily call him a nut. Eccentric, maybe. And what are you griping about, man? The four bills I gave you to haul this thing down here came from him."

"Next time, keep it. And what's this shit? Says on the shipping invoice it's a 'anteekee' footstand," Emmersom remarked. "What dah crap's a foot-stand, man?"

"It's a," Jason began. Then he frowned. "Don't ask unless you want to hear a lot of shit about King Richard's ransom note."

"Shee-it." Emmersom chuckled, lit a butt. "Well I'll tell ya what it ain't. It ain't a box full'a drugs."

Jason looked at him. "Yeah?"

"That thing weren't off the pallet one minute 'fore the Harbor Police were all over it with them dope-sniffin' dogs of theirs. And the mutts could-n't'a cared less about it. Couple of 'em wouldn't even go near it."

Interesting, Jason thought. A bit relieving too. Everything was fine...

So why didn't he *feel* fine?

"Anyway, thanks, man," he offered. "Thanks for getting this big hunk of shit down here. I'll see ya in a few weeks."

Emmersom smiled again, shaking his head. "Shee-it. A fuckin' *foot-stand*?" Then he left for abovedecks.

Two hours later, Jason and Anna had topped off the fuel and water tanks and were underway.

Yeah, Jason thought at the helm, watching Anna bend over the mooring box. *Everything's fine*.

«« — »»

Jason had taken the first salon aft of the bridge, giving Anna the first full shift at the *Betruger's* wheel. It was night somewhere off the Washington coast. His stateroom was lit by a red night-vision light. It gave a ghoulish feeling to the room. Naked, he climbed out of the king size bed and stretched. The cabin door opened. Anna was illumined in red. Her blonde hair fell behind her shoulders. She wore jeans cut off above her pockets which revealed tight thighs and muscular calves. Whenever Anna stood up she flashed bikini lines.

Jason didn't see his pants. "My turn," he commented.

"Ja," she said, stepping toward him. She crossed her arms and skimmed her T-shirt over her head. Her long fingers lightly slid down her shoulders and over her breasts. They stopped for a moment to linger on the nipples. She stroked the valley between and the bottoms of those domes and moaned, "Ja, your turn."

Jason could feel himself stiffen in the night air as Anna's hips swayed from side to side. Her cut-offs slid down. Then those long elegant fingers slid through the dark patch between her golden red thighs. "Ja, your turn."

She took his hands and placed them on her breasts. They were round and firm; the nipples raised beneath his caresses. Anna's fingers ran down his sides, then up to his erection. He moaned as she descended, lightly kissing his chest, nipples, the underside of his ribs. Her tongue tickled him above his hips. Lower, she explored. Her hair teased his penis. She kissed the inside of his thighs, then her tongue was working around his circumcision...

Jason moaned and lay back on the bed as her tongue, teeth, and lips worked in unison. The cool air struck his member as Anna released him and kissed her way up his body, gently massaging him with her breasts. "Ja, your turn."

Thank God for autopilot, Jason thought.

She straddled his hips and bore her sex down atop him. Jason thrust his hips upwards into a very wet, hot Anna. They both moaned... He ran his hands over her breasts as her gyrations became manic. "Ja!" she cried. "Your turn!"

Then her lips pulled back to reveal elongated teeth that looked sharp as roofing nails.

Jason screamed as she bit into his neck...

He leapt awake with a hollow cry, bathed in sweat. The engine's drone was soft, hypnotic. A slight swell rocked the vessel. *Jesus, what a dumbass dream*. In the dark stateroom, Jason felt around for his jeans. An LED clock read 1:40 a.m. Out in the companionway he tugged his shirt over his head and watched Anna on the helm. They were in a following sea. The port aft end of the vessel would raise slightly, then dip. Their motion was constant. If it had been an oncoming sea, he would have felt a bumping motion.

Jason steadied himself along the bulkheads as he walked aft to the master stateroom. If there was something loose in Lethe's crate, a following sea might cause the container to slide and damage the bulkheads. The stateroom was easily larger than his. Its king-size bed sat in a recessed floor, and was topped by a canopy whose floral design matched the bedspread. By comparison, the oblong box which sat in front of the bed seemed small. Jason circled the box looking at how it sat. So far it hadn't moved. He squatted down and tried to see what it would take to move something this massive. His arms and legs strained at the smooth, cool, dead weight. His face grew hot, temples pounded, a groan escaped him; but it wouldn't move. *Shit,* he thought. *Maybe it is Emmersom's Uncle Albert.*

The container was 7 X 3 X 3, exactly. *Footstand, huh, Lethe?* It was time to see this mystery cargo. Jason gripped the under side of the lid and grunted. The cold metal lid wouldn't move. Again he walked around the container, running his fingers under the lip. Nothing. No seams, no welds, no latches of any kind. This was turning into a weirder trip than he thought.

He considered using a crow bar to pry it open. Out of nowhere he was swept by a wave of nausea. His knees buckled,...*ashes to ashes, dust to...* He clicked off the light and closed the door behind him as he ran for the deck. The cool ocean air braced him and the moment passed.

It was quarter of three in the morning when Jason relieved Anna. She was grateful to be off early. A million faint points of light speckled the black heaven. The Pacific Ocean mirrored the dark void of space as the *Betruger* plowed its way through the sea. Jason's heart slowed to a steady beat. Calm took control as he reestablished their position.

An hour later, they were just south of Seattle when he noticed Anna on the side deck staring out into the ocean. *What's she doing up here now?* he wondered. *She only went to bed an hour ago.*

"Couldn't sleep?" he called out.

She didn't answer. She kept wiping her eyes. When she finally turned, he was startled to see her so wan. She looked like she did in the dream. And when he finally asked what was wrong, she said something about a bad dream, too. Her face was that of a child, who after waking from a nightmare, didn't want to go back to sleep.

(ii)

Called him Wire. Smalltime thief, bigtime headcase. Lotta crank 'n speed 'n angel dust had turned what was between his ears into bad meat. Got the nickname in K.C. Detent—doing eighteen months on a GTA—on account he was skinny, like a piece of wire. Earned some more nicknames he'd just as soon forget on his second sendup: "White 'N Tight" and "C-Block Boy-Cherry." That was at Walla Walla, the state slam. Had to do three on a nickel for burglary. Fuckin' animals. Lotta times the players traded him between block bulls for cigarettes. "You my bitch t'night, White 'N Tight!" he'd been told too many times. Wire's poor bowel had been the depository of many an ejaculation.

Raped lots of chicks in his day, and killed two guys once on a burn pickup, back when he was dealing. Fuck dealing nowadays—too many cowboys, and a lotta fuckin' Jamakes had taken over. This county, shit, first offense dealing coke or frog got'cha a mandatory pound in the state cut, no parole. Ain't no way ol' Wire was going back to that shithouse. Jacking was a safer gig if you'd got it up the ass many times as Wire; some of those players had cocks big as fuckin' rolling pins. He'd been jacking small stuff five years now and was doing all right, had a coupla good fences in SeaTac. Boat shit was always big in the fall, ya rip stuff in the fall that people'll want in the spring, give the shit time ta cool down. And a town like this, shit, one fuckin' marina after the next, boats all over the fuckin' place. Pretty penny numbers was shit like fishing sonar, depth-finders, and these new digital map things, whatever the fuck they were. CD-Rome, something like that. Ya keep active, ya do all right, plenty of dust money, which was fine for Wire.

Carried a small folding knife—an Almar. Sharp stuff, it'd do the job. Had a three-inch blade so if the pigs shook him down they couldn't burn him on the knife laws. Anything three-inch or less was in the books as a penknife. Didn't sound big, but ya hold one to some chick's throat and she'll bend over fast, Wire could tell you. Figured he owed it to the system ta rape chicks, after all the times he'd gotten raped in the joint. So fuck it, he didn't give a shit long as he got a nut off.

With boat shit it was easy down here at Shilshole most of the boats belonged to Boeing engineers or Microsoft execs who used their boats one or two weekends a year. Lotta the marinas let their security contracts expire end of October, so usually he didn't have to worry 'bout any of these night watchmen chumps. Wire parked by Charlie's and walked over to B-Dock at the big marina next to the restaurant. Figured he'd hit a row of cabin cruisers.

Didn't figure on seein' the chick.

Off-the-wall shit. He was about to shag a padlock when he felt something weird. Weird night, too. Cold and real breezy. The moon was real low and white. Wire turned, crowbar in hand, then he hunkered down in the coaming.

What the fuck?

See, this chick was standing at the end of the dock. Buck naked, too, which didn't make no sense 'cos it was *cold*. She looked wet. Had this split-tail just come out of the water? *Naw, that's fuckin' impossible, she'd freeze ta death.* Wire's drug-cooked brain was at least functional enough to realize that.

But she was *beautiful.*

Wild red hair, dynamite body, legs, hooters. This chick was one hot number. *So what the fuck's she doin' standing naked on a fuckin' pier in the middle of the night?*

This was a good question. Wire, however, did not deliberate upon it. All he knew was this: he was gonna get inta this chick's shit good. Oh, yeah. He was gonna do a cock number on her like she'd never fucking forget.

She was just standing there straight as a mooring stull, staring up into the black sky.

Wire was getting hard just looking at this weird chick. Her skin was white, almost like light. She had the big dark stick-out kinda nipples and an ass that wouldn't quit. Suddenly she turned and stepped onto one of the boats.

Wire made his move. Fuck the fuckin' inordinate inexplicabilities, he was gonna *get down.* He opened up his Al-Mar and snuck past the dock. The moon made his shadow look like a slinky wire.

She'd climbed aboard a 24-foot cabin cruiser called WE'RE AWEIGH. Nice looking boat, and well-equipped. Maybe when Wire was done plugging this broad till her shit came out her ears, he'd knock the boat over for its depth-finder 'n shit. Two birds with one stone, ya know? But when he peered over the gunwale, he couldn't fuckin' believe it!

The chick was doin' the job herself!

Wire couldn't see what she had, but she was breaking the lock off the door to belowdecks. Just like that—*Crack!* and it was off. Then she stepped down into the cabin and turned on the light.

Wire couldn't make heads ner fuckin' tails of this shit. *Naked chick, wet like she just come outa the water, bustin' into boats.* But if indeed she were a fuckin' thief, like Wire, she was not possessed of much between the head-handles. Gotta be plain-ass stupid to turn on the cabin light when you're jacking shit off a boat at midnight.

She was looking for something, Wire realized next, not jacking. She was rummaging through the cabin slots, tossing things to the floor. Towels, sandals, tubes of suntan lotion, shit like that. She was bending over, and Wire was gandering that big beautiful tail-end on her, and he could see that gorgeous rack of tits swaying back and forth as she continued to rummage. All he could contemplate was this beautiful body and what he was gonna do to it in about two seconds.

But what was she looking for?

Clothes, he realized then. She'd found a pair of cutoff jeans, and slipped into them. Then she found a T-shirt that said THE KORT HAUS TAVERN on it. Before she could put it on, Wire stepped over the sheer line and thumped down into the cabin.

The chick turned, unsurprised. Wire stared at her rib melons, his thumb running along the smooth steel of his Al-Mar.

"Hello," she said.

Wire's sneer went lax. He felt funny all of a sudden; he felt prickly. There was some scent that reminded him of animals or something. "Them shorts, sweetcakes? Get 'em the fuck off," he articulated. He turned the knife, which glinted meanly.

"Are you a sinner?" she asked.

What the fuck was this shit? "Get the fuckin' shorts off, honey, or I cut 'em off. I got no time ta fuck around. We can do this hard or easy. Your choice."

The chick smiled. "Easy," she decided.

Oh yeah, oh yeah, was the only thought that could traverse Wire's PCP-pocked gray matter as she stepped back out of the cutoffs. Wire gaped. He'd raped tons of chicks, some of 'em real hot numbers, hot bods, but never anything like this. Uh-uh. This was some cut of meat. Just looking at her Wire thought he might blow his juice right in his grimy jeans. The mere outline of her in the cabin light, the sleek curvy shape of her—Wire had never fathomed such an intricate and concise ideal of fuckin' physical pulchritudity.

But that all-of-a-sudden funny feeling began to grow, like some fucked up heat way-way down in his gut. What was it? He tried to concentrate, he tried to look at her face, but he couldn't see it, not really anyway. There was something about her eyes—huge, rich dark-brown or dark something, he wasn't sure—that obscured him, and more and more it did indeed seem that she was made of light. She was so fuckin' gorgeous he coulda shit.

But what had she said? Are you a *sinner?*

"You don't need that." She meant the knife. "It's been a long time for me."

"The fuck you talkin' about? I—"

"Come here."

Now something was *really* fucked up. He was staring at those high, big-as-croquet-balls tits on her, that dynamite flat waist and big dark bush. He felt summoned, he felt screwed in the eye by some overpowering call of desire. Next thing he knew, Wire—a sociopath, an amoral streetscum thief and rapist—was making out with this chick *bigtime*. They both seemed to melt together onto the cabin floor, swooning in each other's arms. This wasn't no fuckin rape—this was passion, something quite foreign to Wire, so foreign, in fact, so remote from the scope of his scumbag drug-infested brain-cells-fried-like-bacon life that he could scarcely fuckin' contemplate it. She was all over him, her warm sweet lips dressing him with kisses as she peeled his duds off. Her tongue slipped around in his mouth, and those big dark nipples got so hard they felt like pebbles against his chest, and all Wire could do was lie back and let this tough, brick shithouse chick smother him with her kisses and caress him into a vortex of pleasure like he'd never known.

She reached down—her hand was so *hot*—and all she had to do was lay one finger on Wire's torqued-up throbbing works, and that was all she fuckin' wrote. Wire's spunk shot out of him before he even knew he was coming. *Aw, fer shit's sake!* Some rapist! He felt like a fucking idiot. Yeah, ol' Wire really tore this bitch up, huh? Yeah, he really jammed it to her. *Blow my nut before I even get it in her stuff. You'd think I was some fuckin' thir-teen-year-old or something.* Regardless of the circumstance, he felt absolutely fuckin' humiliated. "Don't worry," she consoled. Her hands stroked him, caressed him. Had he been a bit more introspective he'd have realized it was the first time he'd been really caressed in his life. "Time means nothing," she said.

"Huh?"

"We have lots of time."

Even her voice drove him nuts. Darkly sweet. Softly coarse. She gently turned him over on his belly, straddled him, and began to massage his back. Yeah, this was all right. So he'd blown his first load kinda fast? Like this she'd have him up again in no time. Her fingers felt like electric heat working deep into his shoulders and along his spine.

"Does this feel good?"

"Yeah," Wire moaned. "Oh, yeah, baby, that's nice."

Did she giggle?

"Cadillac misses you."

Wire's thought processes took a hike. His eyes bulged.

"And so do Sliphammer and Percy," she said.

Suddenly he wanted to vomit. He couldn't move, he could only lie there now in terror rigid as an iron rod. What she'd said—it was impossible. His mind became a sewer of memories: all those horrid hot sweat-stinking nights splayed out on some crusty bunk, on his belly.

Cadillac. Sliphammer. Percy.

They were some of the players who'd butt-fucked him back when he was in the state slam. The biggest of them, guys with cocks like radiator hose. Every night these fucking bulls gave it to him. Every night for three fucking years.

"White 'N Tight," she said, and then her voice, that creamy rough sexy dark syrupy voice oozed into hideousness...

"Yeah, we'se gonna bust you up right in yo' boy-pussy, we'se gonna work yo' ass."

Wire was screaming. The giant black hand gripped the back of his neck and mashed his face against the floor.

"You *my* bitch t'night, White 'N Tight," Cadillac said.

SEVEN

BANG!

(i)

By midnight Concannon's was packed. Chatter, laughter, and the aroma of halibut fish & chips swirled in the air. It was one of those nights, Locke supposed: they arrived in droves—the downtown restaurant crowd, armies of beer snobs, and revelers in general. It gave the pub its spirit; this was no pit stop for singles but a consortium of cool and happy people. Carl jockeyed drinks like a madman. Music beat in the walls. In no time Concannon's rocked in frolic.

Locke sank in despair.

It didn't take him long to get drunk. How many pints had he had? Six? Eight? Alcohol pursued his despair—it always did. *I'm becoming a drunk,* he drunkenly considered. Each beer delved further into his memory of Clare.

He felt locked out of the crowd's revelry. He felt totally alone. *Where is she now? What's she doing? How come she doesn't come here anymore?*

Because you're here, asshole.

Was that it? She didn't want his love anymore. She didn't want him in her life anymore. She didn't even want to be in the same room with him.

Is that it?

Locke ordered another pint.

Lehrling was trying to make time with two waitresses from The College Inn. "I'm a novelist," he bragged. "Big deal," they both said at the same time. "I have five million books in print," he tried again. "Oh, we care?" they both said again. Eventually they picked up their Nordic Wolfs and moved across the bar. Then a girl from the art college sat down next to him. "Hi, my name's Dan Quayle," Lehrling said. "Can my father buy you a drink?"

That one seemed to work.

His friend occupied, Locke was left to his thoughts. Before him lay balled-up examples of his current work, on bar napkins. *Exorcism,* he remembered Lehrling's advice. He wrote another one:

> Through twilit nights my love still soars.
> I am forever and ineffably yours.

He crumpled it up at once and ordered another beer. What good was poetic exorcism if it didn't exorcise? Perhaps Locke's love was so great it could *never* be exorcised. Perhaps his love for Clare would be in his heart forever.

Every now and then he craned around. Couples holding hands. Couples kissing. Couples in love. Was the whole world in love tonight? Even Lehrling was making it; the art school girl had her arm around him!

> Kissing couples, holding hands,
> passions swirl in glee.
> Everyone's in love tonight,
> everyone but me.

Forlorn asshole.

Could anything feel this bad? The beer entombed him in regret. If he had no feelings at all, then at least he could cope with himself. But how do you get rid of feelings? How do you *kill* your feelings?

"How do you kill your feelings?" he muttered aloud.

"Wish I knew," a voice muttered back.

Locke's gaze flinched up. It was White Shirt. He'd come back from the john to find his barstool gone. He stood next to Locke at the rail, pasty in inebriation. "God on high, I wish I knew."

Locke launched into more scribbling:

> Once upon my love,
> once upon my glee,
> once upon the resplendent promise
> of all we were meant to be.
> God on high, forgive my grief,
> and kill my feelings—I beg of thee.

White Shirt stared crosseyed at the bar napkin. "A poet, huh? That's not bad."

It sucks, Locke augmented.

"But I don't think God does stuff like that, do you?"

Locke shrugged.

"If there even is a God. Well, I'm pretty sure there is." White Shirt wobbled in place. Carl had stopped serving him an hour ago. Some goateed guy on the other side got up and left. White Shirt began drinking what was left of his beer. "My girlfriend broke up with me." Then he paused to stare up at the rows of pewter beer-club mugs hanging from hooks on the ceiling rafters. "I still love her."

Locke didn't want to hear this drunken carbon copy of himself spout his sorrows. Was love relative? Was grief?

White Shirt gulped, digging in his pocket. "We were going to get married. She gave me the ring back last week." He opened his palm to reveal the ring. "Fourteen hundred bucks. Can you *believe* that? I must be the sucker of time immemorial." Then he leaned forward and pitched the ring into the waste can behind the bar.

Locke's brow elevated, but he said nothing. It wasn't any of his business.

"Yeah," White Shirt bumbled on. "I wish I could kill my feelings, all right. Love's a killer." He gulped again and staggered away, in search of more abandoned beer.

Love's a killer.

Locke tore the poem to shreds.

"Hurry up please, it's time!" Carl shouted, quoting T.S. Eliot as an announcement of last call.

Time, Locke thought. He scribbled:

> Time means nothing,
> time means nothing to me.
> Heralds in ashes, heralds of love,
> vagrant angels peering to me
> the poet in his shroud of feelings,
> his extant heart, and fallow amour.
> I mean nothing.
> I mean nothing to her anymore.

Lehrling, who was still making time with the art student, turned and rolled his eyes at Locke. "I don't believe you, man. When I told you you gotta write about it, I didn't mean *here, now.* Only dejected idiots write poetry on bar napkins."

"I'm a dejected idiot," Locke mumbled.

"What's wrong with your friend?" asked the girl from the art college.

"Don't ask," Lehrling replied. He leaned closer to Locke. "Stop moping. You're supposed to be having a good time."

He was having a good time, all right. *I mean nothing to her anymore,* he thought. Was *that* the realization of truth that would end his despair, that would exorcise him? Was that what he'd been refusing to admit for the last three months?

Locke wanted to cry.

"Last call for alcohol!" Carl shouted. Lehrling seemed disgusted with Locke. "You want a last beer?"

"I want Clare back," Locke said, chin in hand. "That's all I want."

"He looks so sad," offered the art student, with doleful brown eyes beneath blonde bangs.

Lehrling frowned. "He's just drunk. He doesn't listen to advice, he'd rather mope."

"I still love her," Locke warbled. The beer had caught up times ten. The world tipped. "I'd do anything to get her back."

"Cheer up," the girl said. "Maybe you can work things out."

"Don't even say that," Lehrling complained. "You'll get him going again."

Work things out. Right. I mean nothing to her anymore. She doesn't want to work things out—because she doesn't want me.

Locke made to stand and started to fall over. Lehrling, swearing, caught him. "It was nice meeting you," the art girl said to Lehrling. "I can see you've got your hands full with your friend, so maybe we better get together another time."

Lehrling, still propping up Locke, looked frantic. "No—wait, I—"

"'Bye," bid the art girl, and walked out of the bar.

Lehrling ground his teeth. "Thanks, buddy! Thanks a lot! She was going to go home with me."

"Sorry," Locke blundered. "What do you think Clare's doing right now?"

"Just shut up, you drunk horse's ass." Lehrling helped Locke out of the bar. He led him out the back way, into the parking lot along Meridian, then propped him up against the brick wall. "Listen to me, Locke. You've got to get your shit together. You're letting this Clare business turn you into a perpetual fuck-up."

Locke tried to mouth a response, gave up, and nodded.

"You can't let a woman ruin you. You've got to face facts. It's all over. Live with it. Move on."

"Yeah," Locke managed.

"We'll talk about it tomorrow, you're too drunk now. Get in the car, I'll take you home."

Locke glanced at Lehrling's Volante. His drunken vision made the sleek car look warped. "No, I'll walk. I need the air."

"You sure?"

"Yeah, it's just down the street." The cold air began to revitalize him. "And sorry I messed things up with the art girl."

"Don't worry about that." Lehrling opened the car door. "Call me tomorrow."

"Sure."

Locke remained propped against the wall as Lehrling drove off. The car sounded like a purring animal. A few minutes later the lot was empty.

He hated being drunk; it made him feel defenseless against himself. The cold air bit into him, but he didn't feel it. He felt warm, instead, warm and prickly in despair. He gazed out into the open night and realized that Clare was out there somewhere, oblivious to him. The notion made him feel nonexistent.

Maybe I'll go home and kill myself, he thought almost frivolously. It wasn't a serious thought—suicide was for dopes, and, besides, he didn't have a gun. But still, the thought had surfaced, and he had to wonder why. Moonlight bulged in his eyes. *Love's a killer,* he recalled White Shirt's manifesto. Locke thought about that.

Instead of walking toward home, an unknown penchant urged him to stagger back down 45th, away from home. *Where am I going?* came the clear question. *I don't know.* A quest for more alcohol? Maybe. Concannon's set last call ten or fifteen minutes early—"bar" time as opposed to Pacific Standard. Drunks often manipulated this, Locke knew. But he also knew that wasn't the reason...

It was something else that drew him in the illogical direction. Was it a presage, then? An intuition? Locke didn't believe in any of that. But then—

He stopped, afret, at the corner next to a long-since-closed Chinese carry-out called Fuji's. Footsteps snapped in his ears. He passed a comics shop, its dead front window sporting a sign: GOON ACTION FIGURES! ONLY $50! *I'll pass,* Locke thought. Again, without a logical acknowledgment as to why, he ducked behind the brick corner, let his eyes survey the street. Light rain pecked at his head; it ruined the scope of his vision into a mural of tiny slits. There was another bar down here, wasn't there? *I've lived here all my life. I should know, shouldn't I?*

Yes, there was another bar—well, a "wine bar" really, some nose-in-the-air pinkie-raising joint called The Cellar. Got lots of great reviews in the *Post-Intelligencer* and *The Stranger.*

Locke didn't get the big deal with wine. Crushed and rotten grapes were cool? He didn't think so. They also served *foi gras* on lemon grass toast points, and quail tenders in mustard-sorrel sauce. *Give me a Dick's Deluxe and a beer,* Locke thought, still unable to gauge what notion had brought him here.

But then he knew...

Maybe *God* had urged him out here. White Shirt had said he believed in God, hadn't he? But if so, then what kind of sense of humor did God have?

For when Locke peered through the rain, the first thing he saw was this: Clare hand in hand with some guy...

Some guy in a brown suede leather longcoat, short dusky blonde hair, a primped goatee. Skinny, almost svelte; black silk shirt and black slacks. Locke almost hurled. *What? She dumps me for some wussy eurofag lawyer? Fuck! This guy's middle name must be Creamcake!* Probably one of the goddamn associates in her firm. Probably just a paralegal himself, spending all his money on clothes...

But then his gaze focused more sharply, onto Clare herself.

The white blonde hair a little shorter, the same aqua/white cotton tank dress she'd worn on their first date—a simple ferry ride across the sound to Bainbridge Island—and an apricot talbard coat. And—

And the same Bvlgari earrings I bought for her on Valentine's Day!

But none of that—none of the primal jealousy or meat-head ex-boyfriend covetousness—mattered, when he looked a bit harder...

And it all came back.

Still...so...beautiful...

How could he describe this? How could he ever define it to himself? It was his whole world walking across that street right now, a completion of everything that meant anything at all...

It was his truth.

I still love her...

They crossed the street, obviously having just had their fill of fussy and motherfucking gooseliver on toast. The blonde guy was saying something, then Clare tossed her head and laughed. Her face *glowed*—Locke knew, with the same love it used to glow for him.

But not anymore.

This guy was the wine-snob, caviar-eating hump she'd left him for? The primordial instincts poured in. *What's he got that I don't have? Why'd she dump me for him?*

More, more.

Is he better than me? Is he a better lover?

What was the catch?

Then he saw it.

They sauntered to the corner, oblivious to the drizzle, then they stopped. The blonde dork whipped out his keys, then opened the passenger door to a cherry-red Corvette LT-5, fifty-grand worth of wheels. He slipped in, then they were driving away down 45th, Clare's hair shimmering in the drag.

Locke backed up, stunned. That was it, wasn't it? *That's what it always boils down to*... Not love. Not faithfulness or endearment.

It's money! It's cars! It's suede leather coats, wine, and black silk shirts!
All an antithesis to everything Locke held sacred.

But the vision, the glimpse of her, blinded him. *I'm a fuckin' poet who works a day a week at a goddamn bookstore…* The real world was material, and that excluded him exclusively. *What woman in her right mind would want to spend the rest of her life with a penniless fool?*

Yeah, cars and cash—that was reality, and why shouldn't it be? Locke didn't have any of the things that real people wanted, so—

Why should she want me?

It all dragged him down, further than ever before. Maybe he was just full of shit. Was his perception of truth just a selfish impulse? Locke looked down the wet street again—the red Corvette was gone, and so was Clare—but all he saw was the long black avenue of his failure.

He had to face it. He'd never add up. Not in *this* world.

He stood for several more minutes, sucked in the cold night air and the clouds calmly spitting on him. The city was abed; the houses along the side streets stood black. Black shadows pooled across the parking lot.

Locke walked back the other direction, toward where his half-soused brain told him was his apartment. Concannon's was kicking people out. When Carl said Last Call, he wasn't fooling around. Locke hiccoughed, then stumbled around the corner and crossed the parking lot. *Just get your drunken ass home!* he thought. His balance slipped, equilibrium short-changed. He almost fell when his foot buffeted a curb slab.

"Drink much, Locke?" he asked aloud.

He'd only taken a half dozen steps across Concannon's emptied parking lot when he heard someone say: "Hey."

He'd been wrong, the lot *wasn't* empty. A single car remained parked in the corner, in rain-spotted darkness.

"Yeah?" Locke called out. The dismal weather seemed to suck all the vitality from his voice. "Who's that?"

"Come here, I need to talk to you."

In any city you don't approach faceless voices at night, not that Locke had any money for muggers. But he felt no fear. Was it his drunkenness, or an insight?

Another step and he made the car: a shiny black Firebird, one of those Formula models; its waxed lacquer hood looked like polished obsidian. Locke's eyes adjusted in the pallor of the streetlight.

Sitting at the wheel was White Shirt.

"Figured it out yet?"

"Figured *what* out yet?" Locke queried. Suddenly his curiosity overwhelmed his inebriation. His face smacked of the wet cold.

"How do you kill your feelings?" White Shirt looked past Locke's shoulder, at the moon. "I know the answer. God just whispered it to me, just now. Think I'm lying?"

Locke was insensate. "What's the answer?"

"Transposition, man."

"What?"

"Metamorphosis."

Christ. Reason snapped back, and maybe even a trace of sobriety. "Hey, you're pretty drunk. You should call a cab."

White Shirt ignored the comment. "You still love her, don't you?"

Locke stalled in the cold. White Shirt must've deduced his plight by reading the poems he'd written on the napkins. "Yes," he eventually said.

"I know the feeling. That's the transposition. That's the link, I guess."

The link?

The darkness rose again in Locke's heart, like the darkness which now idled about White Shirt's head.

An aura. A black aura.

"That's what makes the two of us the same."

Locke stared.

"And we want to know how to make it go away, don't we? We want to know how to kill our feelings."

Locke's heart seemed to seize. His joints locked up.

"I can show you."

Locke didn't know from guns. He only knew that the gun White Shirt was suddenly pointing at him was *huge*. The giant tarnished revolver looked like it weighed ten pounds. Locke thought he could've stuck his entire thumb into the end of the barrel and there'd still be play.

"Don't move, Locke. Listen."

Even in the swift, bracing terror, Locke caught the illogic. "How do you know my n—"

"I'm not sure what this is about. It's… funny," White Shirt seemed to muse to him. "'Heralds in ashes, heralds of love. Pewter mugs dangle up above like the hasp on my soul's broken lock.'"

Then White Shirt smiled.

Locke remembered the beer-club mugs hanging from the ceiling over the bar. He remembered how White Shirt had been staring at them…

"It's kind of like that," White Shirt said next. "But this isn't a herald, Locke. It's a portent. A warning, I guess."

"A *warning*?"

White Shirt's arm didn't waver against the big revolver's weight. His eyes gleamed like diamond chips. "Love is a great power, did you know that?" He chuckled. "Of course you do. But it's also like a summons. It calls to things. It calls to things that are alike. Doesn't matter if they're good or bad—you know what I mean? Maybe it's primordial or genetic. I don't know. It just calls to things that are alike."

Locke's eyes felt stapled open. "What things?" he asked.

"Sometimes wonderful things. And sometimes the worst things you could ever imagine."

Lunatic, Locke realized. *Madman.* This guy was going to kill him. Locke figured his only chance was to drop to the ground and try to roll...

White Shirt cocked the pistol, as if he'd sensed the calculation. The click of the hammer sounded like a piece of tinder snapping.

"People are whispering to me," White Shirt informed him. "That's part of the summons. They're using me, I suppose. 'Into heaven or the saddest realm of nether... my love for you goes on forever.'"

Impossible. The poem he'd written yesterday, and had later thrown out. How could White Shirt possibly quote a poem he'd never seen?

"Arrivals," the gun-wielder went on. Behind them another ambulance roved slowly down the street, its lights throbbing but its siren off. "He's coming, Locke." The gleam in White Shirt's diamond eyes flicked out. "He's coming soon."

"*No!*" Locke lurched forward and yelled.

White Shirt, his face touched by the saddest smile, plugged the gun barrel into his left ear, and—

"*Jesus Christ don't do it, man!*"

—squeezed the trigger.

BANG!

The bullet made its exit through the right temple, and in the process evacuated the entirety of White Shirt's skull, leaving hanks of brains and viscera pasted to the passenger side of the car's plush Scotch-Guarded interior.

EIGHT

THE SECOND
ARRIVAL

(i)

The new dawn left him awash in light the color of despondency: death-like, pale, drained. North Precinct Homicide Captain Jack Cordesman stepped onto the coaming of the 24-foot cabin cruiser called WE'RE AWEIGH. Another 64; they always got them early in the morning. TSD floodlamps blazed in the entrance, behind intent shadows. Cordesman went down the short steps of the companionway, then stopped, forced to glance down at the atrocity. *What kind of a world is this?* he thought.

"Kenneth Parker Ubell," the uniformed first responder told him. "Also known as 'Wire.' We been looking for this fucker a long time."

"What, he's skell?"

"Scumbag across the board, sir. Word is he's pinching for the fences in south county. Done county time on a GTA and a stint in the state cut—multiple counts of armed burglary. ID'd him through the latent datalink in my car. Hell of a machine, Captain."

Technology. Wonderful. A Hair & Fibers guy was studiously vacuuming the carpet, while another fumed for latents around the forward cabin. But Cordesman was still staring, still not quite sure how this thing at his feet could be human.

The uniform prattled on. "Got about ten outstanding warrants. A dust burnout according to our squeals; used to deal coke before the Jamakes moved in, and the word is he snuffed two of our inside stools on the DEA jam we had going a couple of years back. World's better off without him you ask me."

So the guy was skell. Fine. *What goes around comes around.* But what had happened? Who had done... *this?*

The smell was extraordinary. Cordesman hadn't smelled anything like it since that time the Jamakes had left a couple of movers hanging upside down in a project laundry room. Bellies slit open. Guts on the floor. Cordesman pitied the janitor. The odor spiked him: fresh offal, excrement, fresh blood. Kenneth Parker Ubell, alias Wire, or what was left of him, lay nude upon his side. His innards had been expeditiously hauled out of his abdominal cavity, as though someone had been searching for something lost among the crowd of organs. The cabin had been decorated; Cordesman thought of a high school party adorned with crepe paper, only in this case the crepe paper was the majority of the small intestine, hanging from the low ceiling. The rest had been thrown around. And his head... his head...

"Somebody did the job on this guy," the uniform remarked.

"Even bad guys have bad days." Cordesman surveyed the cramped cabin, careful not to step past the evidence line. Wire's clothes lay aside, unbuttoned, not torn. "I don't like the clothes."

"Sir?"

"I mean what the fuck happened here? What, this guy was busting onto the boat for stuff to pinch, then somebody caught him? Suddenly the perp's the victim? And why take off his clothes?"

"He was raped," a tight, nasally voice answered.

The figure aft turned. It was Jill Brock, Deputy Superintendent of Technical Services, a.k.a. Evidence Section. She wore booties, acetate gloves, and a hairnet, to prevent erroneous fiberfall from contaminating the crime sector. "Good morning, Captain," she added.

Cordesman made a face. "What do you mean *raped*?"

"The crime of forced sexual intercourse without consent."

"I know what rape means, Jill. Usually it's women who're raped, not guys."

Jill Brock shrugged. She was skinny, bony, pallid. "Changing times, sir. You ever walked through Broadway? I'll bet a lot of the fellas there would turn you on. This guy's an ex-con. Lots of 'em get turned in the joint."

"How do you know he was raped?"

"Non-reflexive rectal dilation, giveaway sign. Happens a lot in the bigger cities and the state cuts. Washington, Baltimore, your old stomping grounds. Death by asphyxia, choked to death during the act. You want to see his asshole, Captain?"

"No thanks. I gotta drive."

"My guess is he was working with a partner. The partner turned on him during the job."

"Come on, Jill," Cordesman objected. "His partner *sodomized* him and then tore him up into a cold cut platter?"

Again, Jill Brock shrugged.

"Any prints?"

"All over the place, sir," she said, grasping a CRP portable ultraviolet spotter. "Got a lot of funny fall too, long red pigmentation, along with some kinks. Ask the owners if any redheads or number ones have been on the boat. I'll run the jizz, the prints, and the scale-counts fast as I can, and cross-reff them through the department intranet. And another funny thing, no tool-marks on the lock."

Cordesman looked at her warped. He wasn't buying the "partner" rap. Wire was skell, but he was smalltime. "And what about his head, Jill?" he inquired. "What happened to his head?"

"That's the weirdest part, obviously. I've never seen a cranial insult anything like this. Don't know what kind of thing could pry off the top of a man's skull. The point is his brain's gone."

"His *what* is… *what?*"

"His brain's gone," Jill Brock matter-of-factly repeated.

"You mean blown out?"

"No sir. There's no gunshot evidence. Somebody took his brain."

Cordesman needed a drink. Yeah, a Fiddich, rocks. Make that two. He'd quit years ago but right now he wished he hadn't. He stared openly at her, and at the revelation. "Jill, people don't take brains. They take exams, they take vitamins, they take vacations. But they don't *take brains*."

Jill Brock shrugged. "Tell that to this guy, Captain. 'Cos somebody sure as hell took his."

(ii)

Wire's brain tasted exquisite.

(iii)

Stillness had settled on the Sound. Fog lay upon its waters like a fallen cloud, obscuring the shore. The sweet, stagnant smell of the bay lulled him, along with the droning, vibrating diesels. A raw mist chilled his face. It made him shiver under his foul-weather jacket, his nerves on edge, he felt coiled like a high-tension spring.

Something set his senses on high.

Not too much longer…

It was 9 p.m., 2100 to the military. Their course lay towards the Ballard Bridge and the Fisherman's Terminal, just south of Golden Gardens. The lights of the homes on Sunset Hill shone as clearly as any beacon drawing the *Betruger* to Elliot Bay. As they neared the mark, he could see the light reflecting from Harbor Island with its smoking chimneys spewing and glowing smelters, and downtown Seattle with the huge Christmas star in place on the old Fredrick & Nelson's, and finally, their destination, the festive string of lights that delineated the Terminal.

With the buoys a hundred feet on the *Betruger's* stern, Jason brought the starboard engine to idle. A distant green light swung past his bow. The *Betruger* was in the bay. Looking up at the Ballard Bridge they took a left into the terminal. Twenty minutes later, he guided the vessel to the dock with the engines alone. The captain of a passing ferry gave a noncommittal wave as his passengers gawked at the immense and exorbitant yacht that was coursing along. The ship slowed to a dead stop in front of the marina's north "t." With the forward starboard engine thrusters, Jason closed the gap between the bow and the pier. Anna, about as talkative as she always was, tossed a hauser to the dock girl. Jason got a good look: short honey-colored hair and tan muscular legs made him wonder just how long it had been since—

Well, last night didn't really count, did it?

Dreams didn't count...

The *Betruger* fought against the aft thruster as it forced the stern near the dock. Anna was setting spring lines while Jason wondered about how to get into the dock girl's pants. The way he felt now, he'd have more luck; Anna wasn't biting. In fact, she'd weirded out for the whole trip, barely said a word. But the entire trip *was* weird, Jason had to admit. Sometimes you just felt things, and this had never felt right at all.

Lethe.

Fuckin' weirdo, Jason had no problem articulating. *His money's green, sure, but what kind of guy hires you to take his one-point-five-mil yacht up the coast, says he'll meet you at the marina, but doesn't even leave a number so you can call when you pull into the dock?*

A fuckin' weirdo, that's who.

Oh, well. Why worry? They were tied up now, they'd arrived at their destination, and there was no sign of Lethe on the pier. *I wonder how long we'll have to wait for this screwball?*

«« — »»

He drained the last of his Beck's in the galley. His watch read quarter of eleven. *Women,* he thought. *They take forever and a day.* But, hell, he'd given her enough time; he rapped twice on Anna's cabin door. Nothing. He held his breath, but all he heard was the sound of his own pulse. "Anna?" he called. "We better get topside. Your gear ready? I'm sure Lethe'll be here any minute—it's getting late."

Nothing.

"Anna?"

No running shower, no hair dryer, nothing.

He knocked again and gently opened the door. The cabin was dark, the bed made. *She ain't here. She's already topside, and I'm standing here talking to a friggin' door!*

A soft red light escaped from under the door to the master cabin. Jason could hear a soft rustling noise. *Why would she be in here?* he wondered, then he gently opened up the cabin door. "Anna, what are you doing in here? Looking for Focke Wolfs? Come on, getten zee lead out," he tried to joke. But—

The joke ended when he looked ahead.

A single glimpse showed him the steel crate. Its lid, somehow, had been pushed off, and then another glimpse showed him what was inside.

The veneered, dark wood. The plush white pillowed interior. The lined lid cocked open—

Footstand, my ass! That's a coffin!

But what his *next* glimpse showed him was infinitely worse.

Sprawled across the floor lay Anna. Her long blonde hair lay spread around her head, a macabre halo. Someone in a white suit crouched over her...

Anna's limbs twitched as her glassy eyes stared past the ceiling.

"What in God's name..." Jason muttered.

The head of the figure in white jerked up. A shock of salt and pepper hair hung across the sharp planes of his face. Black eyes bore into Jason's own.

Lethe smiled, blood ringing his mouth.

Anna's T-shirt was sopped with blood, pasting the material wetly to her breasts. More—fresher—blood eddied in feeble pulses from her gnawed-open throat. Even in the red light, she looked anemic.

Rage launched Jason forward. He charged Lethe, raising the first thing in hand's reach, a small fire extinguisher. "You fucker! So help me God I'm gonna split your head!" he promised, then caught Lethe squarely in the temple with the extinguisher, behind a good, hard swing. The impact made a tuned *crack!* Lethe's head snapped back violently.

Then he looked at Jason and laughed.

Jason rammed a right so hard his hand hurt. Lethe's head snapped back again, and then he laughed again.

A blurred backhand sent Jason flying into the port bulkhead; air and spittle exploded out of his mouth.

Jason's mind dimmed. A chuckling could be heard.

Christ. I gotta get outa—

The hands which next ringed his throat felt like an iron collar. Jason's vision swam as the pain became acute. His arms flailed at Lethe's head. Snapping sounds ground from Jason's throat as, very quickly, his larynx was crushed. He could taste his own blood rising from his collapsed throat, and in a surprisingly neutral sensation, he understood that he was about to die.

The protruding bones of Jason's neck emerged through his flesh, passing between Lethe's fingers. The universe closed around the vampire's face.

The next thing Jason saw was the ceiling. He could see Lethe talking but he couldn't hear the words, and he could feel blood running into his ears.

Yeah, I'm dying, he thought. *This is it, the Golden Hour. Shit...*

Lethe came back into view. His arm was wrapped under Anna's breasts, lifting her like a limp doll. His lips mouthed more soundless words.

It looked like he said *drink.*

Then he dropped Anna on top of Jason.

The soft blonde hair fell across Jason's face, her firm breasts pressed to his chest. He'd always imagined that she would feel like this, and what a thing to recall now, dying, with his throat crushed. A sensation, at any rate. Yes, a nice sensation to die to.

But then Anna's lips closed on his throat.

NINE

PARTY

Lehrling stopped out front, the rather infamous building on Third Avenue. "You go on in, I'll park the car and wait for you in the waiting room."

Locke nodded. His head ached with each nod. "What do you think this is all about?"

"It's nothing, man. Go on in."

Locke got out of the Volante and closed the door. He walked up to the Public Safety Building stepping past the trio of winos who sat passing a 40-ouncer of Rainer Ale on the steps in the futile hope that they'd be picked up for vag by one of the passing patrolmen and wind up with three hots and a cot for a few days. Locke took the elevator to the 4th floor and wandered down the hall till he came to a small sign that read in white tactile letters: SEATTLE POLICE DEPT., HOMICIDE /ASSAULT UNIT—NORTH PRECINCT, with an arrow indicating a right turn down the hall.

Locke felt weird. Walking into a police station. Just upstairs was the City jail. It was something he'd never done before. Images from TV surfaced: cops striding back and forth from the booking room, stray banter, phones ringing, typewriters clacking. A bald sergeant with a mole like the end of a finger looked blankly up from the desk.

"I'm here to see a Captain Cordesman," Locke said.

"Locke, the suicide?"

Locke didn't like the way he'd worded it. "Yes, I witnessed a suicide last night."

"Down the hall to the left," the sergeant said, looking back down at some papers.

Locke was surprised they hadn't searched him, or at least signed him in. He could be a nut for all they knew. He could have a gun or a bomb or something.

CAPTAIN J. CORDESMAN, a plaque read on a milky glass door. HOMICIDE. "Come on in," a voice invited before Locke could even knock. No doubt the room's occupant had seen his outline in the glass.

Locke entered a cramped office. A slim figure rose behind a dented desk heaped with reports. Coffee bubbled on a burner.

"I'm Cordesman," the guy said. "Thanks for coming down. Have a seat."

Locke sat, distracted. This guy was a cop? He was skinny and had hair to his shoulders, hadn't shaved this morning, either. A crumpled tie adorned a crumpled dress shirt. "Want some coffee?"

It looked like pitch percolating on the burner. "No thanks," Locke said.

"So you're a poet, huh?"

"That's right."

"Interesting." Cordesman lit a Camel, cocked a brow. "You all right? You sick?"

"I'm hungover."

The cop seemed to smile, as though remembering something. "How many did you throw back?"

"I don't know, eight beers, ten. I wasn't driving or anything."

"Always drink that much?"

Locke frowned. "No," he said. "Why?"

"Just curious. I guess all poets drink."

What was he getting at? "You called me down here to ask me how many beers I had?"

Cordesman sucked smoke. "I'm just trying to determine how accurate your sense of observation was last night. How come you didn't have a bar tab?"

"Huh?"

"A bar tab, you didn't have one. We checked."

Why would they check that? Locke hadn't done anything wrong. "A friend of mine paid."

"Lehrling. The novelist."

"Yeah."

"But he didn't see the guy kill himself?"

"No, he'd already left."

Cordesman nodded and tapped an ash. A Glenfiddich ashtray on the desk sat clogged with butts. "How well did you know Roderick Byers?"

"Who?"

"The guy, you know. The guy who killed himself."

White Shirt, Locke associated. "I never knew his name. Never saw him before."

"So you were just walking out of the lot and you happened to look and see this guy do it? At night? No lights in the lot?"

Locke was beginning to dislike the sound of this. "The streetlights were on. Didn't you check that too? And, no, I didn't just happen to notice the guy. He called me over."

"Called you over? To his car? But you just said you'd never seen him before. Didn't you say that? Just now?"

Why is this guy grilling me? Locke wondered.

"You nervous, Mr. Locke? You're sweating."

Was he? Yes, suddenly he felt icky, stuck in his own heat. "I'm hung over, like I said," Locke excused. "And I'm a little shaken up."

Cordesman tittered without smiling. "Understandable. Who wouldn't be, I mean, after seeing a friend commit suicide?"

"He wasn't a friend. And when I said I hadn't seen him before, I meant I hadn't seen him before last night."

"Ah." Cordesman crushed out the Camel and fired up another. He pushed strings of his long brown hair off his brow. "Just tell me everything that happened."

It felt grueling to replay the scene to himself. He told Cordesman how he'd noticed White Shirt and the girl arguing in the parking lot, and later how White Shirt had told him that the girl broke off their engagement. "So after the bar closes, I'm walking across the lot to go home, and he calls me over to his car. That's when he killed himself."

"That's all, Mr. Locke?"

"He said some weird things. And at first he was holding the gun on me."

"Why?"

"I don't know."

"He try to rob you?"

"No."

"Then why did he hold the gun on you?"

"I don't know!" Locke shouted.

A clock was ticking. Cordesman laxed back in his chair, smoking, looking at Locke. In the window behind him, clouds engulfed the sun. "Relax, Mr. Locke. I'm not interrogating you, I'm just—"

"I know. Trying to determine the accuracy of my state of observation. Sounds like interrogation to me."

"What 'weird things'?"

"I don't know. He was drunk." But what *did* Locke remember, like exactly? White Shirt had said... *Transposition, man. Metamorphosis.* What could he have meant?

You still love her, don't you? White Shirt had asked.

It must've been his imagination. "He said something about portents, warnings. He was drunk, and I don't remember it all too well. I was drunk too."

"Portents. Warnings." Cordesman seemed to fix something to that. "What kind of gun did he have?"

Locke rolled his eyes. "Look, Captain, I'm a poet, not a gunsmith. All I know is it was a gun. And it looked big, bigger than the ones in the movies."

"It was big, all right," Cordesman explained. "A Webley .455, an antique. The British manufactured them for their officers in the Boer War, they wanted a sidearm that could take out a drug-crazed native with one shot. Fires a bullet half an inch wide."

"I'm edified in knowing that," Locke said.

Cordesman then laughed mirthlessly. "I guess if you're going to kill yourself, that's the piece of hardware for the job."

Locke felt cruxed, irritated. Sweat trickled at his armpits.

"Parity," Cordesman said. "Do you know what parity means?"

Locke eyed him. "It's a connotative noun that means equivalence or resemblance, in status, nature, amounts, things like that."

"Exactly. Similitude, right?"

"Yeah."

"Well, there's a parity here, Mr. Locke, a *similitude*. There often is when a violent death is involved. And I think you're aware of this parity, but you're not mentioning it for some reason."

"I don't know what the fuck you're talking about, Captain," Locke said.

"Byers was a poet."

Byers. Locke still had trouble with the association. His name wasn't Byers to Locke, it was White Shirt. But—

A poet?

"I didn't know that," Locke eventually said.

"No?" Cordesman lit yet another Camel. If he didn't get to the point shortly, he'd die of lung cancer right here in the office. "He was a professor of English at Evergreen State. Had several dozen books of poetry published. Hardbacks."

Locke kind of crinkled his nose. *Probably just little college hardcover house, and small-press publishers.*

"Random House," Cordesman added. "For a poet, this guy Byers was a big gun. No pun intended. Big reviews in the *New York Times,* the *Post's Bookworld,* all that. Gotta $50,000 advance for his last book. Sounds like pretty good money to me. You get that kind of money for your poetry, Mr. Locke?"

Locke crinkled his nose some more. "No."

Cordesman nodded. "Strange, though, isn't it? The guy's a big-name poet, and you've never even heard of him."

"What's a big name? Poetry is poetry." Locke couldn't help but add, "And $50,000 advances for poetry books are very atypical."

"Still, it's weird. You didn't know him, yet he called you to the car to tell you something. How do you account for that?"

"I can't account for it."

"It's almost like he waited for you. He waited for you *specifically*. To tell you 'weird things.' My question is this, Mr. Locke. Why? Why you?"

"I told you, I don't know. And what's this got to do with parity?"

"Byers was a poet. You're a poet. Byers' girlfriend recently broke up with him. Didn't your girlfriend recently break up with you?"

Locke stared at him.

"I'm an investigator," Cordesman replied to Locke's stare. "I investigate death, and any potential detail surrounding death. It's my job, Mr. Locke. I ask around."

Locke, at once, felt trespassed upon, molested.

"Clare something, right?" the policeman continued. "A paralegal?"

"What's my private life got to do with the suicide?"

"Parity, remember?"

Locke continued to stare.

"You and Byers have a lot in common."

"So what?"

Cordesman gave a shrug. His crumpled tie had an embroidered half-moon on it, flecked with ashes. He smiled crookedly. "I don't know, I just have this feeling that Byers was specifically drawn to you, via similitude. Kind of weird, huh?"

"Yeah, kind of weird." *Similitude,* the thought returned to Locke's mind. His mind felt clogged, like the ashtray. Now Cordesman seemed to be looking at him in some sort of precision. "Two poets. Two jilted lovers." The cop held up a small photo of White Shirt. "Hell, you two guys even look alike."

Did they? *Bullshit,* Locke thought, and even if they did, what was the big deal? "I don't know what you're grabbing at."

Cordesman's lips pursed, as if sucking on something, a thought, perhaps. Or a conjecture. He got up, walked around behind Locke, closed the office door, and returned to the desk. A sheet of blank paper had been pinned to a cork board beside the window. The policeman lit another cigarette and returned his gaze to Locke.

"You know the old phrase. Opposites attract? Well, in my business, that's almost never true. In my business—"

"Parities attract," Locke guessed.

"Yes, and why? I think people, and their interactions, are sort of…magnetic. In lots of ways. About ninety percent of the homicides in this country are committed by perpetrators who have things in common with the victim. Same for rape. Same for most violent crimes."

"Is there a point to this?"

"Oh, there's a point," Cordesman continued without pause. "There's something in the human psyche, I think, that has a mutual effect. If you'd been investigating murders for as long as I have, you'd probably know what I was talking about."

"This wasn't a murder. It was suicide."

"Well, suicide is murder. The murder of oneself. It's still a crime. And what is crime really about? It's about the failure of personal interactions, isn't it?"

"If you say so."

"I think that people are *called* to commit crimes. Does that sound absurd? I think people are *summoned*."

Locke's throat felt parched. Hadn't White Shirt said something about a calling, a summons?

"Why did you do it?" Cordesman asked.

"If you're accusing me of murder, I think I better call a lawyer."

"No, no, I'm sorry. Byers killed himself. We n/a/a'd his hands last night, our TSD people. We've proved that he killed himself."

"Then why did you ask me why I did it?"

Smoke gushed out of Cordesman's smile. "I meant why did you write that word on the inside of Byers' windshield?"

"What word?"

"Come on, Mr. Locke. There was writing on the inside of the windshield, in blood. In *Byers' blood*."

"Well, I didn't write it."

"No?"

"No."

"Then who did?"

"He must've written it himself."

Cordesman laughed. "What? After he shot himself?"

"Why not? He could've written it before he died."

"That would be clinically impossible," Cordesman countered. "Death was instantaneous. The Webley slug created what forensic people call a counter-cou-vacuum. It sucked his entire brain out the opposite side of his head. Byers *couldn't have* written it. He was dead."

"Someone else must have, then. Between the time he killed himself and when the ambulance arrived."

"In five minutes? Christ, the hospital's just a couple of miles away from the Concannon's parking lot."

"Then when I went back inside to have the keep call," Locke guessed.

"Unlikely. We're talking minutes here, Mr. Locke. Somebody just happened to be walking by at two o'clock in the goddamn morning when you just happened to be back inside having the barkeep call the ambulance? And this somebody just says hey, that dude just blew his brains out in his car so what the hell I think I'll just write some funny word on his windshield? In his blood?"

Locke could not assess this. It was too fast, and there was too much he didn't know. "Listen, Captain, I still don't know what the hell you're talking about. I didn't write any *word* on the guy's windshield. I wasn't even aware of it."

Cordesman's keen, analytical gaze went suddenly flat. Was he disappointed? "No, Mr. Locke, I guess you didn't. Maybe you didn't. But I'd really like to know who did."

Locke sat in the silence, trying to untie the knot of feelings and questions. "What was the word?" he finally asked.

The gaunt policeman turned to the cork board, where he'd posted the blank sheet of paper. He picked up a red magic marker, which squeaked as he hastily wrote:

SCIFTAN

TEN
ENCOUNTERS

(i)

It goes on forever. Why?

I'm a monster. I'm hideous. I ate a man's brains last night and I liked it. There's something—some gravitation, some force—that wields us in some way. It's not fair, I don't understand it.

Why am I like this? Why do I do the things that I do?

I guess I'm just in one of those moods. Women get that way sometimes— ha—Maybe it's that time of the month. I'm a bitch. I want to kill.

Good and bad. Beauty and ugliness. They're words, they're relativities. Why can't I be like everybody else? I'm not allowed to be, it's my providence. We all have a providence, don't we?

The man on the boat—whose brains I ate like a rich meal—he had some money on him. I bought some clothes at a store called The Gap. Do I look pretty now? Will people look at me and say "There's a pretty girl"? Maybe. But beauty's skin deep. What a trite phrase! They wouldn't think I was pretty if they could see what I look like underneath.

I almost wish that they could.

«« — »»

I know what I'm looking for now. I've always been looking for it—something true, something real. It's my only salvation, and it never ends. Never, never… It's like the Sartre story: what we need the most—to be happy, to be free—is the one thing we can never have. Vicious cycles. I want you, you want somebody else, somebody else wants me.

I want to be loved. Don't you? Doesn't everybody? Sometimes I laugh about it, my hands outstretched to the moon at midnight, with some peon's blood running over my breasts and down my legs, making myself come with my own fingers in this black chasm that's my life. I want to be loved. But the only man on earth who loves me is the only man who has the power to destroy me. And he will. Someday he will. Because the closest feeling to love is hate.

«« — »»

Men are so stupid, even immortal ones. See, I dumped him. It was a long time ago, and he's found me and brought me here. He's got this idea in his head that when I see him again, my love will return. Stupid, stupid! Only men can conceive of stupid things like that. And when he finally realizes that my love for him is dead—

He'll kill me in the worst way imaginable.

I'm not very happy right now. Can you tell? I guess I'll go and find something to do.

Something that will make me happy.

(ii)

Locke sat at his typewriter. It was 9:00 p.m. He'd been trying to write for hours, but the only payment for his efforts was the blank sheet of paper that stared back at him from the platen. It mocked him with its intractable blankness—*Poet, where are your words...*

Uninvited thoughts drew him back to his many talks with Lehrling, who'd told him he considered "writer's block" to be the excuse of the "candy-ass dilettante" and Locke had nodded, agreeing with him. That had been a lifetime ago, when he had a muse named Clare; there had been no ending of words then, he could fill volumes, but now—

Now there was only the awful whiteness of the blank page which lolled out of the typewriter carriage, the page as empty as his life, his spirit.

He glanced out the window, the street beckoning him.

A long walk, a tall drink—something hard. The vision of a chimney glass of Tullamore Dew barged without welcome into his consciousness. He was drinking too much, or maybe not enough; but in any event the idea of staring any longer at the blank paper seemed abhorrent.

Next, he was out walking into the tepid night. He looked up at the stars. So much to see, or was there? Many saw inspiration, others—writers, perhaps—often saw their muse, while still others viewed a vast and fascinating panorama of possibilities. Like that bizarre San Diego coterie who'd seen a UFO coming to take them to a better world, but only if they killed themselves. Locke wondered what Lehrling saw when he looked up at the stars.

Dollar signs and women's phone numbers? Locke looked up and saw the moon, a baleful, malformed eye staring back at him with a cold dispassionate gaze. The stars themselves seemed empty and devoid of possibilities; just a vacant gulf that made him feel trapped and twisting in a net of isolation.

People are out there right now, he realized. *Laughing, kissing, making love...* But for Locke there was only the dull sensation of being utterly and completely alone. His future seemed behind him, a spot on the night's horizon too far away now to go back to.

Gems glimmered suddenly and he stopped. Hawberk's Jewelers, the narrow store where, in the past, he'd often stopped to peruse their selection of engagement rings. Clare had been with him once and pointed out a beautiful band with a small diamond in a heart-shaped mount. Now, of course, the store windows were blank, the window displays stripped of their true adornments until morning, leaving only the baubles and paste and slender mannequin hands with nothing on them.

The shit that's worthless, Locke thought.

Like his muse, and the way his life felt now.

The shit that no one would bother to steal.

Locke found himself across the street from Concannon's, the neon sign of a leprechaun holding a martini glass winked at him as if in recognition. *I'm so broke I can't even pay attention.* Maybe Lehrling would be there...

The tavern stood quiet for mid-evening. Only a few people sat at the bar, the lone drinkers who had lingered long past happy hour. Stockbrokers and junior partners for the most part; twelve-hour days of cocaine-driven screeching intensity followed by the usual five hours of power-drinking to mellow out and hopefully snatch a few hours of dreamless sleep before climbing back on the Sisyphean economic treadmill. A lone man stood at the dartboard, playing a solitary game; and there at one of the tables, Lehrling, and a companion...

Someone's getting lucky.

The blonde seated with Lehrling was almost a stereotype of Aryan beauty—reminding Locke of one of the girls from the beer commercial featuring "the Swedish Bikini Team"—she sat pressed against Lehrling, his arm around her and her body-language leaving no doubt that some rapport was growing which would eventually lead them both to bed later. It astounded Locke—this girl was drop-dead gorgeous, and Lehrling, though a witty enough conversationalist, was certainly no one's idea of a movie star, unless of course the movie star in question were like, maybe, Charles Grodin. Locke glanced at the mis-matched couple again and Lehrling met his gaze and nodded toward the bar making a writing motion which indicated that Locke should charge his drinks to Lehrling's tab.

What a man.

Locke returned the nod, took a seat at the table nearest the dart board to watch the solitary practitioner of the ancient game.

Carl wasn't behind the bar tonight and the waitress who took his order for a Tullamore Dew and water seemed exasperated when directed to charge his drink to Lehrling's tab. Locke sat and watched the dart player; a tall man of indeterminate middle age, dressed in a fine charcoal gray suit. He played as though the remarkable precision of the game came as naturally as breathing. Locke had played casually before counting down from 301 to hit zero exactly on a "double" got on his nerves; he'd thought it the most frustrating game he'd ever been exposed to: hit a target a quarter of an inch wide to start the game, the "double" ring and then finish by hitting the appropriate "double" to bring one's score to zero... The precision involved was maddening; that's why Locke had quit.

But now he watched the man take careful aim and throw, double twenty; a lucky first dart "on," he thought, then in rapid succession: two darts sped unerringly to the treble twenty; a "160" on...

This guy's real good or real lucky.

Immediately, Locke's interest was piqued. He watched the man retrieve his darts and quickly throw a treble seventeen, treble eighteen and then the double eighteen: a perfect game...

Christ! Locke thought.

Gathering up the darts, the man came over to Locke's table and, reaching into his pocket, produced a crumpled bar napkin and placed it in front of Locke.

"I believe you dropped this the other night, and what with the small drama that took place outside, I neglected to return it to you then. You have a rare gift for true poetry, Mr. Locke." The man spoke in a soft voice that betrayed just a hint of accent.

"Well, thank you. I'm afraid that this little snippet isn't really among my more serious works, but thanks for returning it, Mr.—"

"Lethe, my name is Lethe." The tall man proffered his hand, long piano-player fingers, a solitary onyx ring on his index finger. Locke shook hands and gestured for the man to take a seat; he was surprised by the tensile strength in the returning grip. This was not the macho-see-how-strong-I-am handshake of one of the pathetic ex-high school jocks, but instead almost a restrained, controlled strength, as though Lethe was far, far stronger than his slender frame would indicate.

"That's quite a grip you have, Mr. Lethe," Locke said smiling. "Musician or athlete?"

Lethe chuckled, "I'm glad you didn't guess woodworker or stone-mason. Actually I've a number of interests, many of which require a good deal of physical discipline, but that's not what motivated me to stop by and chat; I hadn't intended to discuss my frivolous hobbies like tae-kwan-do or the *klavier*. No, I wanted to talk to you more in my capacity of, shall we say, a patron of aesthetics. You see Mr. Locke, I'd like you to write a book."

Locke nearly choked on his drink. He'd heard of deals struck at upscale parties and writers' conventions, but this had to be some kind of weird angle. *Is this some sort of gay come-on?*

"You're a publisher then, Mr. Lethe? Which house do you represent?"

Lethe smiled and signaled for the waitress before replying, "No, no I'm not with one of the New York houses; I'm more of an aficionado of literature; particularly that in which the author is able to capture the true feelings within the human psyche. Not the crass sort of popular drivel that your friend over there churns out." He gestured dismissively towards Lehrling. "What I'd like for you to do is create a small volume of your work that I could have privately published in a suitably ornate edition for my library. There's an old fellow out on one of the San Juans that does exquisite handmade books, and has in fact prepared a few choice volumes for me previously." Lethe paused and took a sip from his drink.

"You mean a vanity press sort of thing?" Locke frowned. "Of course I'm flattered, but I really do try to focus on wider circulation, no offense intended." Locke looked over at Lehrling's table again. The blonde seemed to be doing her best to force her tongue down his throat. *How the hell does Lehrling do it?*

Lethe followed Locke's gaze and chuckled, "Well, crass commercialism and a gift of gab does seem to have some rewards, but I rather doubt what we're seeing there has the same depth and power as love, loss, and the other subjects you write so well about. I'm not basing my proposition, of course, on a single poem—I've read your work extensively."

Locke turned a suspicious brow. "Is that right? Where?"

"*Calvert, Gothic Light, Mynd.* Oh, and your 'Preceptor' piece in *The Phoenix* was exemplary, as was "Exit" in *Cosmopolitan*. Quite a lofty sale, I'd say."

Locke had sent back the $300 that *Cosmo* had paid him, but that wasn't what grabbed him at the moment. *This guy's for real,* he had no choice but to conclude. *He's read my work...*

"While I'm certainly not able to compete with Random House or Penguin," the articulate man went on, "I am rather...ample of means. Would you consider, say, $10,000 a substantial enough fee to ignore the 'wider circulation markets' for this particular project? Reprint rights, of course, revert back to you. Immediately."

Locke was stunned—$10,000 for a privately-printed limited edition! *Robert Frost and John Updike didn't get money like that!* "That's more than generous Mr. Lethe," he close to stammered, wondering if he should pinch himself awake. "I don't know what to say. I, I…"

"I know, you don't want to make any hasty decisions, and you must talk to your agent. Not to worry; there's no pressure—here, take this, as shall we say, an advance. If you decide you don't want to pursue this project, well, then just consider it a token gift from an admirer of your work." Lethe passed a small sheaf of bills across the table and rose to depart.

Locke stared at the five matching engravings of Benjamin Franklin that smiled knowingly at him from the table. *Five-hundred dollars, is this guy whacked?* Locke slowly slid the money across the table uncovering the man's somewhat old-fashioned calling card which read in stolid print:

A. Lethe
Todesfall Rd.
North Bend, WA
888-0776

A Microsoft millionaire? Locke wondered. North Bend was a small suburb to the East with incomes ranging from just above the poverty line to palatial estates that had been carved out of the bucolic countryside by the cyber geniuses of Nintendo and Microsoft. Yet North Bend was still small enough that its Post Office tolerated quaint anachronisms such as no street numbers. Perhaps this strange commission was the beginning of a turn for the better, a fresh start, a new day in his pocked life. Feeling expansive, Locke signaled the waitress to bring a round of drinks over to Lehrling and his beauteous companion. The waitress scowled at him when he gestured to Lehrling's table.

It was empty.

Oh, well, Locke thought. He looked at the money in his hand. *At least Lehrling's not the only one who got lucky tonight.*

(iii)

Lehrling groaned with pleasure and subtly shifted his position, the silken ropes that held his wrists to the bed-frame were smooth enough to preclude any chafing even if things got a bit more energetic. He couldn't believe this good fortune: he'd met the girl, Anna, only by chance at Concannon's. She'd bumped into him and dropped her wine spritzer whereupon he'd quickly taken the blame and offered to buy her another. From that point on the evening had moved along at a delirious pace that was much better than anything he could have contrived to orchestrate. The language barrier had been dissolved by the solvency of several more drinks, and Anna had begun to display such a degree of passion and enthusiasm that Lehrling thought a hasty exit from the pub to be in order.

Pay day, he thought.

He'd had lots of pay days—the "Rich Novelist" persona served him well—but this was a bit more than a typical bar floozy. This was prime turf.

Upon inviting her to his place for another drink, Anna had responded with her usual reply of "Ja ist gut!" and Lehrling had negotiated the winding drive to his Laurelhurst condo in record time. After arriving he'd barely time to mix them a couple of Champagne cocktails before she was leading him to the bedroom. Anna had apparently gone out well-prepared for a carnal frolic, from her backpack she'd produced a couple of pieces of silken cord and a small wooden paddle; she bent over and wriggled her firm buttocks at him and indicated that she wanted to be tied up and spanked. Lehrling complied with her request, though he was more than a little disconcerted by her yelps with each stroke of the paddle. It was obvious the spanking was bringing her to the point of orgasm. On about the fifteenth stroke she convulsed and shuddered, gasping "Aaah...gott!"

Kissing her on the neck, Lehrling untied the cords and made to turn her over. She quickly rolled over on top of him saying "My turn, ja?"

Uh, ja, Lehrling thought.

She scooted up on the bed, lowering a pristinely blonde muff over his face. At the same time, though, she tied his wrists to the headboard. Lehrling began lapping at her sex as she rocked back and forth on his face when...

Did he hear something? He thought he'd heard the front door open, but of course that was impossible. Not with the Arrowhead alarm system, and the motion detectors in the foyer. *The only door opening here is hers...*

He lost himself in Anna's wet musk as he felt her hand reach back and grasp his cock. She climbed off of her perch and began running her tongue up and down his chest, all the while gently tugging his erection—Lehrling closed his eyes at the tensing pleasure, reveling in the sensation of her tongue and lips traversing every inch of his chest and belly, finally coming to his groin. The lips, then, with an almost painful slowness, worked their way up the shaft, toying with him, a tease of flesh. This was exquisite torment. *Tough life, huh, Lehrling?* he joked to himself.

Then she finally took him into her mouth and began to suck...

"Now, Anna..."

Lehrling's eyes shot open at the sound of the man's voice. A tall figure stood in the doorway, features indistinguishable in the darkness; however, the shock of an intruder in his bedroom paled in comparison to the blinding white-flash pain as Anna's teeth came together and precisely bit the corona off of his penis. Lehrling jerked so violently that both wrists dislocated.

Blood gushed. The red smile showed him what she was doing...

Chewing. She was chewing his glans, vigorously, as one might chew a tough piece of clam meat.

Then, so to speak, she went back to the well, and sucked some more.

Teeth, with the exactitude of siding shears, bit off the rest of Lehrling's penis in minute increments—biting, chewing, swallowing—biting, chewing, swallowing—until nothing remained but a meager stump. All Lehrling could do, of course, was feel the pain... Coherence was long lost, nothing sapient, no human thoughts in his head, which seemed reasonable. Well, maybe just one, somewhere flitting about in the mad crush of his brainwaves...

—*she's eating my*—

But that was about it.

ELEVEN

INTERROGATION & A SOLITARY WAKE

The knock on the door startled Locke to wakefulness; he groggily threw on his bathrobe and glanced at the top of his dresser, where the money and calling card remained, fanned out like a winning poker-hand. Yes, one could be true and be financially rewarded at the same time it seemed. *Right?* he asked himself. The knock came again, jarring him from the first positive mood he'd known in quite a while.

Locke opened the door to see a grim-faced Captain Jack Cordesman, accompanied by another man whose off-the-rack coat and scuffed *Volume Shoes* loafers readily identified him as one of the hippish-detective's brethren in law enforcement.

"May we come in, Mr. Locke?" Cordesman seemed stern, distant—not much like the refined wiseacre Locke recalled from their first meeting.

"Is there a problem?" Locke was puzzled. Cordesman, in spite of his previous method-acting, had seemed satisfied that he'd had nothing to do with White Shir—er, Byers' suicide.

Why are they here?

"You're not under arrest, and we don't have a warrant, at least not yet... We would like you to get dressed and come with us, there's something we'd like you to take a look at." This from Cordesman's companion, a man who seemed completely devoid of emotion. In another setting the Jack Webb monotone would have been hilarious; in this context it seemed to possess something of a creep-factor. Locke glanced at his clock, 9:38 a.m.

"Captain Cordesman, can't you at least give me some idea what it is that you're after? I work quite late you know—"

"Work late or drink late?" the captain slipped in, one eye on the empty sheet that hung out of the typewriter.

I'm not in the mood for this. "I can juggle mangoes late and whistle

Dixie but I don't see how that's any of your business. So why don't you and
Major Hochstetter there turn around and—"

Evidently Cordesman wasn't in the mood for it, either.

"It's like this Locke, you get dressed and come with us now, freely and
of your own accord, or we'll..." The captain paused. "Let's see, how can I
say this with eloquence? Ah, I got it. We'll grab you by your hair, drag you
out of your palace, and throw your ass in the county detent with a bunch of
guys who'll just be tickled pink to have a real live poet in with 'em to help
the time go by. Those fellas will make you go through every verse of 'Old
MacDonald' from quack-quack to moo-moo before they get tired of your
attributes. In the meantime, we'll be processing your arrest report."

"Oh, yeah? For what?"

"First-degree murder," Cordesman said.

«« — »»

The journey in the unmarked prowler was short and uneventful, other
than the terse introduction of the second man as "Detective Kerr." Both
policeman maintained a stony silence as they headed east on 45th past
Concannon's, past the University, to the winding streets of the Laurelhurst
neighborhood. Locke had a sinking feeling that he knew what the ultimate
destination would be... His suspicion was confirmed as they pulled onto
Lehrling's cul-de-sac.

It was a frenzy of activity, three squad cars, a plain vehicle with city
plates, and a camera crew from one of the local stations. Locke was
reminded of scurrying ants racing about a pile of spilt sugar or roaches surprised by a sudden burst of light.

"What is it, what's happened here? Is it Lehrling? Has there been some
kind of accident?" Locke was suddenly very concerned for his friend.

"We thought you might be able to tell us, buddy," Kerr said.

"Oh, give me a break!" Locke exploded. "Is Lehrling dead?"

Cordesman looked back, a brow cocked. "Why would you guess that?"

Locke felt astonished by this outrage. "Well, for starters, you just
implied I was about to be arrested for murder, and for seconds, we're pulling
up in Lehrling's fucking driveway. So I guess it's reasonable to assume—"

"I was merely citing an abstract possibility, in order to gauge your initial, emotive reaction," Cordesman blandly replied and refaced the window.
"Thus far, I'm not sure how to judge them...which is disturbing."

Locke exploded again. "You fucking mind-game, Gestapo mother-
fuckers can't—"

"Just come with us," said Cordesman.

The car jerked to a halt, then Locke was being led out. The threesome made their way quickly through the crowd of gawkers and newspeople, to the front door of the building with the ominous "Crime Scene" barricade flanked. Two granite-faced uniformed cops stood guard.

The sinking feeling of certainty had already settled hard into Locke's gut. The book offer last night and the inexcusable (and probably actionable) manner by which Cordesman had treated him were blocked out. Locke, in slow dread, ground his teeth, forcing himself to think about nothing.

An odd, slim woman with dark frizzed hair came out the front door. She carried a black bag with the Seattle PD Criminalistics insignia on it, and she looked shell-shocked, even pasty—that or sleep was an infrequent venture.

"Captain, you're not taking a civilian up there, are you?" She looked at Cordesman with and expression of deep concern.

"'Fraid so, he might know something about this, and we can't be sure till we see how he reacts," Cordesman remarked brusquely as the trio pushed past and started up the stairs.

"I've never seen Jill act that way before," said Kerr. "Shit, I've seen her eating lasagna while she's got a three-week floater out on the slab next to her."

"Yeah, and that bothers me too," Cordesman noted.

Another uniform stood at the door to Lehrling's townhouse. Even before they entered, the stench of wrongness, of violent death, hit Locke like a sharp jab to the solar plexus. *God almighty...*

Bracing himself for what waited behind the door, he steeled his nerves and allowed the detectives to guide him almost gently into Lehrling's abode. *God al—*

It was worse than anything he could've imagined... The horrific stink emanated from a sheet that had been draped over the loveseat as a slipcover. A huge shape of dried blood encrusted the sheet, along with ample urine and feces. Saving that, the living room was relatively undisturbed. Lehrling's somewhat ostentatiously handmade book-shelves containing proofs and first printings of all his books stood unmolested, as did his shelves containing valuable first editions by other authors—Crews, Taylor, Tessier, and the like. It was the small bedroom upstairs that provided a vision into a demonic abattoir...

No.

Lehrling's head had been impaled on one of the bedposts, one eye staring sightlessly at them as they stood at the doorway, the other transfixed on the bedpost, fluid leaking slowly to pool on the floor. His hands and forearms were still tied to the headposts by silken cords. They'd been severed just above the elbows. Locke struggled to keep from vomiting, he probably could've held it in had he not glanced down at the body lying just inside the doorway; the body with the chest cavity open and empty, and the horrible wound to the groin; it looked like the whole area had been gnawed on...

Cordesman watched Locke very raptly. "Mr. Locke? I'm sorry about this, but..."

The area of space that had once been occupied by Lehrling's genitals now revealed nothing more than a ragged void of flesh. In a haze Locke dimly heard Cordesman reciting, "—man teethmarks are all over the corpse, and, uh... Jill, would you be so kind?"

The pale woman with the headful off kinky split-ends had just returned with an acrylic clipboard. On the clipboard, Locke noticed at once, was Lehrling's driver's license and gekkoskin wallet in a plastic evidence bag.

"Something worth adding," Cordesman said. "Lehrling's tongue isn't in his mouth anymore."

Locke wobbled, his knees threatening to give...

"The dentoid patterns, as Captain Cordesman has just told you, are human." A distinct eeriness—or a sinus problem—exuded with the woman's discourse. "All dentoid patterns, similarly, will leave salivary evidence. In this case, we used a traxelene field test. Traxelene, simply put, is a genetically-engineered dye that, when in contact with saliva, will register molecular traces of primary salivic enzymatic activity."

Locke could barely hear her, and could barely understand what she was saying. He did notice, however, small smears of some mock-bluish dye-like substance on various areas of Lehrling's corpse.

—salivic enzymatic—

The blanched woman went on, her nasally tone irritating as nails on slate. "What this means, Mr. Locke, is that the perpetrator apparently consumed the victim's penis—"

Dazed as he may have been, this slapped Locke in the face. He jerked the line of his sight to meet hers. He was speechless.

"The presence of primary enzymes, is what she means." Cordesman again, fingering an unlit Camel. "If you bite something when you're not hungry, those enzymes won't be there. Get it?"

No. Locke did not get it. He felt too traumatized to get anything except *out*—

"That's what leads us to seriously suspect that the decedent was subjected to anthropophagic acts," the woman added.

"That means cannibalism, Mr. Locke."

Locke just kept staring.

More: "—sliced him open, then commenced with the manual extraction of major organs, such as the liver, pancreas, spleen. We found part of the liver on the front steps."

"Abstraction, Locke," Cordesman was insightful enough to add.

Then Kerr, not so insightful: "Looks like whoever did this ate their fill and didn't want to bother taking home a doggy-bag."

As Locke fell to his knees, what was left of last night's dinner came rushing up from his stomach to splatter on the floor. He looked up at the ceiling where a solitary word had been written in a mahogany blend of blood and feces.

The word was *SCIFTAN*.

"Locke, hey Locke." Detective Kerr roughly helped Locke to his feet, sidestepping vomit. "Is this him? Is this Lehrling?"

"Of course it is, you flatfoot gumshoe motherfucker!" Locke properly replied. "He was my best friend! He was like a brother! And you know fuckin' well it's him because you got his ID in an evidence bag!"

Kerr throttled back, paused a moment, as if a moment would be enough to absorb Locke's grief. "Were you with him last night?"

Locke couldn't believe what he'd seen, Lehrling dead, vigorously mutilated; these cops thinking he could've had something to do with it.

It was surreal, abominable...

"I saw him last night at the pub, he had a girl with him, but then he usually did. They were getting pretty close so I didn't go talk to them. She was real cute, a blonde, pretty young... She couldn't have done something like this, could she?" Locke needed answers, reassurance that the whole world hadn't just turned into a sociopath's funhouse, that maybe this wasn't really happening, maybe that wasn't his best friend lying here all torn to pieces— *eaten*—by some kind of Dahmeresque creature.

"Sorry about bringing you here, Locke," Cordesman murmured, "but it's that...parity I was mentioning; people around you seem to be having really bad luck lately. Your friend for instance—well, we always say 'it's a jungle out there.' Looks like someone thought he was food..."

(ii)

A silent drive downtown then, to Cordesman's smoke-rank office. *I thought smoking was banned in all public buildings now.* More questions, to the tune of four hours' worth. Seeing Lehrling dead so abruptly was bad enough; being treated like a suspect only compounded the jagged gears of his feelings. "No rubber hose? No bright light in my face?" he asked. At this point, nothing would've surprised him. But instead Cordesman merely asked rounds of the same questions, in different sequences, while smoking perpetually and brushing his shoulder-length hair out of his eyes time and time again. *Jesus Christ, just cut your hair, will you?*

Eventually he wondered when they would ask him to take a polygraph exam, and he even wondered if they were going to advise him of his right to counsel. Gratefully, though, after crushing up one pack of Camels and opening another, Cordesman and his cohort took Locke back to the unmarked car.

"Look, I didn't have anything to do with Lehrling's murder," he nearly pleaded with them in the car. Kerr drove; his brow creased at the statement.

"So you've told us," Cordesman said, and lit yet another filterless cigarette.

"Do you believe me?"

"Of course. We just want to get your story straight. I eliminated you as a suspect the instant you walked into the crime scene. Tarsal plate fluctuation, right-left eye movement, things like that—it's the best lie detector, Mr. Locke."

Locke's backseat fury began to build up like steam. "If you eliminated me as a suspect when we got to Lehrling's, why the hell did you question me for another four hours afterwards?"

Smoke gushed in front of the long-haired head. "By making you constantly repeat your observations from different starting points, it's easier to jar something you may have forgotten. I'd think you'd *want* to assist the police in any way you can. After all, Lehrling was your best friend, or at least that's what you've claimed."

Claimed. He's damn near calling me a liar! Locke wrung his hands together, repressing himself. Figuring Cordesman out made no sense—the man seemed bent on quietly keeping Locke at odds with his own emotions.

They stopped and started along with rush hour; Locke thought they were driving him back home but was surprised when they pulled into Concannon's parking lot and got out, Kerr of the granite jaw and cheap suit, Cordesman pushing hair out of his face.

"I didn't know Seattle PD drank on duty" Locke said, a mirthless joke. "But, hell, if you're buying, I won't tell."

"We'll leave the drinking to you, Mr. Locke." Cordesman jettisoned a Camel butt. "We're just here for a little human discourse."

"Oh, you mean you're going to interrogate, manipulate, and intimidate the bar staff, maybe accuse them of murder like you did me."

Kerr glared, "Why don't you—"

But Cordesman stopped the rebuff with a flit of his hand. "No, Mr. Locke. We're merely going to make relative inquiries regarding this blonde woman you claim to have seen Lehrling with."

There was that word again—"claim"—and everything it implied. The tone bugged Locke, but so did everything about this guy, and now that he was back on familiar ground, he felt a trickle of bravado. "I ought to sue you for the way you treated me today. You goddamn cops think you're hot shit with your big bad badges and guns but I'm a *citizen*. Your job is to *protect* citizens, not *harass* them."

Kerr's glare deepened, a tint of red coming to his brow. "Captain Cordesman has the highest conviction rate of any homicide investigator on the west coast."

"He's also got the longest hair," Locke came back, "and he smokes more cigarettes, but that doesn't give him—or you—the right to shake me down—"

Cordesman bid Kerr to follow, replying but not bothering to return any eye contact. "If you feel that I or any other member of the Seattle Police Department has infringed upon your rights, Mr. Locke, then it is not only your privilege but also your responsibility to report such infringements to the Office of the Chief of Police. Feel free to take legal action too; in fact, and I strongly recommend it, in which case, of course, I would be at least temporarily removed from this investigation—"

"Sounds good to me," Locke butted in.

"—and the assailant or assailants who eviscerated and castrated your best friend would, as a result, never be caught."

Locke smirked, following them toward the ornate entrance. *He's got a pretty damn big ego.* The neon-illumed leprechaun beamed knowingly, as though in possession of the answers to the conundrums plaguing him. The electric martini winked on and off, an almost hypnotic summons to the bar, an invitation to partake of fun, festivity, and most of all forgetfulness. Locke stepped inside and was dismayed to find the Irish pub as lively as ever. No mourners for their departed comrade in evidence, not even many familiar faces. Just last night Lehrling had sat here, had joked and flirted and drank here, and was now irrevocably taken from their midst, yet no one seemed aware of it.

At least there was one familiar face.

Carl was in his usual spot behind the bar, deftly flipping a cigarette into the air and catching it in his mouth.

"Tom Cruise from hell," Locke said.

"Damn straight. Too bad I'm better-looking." But the tall barkeep's gaze thinned at notice of the police. "Those guys again. They've already grilled half the people who were on last night. Me included, and I wasn't even here."

Locke pulled up his regular stool, stealing a glance over his shoulder. Cordesman and his mascot had cornered the busboy and fry cook near the kitchen entry, Kerr scribbling in a notepad while Cordesman spewed his inquiries.

"They're back to do some more grilling." Locke ordered a Red Tail V.S.B., though he felt an atypical urge to get into some single malts. Maybe he'd have a few later.

Maybe later. Yeah, and maybe *I'm an alcoholic.*

"I take it they've been doing the same with you," Carl supposed.

"Let's just say I feel like a beef and pork combo at Toshi's Teriyaki House."

Carl drew a perfect pour from the tap and set it aside a moment, to "set." He glanced solicitously to Locke. "Still can't believe it about Lehrling. The cops give you any idea who they think did it?"

Locke shrugged. "Shit, for a while they were acting like they thought *I* did it. Maybe they still do. That son-of-a-bitch Cordesman was pulling all kinds of mind-stunts—first he tells me I'm a murder suspect, then he drags me to the crime scene because he says they need positive ID of the body, then I see some funky evidence lady with Lehrling's driver's license in a plastic bag. Which means they knew damn well who it was all along."

"Why'd he do all that?"

"Just to see how I'd *react*."

"Sounds like police harassment to me." Carl slid him the beer. "They were asking me about the blonde girl Lehrling left with. You saw her, right?"

"Have to be blind to miss *her*."

"The long-haired guy's putting it on like *she* was the killer. That 110-pound rack of angelfood cake? Right. If she's a psycho-killer, I'm gay."

Several provocatively physiqued women at the bar laughed; Locke was sure they could all make a first-hand verification as to Carl's heterosexuality.

"It sucks, though," Carl continued, simultaneously preparing oyster shooters and pouring several drafts. "Lehrling was in here all the time, almost every night—"

"He was part of the place."

"And now he's in the morgue."

Locke's mind went silent. In the morgue, yes, but not exactly complete. *In the morgue...with parts missing... Parts consumed...*

A flash in his mind's vision tried to comprehend the scene: Lehrling's body convulsing, blood blooming forth from his groin, his abdominal cavity converted to a psychopath's warehouse of delicacies, organs plucked out as if by voracious melon-pickers, evacuated with glee.

What kind of a world was this? *Not a world*, he decided. *A hock-wad of the gods. Cosmic phlegm...*

The beer, ordinarily a sweet bitter ale, turned sour with the cogitations. Drunks generally turned to their poison for solace but, just as generally, solace was the last thing they collected.

"When's the funeral?" Carl asked, snapping the images. He triple-flipped pint glasses onto the rubber-lined shelf, expert as a Pike's Place juggler.

"There isn't going to be one. Lehrling was an atheist, didn't believe in funerals." More beerside recollections trailed home. "He'd always joke about dying. Said he wants his friends to pay their respects to him here."

"Then I guess you're ready to pay more respect."

Locke glanced in a half-shock at his empty pint glass—he'd downed it in minutes. But just as he would raise his finger for another, the two policemen were standing at either shoulder.

"Can I get another beer before you cuff me?"

"We're leaving now, Mr. Locke," Cordesman announced. "Just wanted to know if you'd like a ride home."

"Thanks for the thought, Captain, but after so many hours in your polite company, please don't be offended when I say that yours is not a face I prefer to look at anymore."

"No offense taken, Mr. Locke."

"You definitely beat the clichés," Locke pointed out. "A police captain who talks about abstraction in human dynamics and has hair longer than a heavy metal roadie."

"It's true that basic ethical concepts are essentially indefinable, but they do seem to denote intrinsic, objective qualities apprehended intuitively." Then Cordesman made a gesture that was the closest thing to a smile Locke had seen. "How's this for cliché, Mr. Locke? Don't leave town anytime soon."

«« — »»

Locke meandered home, up the steps, and next found himself sitting statuesque before the window, trying to make sense of it all—this busted puzzle that was his existence...

First Clare leaving him inexplicably, now Lehrling dead—his best friend—gone... *And who was the blonde girl? She couldn't have done this, could she?* No, only some kind of monster did this thing, so what had happened to her?

Had the killer taken her?

Questions with no answers trickled on him—like the rain—as he cracked open another beer, this one from his own refrigerator—Hamm's, the Poet's Beer. $3.98 per twelve-pack. The gray early-evening drizzle had started, more of a mist actually, a clammy and cloying wetness that gradually soaked through everything. Locke was agitated, confused; what to do... *Call Lehrling?*

No, Lehrling was dead.

He glanced at the dresser, paused midsip on his beer. There it was, like a beacon calling to him from across a dangerous and rocky harbor, the business card lying neatly where he'd left it.

Lethe... He'd call Lethe. The man's offer had seemed sincere, and getting out of town, even a short distance, would be good. *To hell with*

Cordesman, he thought of the detective's order. *This ain't Iraq.* Suddenly it didn't matter anymore, considerations he'd once dwelled upon.

Writing for money. Writing *poetry*, which he viewed as the ultimate art form, in return for financial compensation. Somehow, though, he felt that he was making the right move. Why not engage his skills to keep afloat? Poe had. Blake and Shakespeare and Stevenson and Faulkner had. Perhaps financial solvency would accelerate his muse, lessening day to day worries so that he could climb out of his recent block.

Perhaps it would make him a better poet.

Yeah...

And if this were the case, then he owed it to his art to do it.

Locke never even suspected that he might be rationalizing...

He snatched up the business card, quickly punched in the numbers.

"Ja?" a female voice answered on the third ring.

(iii)

I smell it in the air, I breathe it out of the glint in your eyes. Fear and reason. Sin and redemption.

Relativity.

Human truth and the crudest clichés are all the same in a way. When you're fucking your girlfriend, striving for that "nut," what do you see when you haphazardly notice the moving shadow on the wall?

Do you see love or lust? Do you see proof of the human species as a higher order of life?

Or do you see another animal racing to dump primordial sperm into another available receptacle?

I don't know.

Do you?

They say that existence precedes essence.

I don't want to believe "they" are right.

Because I am not the only one who can breathe it out of the glint in your eyes.

There's someone else.

Someone who does it far better than I do.

(iv)

"Is Mr. Lethe available? It's Richard Locke, the poet," Locke replied, hoping he hadn't misdialed in his haste.

"Ja, chust und minute," the voice replied. A throaty purr conjured up a vision of Dyanne Thorne in *Ilsa She-wolf of the S.S.* Or maybe a fiesty Hans Holbein peasant girl. Locke shook his head at the unwitting imagery. This was probably Lethe's housekeeper, and more than likely some obese, middle-aged German woman.

"Lethe here," came the quiet voice with its hint of accent.

"Mr. Lethe, this is—"

"Ah, Mr. Locke. How wonderful to hear from you so soon."

"I'm calling regarding your offer; I think I'd like to accept."

There, it was out— He'd agreed to write a book solely for money... Was this hackwork? Was it a setting aside of what was real, what was true? Locke didn't know anymore, all he knew was that he was alone, his best friend was dead, Clare was gone, and anything that was different had to be an improvement. It was time for a change.

"Mr. Locke, your timing couldn't be better. I'm having a small get-together here tomorrow evening and we'd be delighted to have your company. Why, there's even a small guest-house that you could stay in for the weekend if you like."

"That's very kind of you, I'd be glad to get away from the city for a few days," Locke went on. "A break in my routine may be just the stimulus I need to get started on this project."

"Bring whatever luggage you like, you can stay at the cottage as long as you wish. I'll send my driver round for you about six if that's satisfactory. I think that this will be a most rewarding weekend. You've much potential Mr. Locke, perhaps much more than you realize."

Without waiting for a response Lethe hung up, leaving Locke's eyes to query the phone. What to do now? *How about writing?* he suggested to himself. *I just got a $10,000 book deal, I can't sit on my ass forever.* But he found the mood, and the motivation, displaced. Lehrling wasn't even cold yet.

Something nearly subconscious took him to his desk. *I know...*

Exorcism. Lehrling had talked about it all the time—

"Catharsis," the novelist had advised only nights ago. "Exorcism. Turn your feelings into art. Write the best poem you've ever written. Then you'll be free."

Catharsis, the displacement of despair via his creative energy. But Locke had dismissed it as a pop psychology, liberal rhetoric. He'd never really bought all of that but he saw the link.

Tomorrow, for the first time in my life, I'm going to accept money for my work. So tonight...

An unheeding glance to the dresser, to a picture of Clare. She seemed to smile back at him through the dead memory.

Tonight I will write the best poem of my life. And then...

Like the prelude of a pianist before the ivory keys, Locke flexed his fingers before the manual typewriter.

He began to type.

«« — »»

Eleven lines, and how many rewrites? *Thirty-five, forty?* Locke never thought in terms of drafts or output; it was irrelevant. The final creation was the only thing that mattered.

It was full dark now. Hours has passed in his creation of the simple eleven-liner in his pocket. What else could he do? It felt like some inkling of closure, or at least self-cognizance. *The last act of the artist before his welcome permutation into hack.* Locke didn't care anymore how he felt about any of that.

The poem was the thing, and that was all.

Well, not quite all.

More of his cryptic poet's empathies suffused into the mix of what he feared might be the final dribbles of his concept of truth. The poem itself was fine—it was as good as he could make it, and it had been a long time since he'd felt that way. *But it's not real.*

Not yet.

Until the conveyance of his muse had been finalized, the poem could never be real. He hadn't created it for an audience, nor had he created it for himself.

There was only one person in the world he'd created it for, and until that person read it, the poem would never be anything more than meaningless black marks on bleached woodpulp.

It will never be real until she reads it.

A numb trek through oblivion—that's how his journey seemed to him— with truth at the end of the line. Clouds like dark mountains crept overhead; moonlight through their valleys, steeped by the atmosphere's ash-gray sky, painted ghost-light about their billows and edges. Locke thought of luminous, warped bones. Bereft of their leaves, the trees on either side of the dead street seemed to extend their branches—skeleton hands clutching for Locke's soul.

Closer, now…

His footsteps, like his resolve, plodded on.

Closer…

The anticipation—and more than a prick of fear—distorted his vision. He began to see Roosevelt Street in rhythms, in skiagraphs, in weaveworks of textures, as though the force of his determination had tinted his blood with some psychedelic. Colors hummed, unreal yet painfully intense. Pots of some otherworldly phosphor seemed to hover at the fringes of his vision, but when he focused…they were streetlights. Truly, this was a poet's night, a fictile darkness of steeped dimensions and hidden heights.

A few more steps through this strange realm, and he was there.

Reality reattained. Locke stood with hunched shoulders at the apartment building's darkest corner. A loiterer, a hoodlum. He dare not look up at the second-story unit—*What if she's standing on her balcony? Christ! What if she sees me?* These very real considerations did not occur to him until this very moment. A neighbor might dismiss him as a peeping tom, call the police. Wouldn't *that* be lovely? *She'll look out her window to see a couple of city beat cops stuffing her ex-boyfriend into the back of a prowl car.*

But he would not be thwarted. *Cowards die a thousand times,* he thought. He'd come out here with the summit of all his truth in his breast pocket—he sure as shit wasn't going to turn around now.

But where to put it? Where must he leave his truth?

Easy! There was Clare's car—the Nissan Sentra—parked cold at the curbside. He could just stick the poem under a wiper and leave. In the morning when she went to work, she'd see it, take it off, read it.

Locke smirked. *Yeah, but if you had any real balls, you'd go inside, walk your ass up the steps, and stick it in her door...*

Suddenly his teeth were chattering. It was cold, yes, but not *that* cold. He was afraid—afraid of being seen, afraid of humiliating himself.

But didn't that really mean he was afraid of the truth?

His hand trembled when he reached into his jacket and withdrew the single sheet of paper, trembled more when he unfolded it. Paled by moonlight, his face looked down at the truth.

THIS, MY VERITY, I PROFESS
by Richard Locke

Glyphs, like signs, like cenotes and ziggurats,
remnants of ruby revelations—they're symbols.
Welcome to my castle in the air; its walls are
muses with garrets through which I peer for
errant truths.
You can't see it, but it's always there.

Providence, infinity, terra incognito? They're all
the same in a way. So up into the ziggurat I go,
through the rive in the interstice, jubilant and
dressed in raiments black.

Swaying the fragrant thurible for you.

Yeah, he thought in a mental sound like a death rattle, or the keen of a rusted mausoleum gate.

Here was his eulogy, and all that he professed. Here was his exorcism, and—

Here was his love.

Solemn as a pall-bearer, and in graven silence, Locke opened the door to the apartment lobby and began to ascend the steps.

(v)

"Don't you ever sleep?" Kerr said.

Cordesman, slouched at his desk, glanced up. He has been ruminating over the dichotomy of epistemological theory and its subtexts involving pure phenomenalism. It made sense but it didn't. If it made sense then, conversely, it *couldn't* make sense. If it was real, then it could only exist in the acknowledgment that most of reality was *un*real. The tenets of the so-called Knower-Known pretext (that an object of knowledge is not a construction of the mind but an independent act of *knowing*) seemed to clearly contradict the functionalism of the theory's major moving part, that being is subjectivism, or the assertion that physical bodies are only complexes of sense-qualities. In other words, matter does not exist.

"You ever read Descartes, or Moore?" Cordesman asked, exhaling Camel smoke.

Kerr popped him a mugshot. "Uh, Clancy sometimes. And a little Grisham. But I've never heard of—"

"It's just philosophy," Cordesman admitted. "It could be nothing but a rooker full of egghead bullshit, but—goddamn—if you look at it closely enough... None of it makes sense, and that fact is what authenticates the sense of it. See what I mean?"

Kerr walked slowly across the smoke-rank office, side-glancing his boss with a concerned tip of an eyebrow. He poured coffee from the little burner on the room's only file cabinet. The stuff in the pot bubbled like radioactive sludge. "Well, no, Captain, I don't know what you mean."

Cordesman winced, aggravated. "We're *cops,* Kerr. Jesus Christ, who is more in the middle of the human condition than us? Our job is to enforce an ideal of civility in a primal scape. Right?"

Kerr glanced over his coffee cup, paused. "Whatever you say, Captain."

"Don't you see? It's functional altruism versus emotive and approbative indefinability. The only way we can be real is for both of these values to be fact."

"Yeah?"

"And if they're both fact then, functionally, they cancel each other out."

Kerr at last took a sip of the coffee, smirked, then spat it out into the waste basket. "Hey, this coffee tastes like paint."

"By now, it probably *is* paint. It's been cooking on that burner since this morning."

Kerr, disgusted, dropped the entire cup in the trash. "And speaking of this morning, that was the point of my comment when I first entered your charming and very fragrant office. You know, the comment that you immediately ignored?"

Cordesman leaned back in his Office Depot chair, drew hard on his cigarette. "Oh, something about sleep."

"Yeah. You picked me up for the prelim site exam at, what? Five this morning? Now it's past two a.m. And this ain't the first time."

"Well, you're obviously not sawing any logs yourself."

"It's all that crystal-meth I've been stealing from the property vault. You ever been down there? Actually I couldn't sleep because of the pending Cone trade."

"Yankees will never trade him, especially to Seattle. If they do, I guess I'll just have to cut my throat. Why go on living? I came close when that shit-for-brains Steinbrenner got rid of Key and Wetland. What'd they ever do for him except win the World Series?" Cordesman, in spite of his conviction record, had only been here since '91; he'd come from a county department in Maryland, where he'd lived all his life. But, even more to the contrary, he was and always would be a Yankees fan. "I see, so you couldn't sleep because you've got steel in your shorts over this trade that'll never happen, so you come *here?*"

"Not exactly. I decide to pour myself a bottle of Adam's since this week it's on sale at Safeway for $4.49 per six—hint, I can only buy it on sale because I'm two years overdue for a step-raise—"

"Oh, shit, I didn't know that. I'll put you in for one," Cordesman said. Kerr was a good cop. He deserved his Adam's. Cordesman remembered the day when he'd drunk it himself—always to excess.

"—and then my phone rings. It's one in the goddamn morning and my goddamn phone rings and you know who it was?"

Cordesman stalled. "David Cone?"

"No, it was Jill Brock, you know, the field chief for Evidence Section. And you know what she says?"

Cordesman held up his hand in dismay. "I don't know. Maybe she told you to forget about the trade because the Yankees are the only team that matter?"

"No, she said, and I quote, 'Doesn't goddamn Cordesman ever read his office intranet?'"

Puzzled, Cordesman stroked an imaginary beard. He'd tried to grow one once but, for whatever reason, the right half of his mustache came out blonde. "Office intra—"

Kerr pointed to the Hewlett-Packard P-6 on the captain's desk. The monitor was off. "Do you ever turn that on?"

"What, the computer?"

"No," Kerr said. "The pencil cup. For the most decorated senior officer in the department's history, and for a guy who could've made deputy chief the day he walked in here but *didn't* because, so he says, he didn't feel that his 'Kantian opportunities' could be 'maximized' in a desk job—and rejected an eleven-grand pay-hike as a result—you sure don't know much, do you?"

"Hey, fuck computers," Cordesman said outright. He lit another Camel off the lit end of the last butt. "I don't fuck with any of that fuckin' computer shit. I've told you that. That fuckin' thing sitting on my desk there—" Cordesman pointed to the beautiful Magnavox .26 17-inch monitor—"is the eye of hell."

Kerr nodded. "Eye of hell or not, sir, you might want to take a quick peek at it every so often. There's a little icon on it that says 'Weekly Multi-Precinct Homicide Blotter.' Then you'll be aware of related homicide evidence among the other three city homicide zones."

Cordesman had profane language on the brain tonight. "I don't give a fuck about the other fuckin' precincts, Kerr. I only worry about fuckin' *North* Precinct."

"I understand that, sir. But when fuckin' evidence in the fuckin' East, West, and South fuckin' precincts directly fuckin' relate to an ongoing homicide fuckin' investigation in the fuckin' North Precinct don't you give a fuck about *that?*"

"Watch your language, Kerr, and yes, I do give a fuck about that. But I don't generally worry about it, for two reasons. One, Ann Arundel County, Maryland, has more homicides in three or four weeks than this entire candyass city has in a year."

"Ah, I see, the blood-soaked big bad east coast homicide cop has looked into the abyss and the abyss looked back."

Cordesman clapped. "That's good, Kerr. At least you've read some Nietzsche—"

"What's the second reason?"

"I expect my immediate subordinate to keep me apprised of relative homicide evidence from other precincts. Immediate subordinates who fail to do that don't get recommended for their step-raises."

Exasperated, Kerr turned on Cordesman's computer. The screen buzzed, then flashed. He dragged the mouse pointer to the LISTINGS menu, then clicked H/A UNIT.

"Read," Kerr ordered his superior officer.

Cordesman read, his face drooping. Kerr plucked the cigarette from his lips before it fell out of his mouth.

"Oh, fuck me," Cordesman said.

(iv)

After the deed—and, no, he hadn't been seen—Locke walked home, that is, he walked home the long way as in about four miles. He hoped the bracing air might clear his head, but not halfway through Fremont, he found himself staring into a bookshop window which sported a handsome display of Lehrling's first-edition hardbacks, all signed by the now-dead author. An ornate, hand-lettered sign read "In Memoriam." Locke scowled—the book-seller had probably received the books as gifts from Lehrling himself, and had now raised the price by over fifty percent. *News travels fast.* This commerce of literature disgusted him, this ghoul capitalizing on his friend's death, but here was Locke himself accepting a commission to pen a volume of poetry for a wealthy eccentric. Contradiction upon contradiction. Where was verity? Was nothing really true any more? *Great is truth, and mighty above all things,* came a lost thought from scripture. Or was he taking the part of the cynic because of his own string of losses? Just an hour ago, in fact, he had creatively acknowl-edged the end of his love for Clare. And hours before that, he'd witnessed his best friend as a gutted, decapitated corpse. *Not a very good day,* he figured.

His trek seemed aimless now. He didn't know where he was going and he didn't want to know. More catharsis? The final trimming of the exorcism? Down one street, then another, cutting through alleys and trash lanes. One moment he found himself loitering about a marina dock near Gasworks Park, and the next moment—in reality over an hour later—he was standing midpoint on the Ballard Bridge, watching late cold-front clouds slither before the night. *Oh, weep for Adonais,* he recited Shelley, looking down at black water. Fishing ships sat motionless in their great slips. *The passion-winged Ministers of thought...* Locke felt lost of such ministers tonight, and lost of all passion. Then, Byron: *All heaven and earth are still—though not in sleep. And silent as we stand in thoughts too deep...*

It seemed pathetic to allow his soul to be so completely demolished by something as simple as a broken love affair. Nothing deep there. Just more human dynamics, as Cordesman would say.

I'll never see Clare again...

All right. Fine. *Get on with your life.* He'd submitted his proof—his poem. He'd taped it to her door. If this was to be a psychical exorcism, why did he feel not all that much different?

The remembrance of Lehrling's guts ripped out didn't help.

A crosswind rocked the bridge; Locke wavered on the narrow walkway, chilled suddenly to the marrow. For some people, creation was life.

But with what would he create now? Tomorrow guillotining his lifelong ideals and taking money for writing?

He'd created with whatever he could. Ashes if need be.

Perhaps ashes would prove the most honest pigment for his whore-poet's paint.

"Hey—"

Locke turned, faced the north side of the bridge from whence he was sure he'd heard the voice. But no one refaced him. "A man's voice," he muttered to himself. He jerked up the collar of the too-light jacket; Autumn in Seattle always sucked. *Poe should have lived here, more fuel for the gloom.* But where was Locke's fuel? The minute drizzle seemed to dissipate into something foglike, and just as he was ready to dismiss the caller's voice as imagined, he thought he saw something—no, someone, standing a good fifty yards ahead.

Just a figure.

He smelled a trace of something awful but it disappeared with the next breeze. *A bum,* he concluded. Ready to make a plea for spare change or a cigarette. But the figure just stood there, barely visible, an entity half-formed of the gelid mist. A metastasis of the night.

"Don't go there…"

Locke's gaze thinned; the figure sharpened, yes, he could see it. What's more, the voice had sounded familiar, no one he knew, but—

Who could it be?

Don't go where? To Lethe's? No one knew about that but Locke himself.

"We know. Lehrling and I…"

Locke broke from the rigid stance, ran forward down the walkway with speed that surprised him. His footfalls clattered, resounding like gunshots. Yet the closer he got to the figure, the more insubstantial it became, until—

He was there.

—it was gone.

Jesus.

Certainly it had never been there at all. Lehrling's death, and the final wounds to his heart over Clare—it was leading him to imagine things, or—

A polite way to suggest hallucination.

Even Locke remained rational enough to consider the likelihood. Wernicke-Korsakoff Syndrome, *delirium auris*, depressive neurosis and hallucinosis. All common symptoms of progressive clinical alcoholism. Admitting that's what he might be—an alcoholic—didn't really bother him.

My brain's a booze sponge.

"Why not just jump off this bridge right now?" he asked himself.

He looked down at the water—a black, endless plain which seemed a mile below him. What would he feel? Nothing, or at least not much, but—

No. I may be pathetic but I'm not a sucker.

A last vestige, perhaps. The last hook still punched through the skin of his inner being.

"Maybe next time," he told himself.

Locke crossed the bridge, headed back toward home. *Hearing voices, seeing things. Terrific.* More time lapsed with the fractured thoughts; next thing he realized he'd passed the Red Hook Brewery, was re-entering Fremont—the full circle. The scenic, lakeside town stood dark, asleep. Even the bars were closed. For the first time, then, he checked his watch and noticed through a start that 3 a.m. was long past. *Time flies when you're having hallucinations,* he thought. He even chuckled. Now, in the mist-drenched night, alone, he wished he hadn't quit smoking. An accompaniment for the mood.

Seeing an imaginary figure on a bridge. A ghost...

But then Locke's footsteps took him up Woodland Park Avenue, past a trailer-sized pub, its windows dark, and of all things, an alcohol-abuse clinic. The mist reformed, seemed to collapse downward from some unseen point above him—living fog. Sentient. And when he turned onto the next street, he halted, peering out.

Two more figures stood in the rainy mist.

He turned around, looked behind him.

Two more blocked his escape.

Locke had a funny feeling *these* figures weren't hallucinations.

A second later—

WHACK!

—he knew beyond all certainty, when one of the figures broke a wooden plank across his face.

TWELVE

FEEDING FRENZY

(i)

Haunters of the dark. There are many more than you might think. What stood in wait on the bridge was an auspice.

But I, not by choice, am more than that.

I watched him come across the other side of the bridge, watched him follow the waterfront road. My senses felt famished. My blood ached. But I too am cursed, like Locke, like Byers and Lehrling, and like my nemesis. Just in different ways.

The gods, evidently, like variety.

A saturnine night, but then mine are always like that. Think of someone famished, one of your homeless, perhaps, one of those half-persons you turn your gaze away from when you see them begging on a corner. Then imagine such a person set down before a steaming buffet but they can't eat because their lips are sewn shut. Or one of your addicts holding the rock in their dirty hand…

But there's no pipe.

Appetite and demand. The constant yearning to be quenched. There are meals all over the place; they're like gnats.

I could sniff its scent in the air—blood and flesh—but none of the soul-rot that was the only thing which allowed me my sustenance. I could taste this one's aura with each breath, a taste like my own blood in my mouth when I bite my lip.

Damaged goods. A damaged soul.

Just like me.

But those other men who converged from both sides of the street?

Oh, yes…

(ii)

T.J. wanted to bust a gut when Craze cracked the wood across the geek's face. The skinny dude hit pavement before any of them could really see it. "Easy pickin's," T.J. said, tossing his empty bottle of 'Bird. What kind of shit for brains must these assholes have to walk the streets this late? But God love 'em, 'cos this was where T.J. and his crew really danced. You need money? Then just wait for some dickbrain like this guy to come your way.

Then take him down.

Simple. Why work when the money walks right up to you and says "Take me?"

As for T.J. himself, whose real name was Thomas Jonathan Cambers (though his rucking pals thought it had something to do with T.J. Swan), he'd left home when he was fifteen—fuck school and all that teachers and books shit. Never knew his father but he supposed his mother was all right. She'd cry and blubber whenever he came home to Tacoma—only when he needed money—and never understood why the regular world wasn't for him. The last time, she'd refused to give him anything so he'd locked her in the basement for a week, thinking the confinement might loosen up her purse strings. Too bad she'd died the first day—hell, how was he to know she was taking heart meds? At the end of the week, he stuck his head in to be socked in the face by the stench, and there was mom, her eyes black, her cheese-mold face, and the squat body bloated up with putrefactive gas. Oh, well. Shit happens.

Never really bothered him much, at least not consciously. At night, though, most *every* night, he had dreams like to make him jerk upright and scream: dreams of himself getting locked in the basement and seeing that fat pile of rot that was mom get up and give him a kiss. Of course, T.J. never told the others about that part. As leader, he had a reputation to maintain.

"Check his shit, Craze. Willy, Marlon, eyeball the street."

They were a rather unique coterie: homeless sociopaths. Willy was constantly drunk or fucked up by drugs, not much good for lookout tonight, but Marlon was okay. And Craze...well, he was just Craze. Streetpersons, the papers called their ilk. The poor and the homeless and the destitute. Well, shit, T.J. would rather sleep under a bridge any day, the rent was just right. When the winters got bad, they stayed at the shelter on 45th; when it rained—showertime. Right now they were cooping in the abandoned church, a good crib. Yeah, it was easier this way; they were their own men. You piss when you want, shit when you want, eat when you want, get faced when you want, no fuckheads telling you what to do. You got a woody, you find someone to fuck.

It was autonomy.

Cops rarely messed with homeless. They didn't want to get their hands dirty. Hell, one time T.J. had gotten picked up for peeking in apartment windows, looking for a good place to leave a peckersnot. "I'm gonna shit my pants, man," he'd said, reeking in the backseat of the patrol car. "No lie, can't help it. Sorry if I get shit in your car, it comes out the leg…" They'd expeditiously dumped him off on Midvale, waving his stink out of their pinched faces. T.J. had no hair at all on his head but a great unruly beard. He wore the same overalls he'd jacked out of one of the Stone Electric service trucks a year ago. Other than that, they all looked essentially the same with their unwashed clothes, food-flecked beards, matted hair. You could smell them coming. Willy limped; he'd had his foot crushed a while back when they'd been busting into a hardware store for crowbars. An anvil or some shit had fallen on him. Fuck doctors. Willy just kept himself juiced till the pain died down—now the foot was half to rot, he kept it wrapped up in a towel surrounded by duct tape.

"Shit, T.J.!" Craze complained. "The motherfucker's only got a few bucks on him, and no credit cards!" *Uh-oh*, T.J. thought. When Craze got his dander up, he was hard to turn off. Craze was schizoaffective and bipolar; all fucked up was another way to put it. They'd lit his brain up for years at the state psych ward with that shock treatment shit of theirs. Why? Claimed he'd knocked some little girl's head in with a tire iron when he was like twelve. Just felt like doing it so he did it. Then he tore off his first piece of ass, at least that's what he said, humping this little Tootsie Roll while her brains squeezed through the fracture. T.J. saw no reason to disbelieve him. Sure, Craze knew right from wrong—he just preferred wrong.

The geek groaned, blood on his face. "Let's do a number, fuck him," Craze said.

"All right, why not?" T.J. authorized. "Come on, drag him home." They each grabbed something and dragged the geek to the old church. *Plop!* went the geek when they stuffed him into the side window. Rusted chains secured the once grand front doors. All the pews had been taken out, all the stained glass removed to be covered over with planks. A variety of unchurchly things decorated their abode: countless empty beer cans and wine bottles. Food scraps, chicken bones. And shit. Lots of shit. A few downed planks let in enough illumination from the corner streetlight.

Craze whipped out his carpet razor, was fixing to maybe cut one of this geek's ears off, or slice off a lip like he'd done to that rich old lady they'd taken down at the Ballard Market last summer. Cut her lips clean off while Willy and Marlon put the blocks to the old bag. Nothing but red teeth showing. Kinda funny.

Marlon lumbered up, picking at his crotch. "Lemme scratch my dick in him first, huh? This shit itches."

"Sure, Marlon," T.J. okayed. See, a couple months ago, they'd busted up a whore on Aurora—this bitch was *all* fucked up on crack—jacked her pussy-pouch for sixty bucks, but that wasn't enough for Marlon. "Shit, man," T.J. warned. Even homeless sociopaths could be possessed of some prudence. "These street hoes got everything going between their legs. You gotta be crazy to dip into that shit." Plus, Marlon already had a case of rectal herpes from the joint. Every time he'd take a shit, he'd holler.

But Marlon, all six-foot-five of him, wouldn't hear of it. This chick was like most of 'em: rack-skinny, little tits on her, and long stringy hair. The usual crack-whore trash for clothes: tight shorts, halter, high heels. Willy and Craze held her down behind the dumpster at Blue Video, but she'd passed out once she got a whiff of Marlon's unwashed-for-a-year crotch. He'd plugged her hard, left his snot quick, then they'd all pissed and shit on her. But Marlon, ever the completist, just couldn't be slaked, the sick pup. He'd scooped up a good rasher of their shit off her chest, then mashed it all down into her face. He pressed down good and hard until she smothered. "Fuck it," he excused himself. "Guess I just got a hair up my ass."

But the joke was on Marlon. Few days later, they wake up under the Nickerson Street overpass, and he's got some big pusser on his dick, the size of a walnut. "Told ya so," T.J. said. "Itches," Marlon replied. "Just like my asshole."

Marlon had been in the Nam. Mostly peed himself and fired his 16 over his head during a fire fight. Said he got captured by VC, got the shit tortured out of him. Had something *all* fucked up with his skin, his chest, legs, under his neck—like hundreds of little holes, and T.J. figured it had something to do with the torture. No reason not to believe it 'cos—shit—anyone fucked up enough to do the shit Marlon did *had* to have had a reason. Willy was another story, though. Kinda quiet, happy to sit by himself with his crack or his Mickey's. Said something once about an aunt or a foster home or something but that was it.

No point crying over spilt Mickey's, T.J. reasoned. The past was the past. So, they'd all got themselves bung-holed one way or another. Only made sense to make up for it now.

Willy sat against the lectern post, picking at his foot and sniffing his fingers. "Hurry up and have your butt-fuck," Craze said, his razor gleaming. "I wanna do me some carving."

"Shit, T.J., I gotta puke," Willy complained.

"Then puke, Willy Boy. It's a free country, and you're a citizen."

"Uh, yeah. You're right." Willy leaned over right there and— *errrrrrp!*—let his belly rip right about where the priest would've stood when reading the lessons. He picked through the vomit, fascinated by the bits of undigested peppers from the macaroni salad they'd ripped off from Safeway.

"Why waste 'em?" He began to eat the bits, clipping each one with what remained of his front teeth.

That's my boy.

T.J. sighed an overwhelming satisfaction. The beautiful night sky showing through the plank gaps, the cool breeze, the whole world open to them. Life was good, and T.J. felt blooming in gratitude when he looked down at his flock.

Marlon was just about to pull the geek's pants down, when—

CLANK!

—they heard the lock bust and the chain fall.

Then the front doors creaked open and the woman walked in.

(iii)

I'd been following him all the way from the bridge. Something about him. I could smell his heart—a sad heart but a true one. I could smell his brain.

I knew he wouldn't suffice, I knew that in a glance. I saw honest passions and grand designs. Tainted in sorrow yet too true to his core.

Then I saw the others.

(iv)

T.J. stared at the woman who'd entered the emptied nave; in fact, they all stared. Their crusted mouths hung open at the incredulity, their black-rot teeth glistening in their grins. Shit, she had no idea what she was in for. Right here, in the abandoned church? Who cared how she broke the door chains—they'd been rusted for years, probably gave way with a quick tug.

Marlon's diseased cock stuck out, his hands frozen above their previous task. "Hell with this fella," he guttered.

"Yeah," Craze said, rising to his feet. His carpet razor glinted like a gem fragment.

"The more, the merrier," T.J. said.

He couldn't believe what happened next. The crazy bitch just walked right up to him and said, "Do you think I'm pretty?"

Pretty? *Shit!* This chick was a piece of work. Dressed like a whore in the tight jeans and top. Chilly as it was tonight, you'd think she was nuts but that was fine with T.J. and the boys. That cold air perked her big tits right up, nipples sticking out like to poke you in the eye. Couldn't see much of her face, though, the way her breath turned to steam every time she exhaled.

I don't give a shit about her face…

"Yeah, you's real fine, hon," Craze said.

"*Real* fine!" Willy added, unceremoniously rubbing his joint through his pants and anxiously tapping his rotten foot. But it was T.J. who made the move, reached out and grabbed her shiny red hair and hauled her the fuck *down*.

What—

T.J. had her about squashed flat against the dirt-caked floor; his hips dry-humping her as grimy hands struggled to get his Stone Electric overalls off. She didn't resist at all—this was gonna be way too easy.

"Come on boys," T.J. said. "Time to get this train rollin'."

"Yeah," Marlon guffawed. "All aboard!"

They raped her for hours, taking breaks between the variety of positions. A tough chick, too. After Craze's first turn he beat the shit out of her good and got to choking her so hard T.J. had to stop him. "Can't be killin' this dish, Craze. Gotta make her last, you know? Fun for the whole night."

Now Marlon was plumbing her good, the biggest of them. Each thrust of the pus-bulbed penis made a sound like Willy scarfing macaroni salad.

"I wanna cut her a little," Craze excitedly asserted himself. "'Kay?"

"Sure, but just a little."

T.J. sat back in attendance, amid garbage, hitting off another bottle of 'Bird while Willy hit off his crack pipe. "Get me hard faster, the rock," he pointed out, sucking the hot gas into his lungs. The light neatly tinted the scene. *Cozy,* T.J. thought. But—

Yeah. One tough chick. She didn't make a sound when Craze started nicking her with the razor, and he knew she wasn't dead because just then her legs went up and wrapped around Marlon's hairy back.

She's…digging this, T.J. realized. *We're raping the shit out of her and she's—*

"More," she breathed under Marlon. "Harder…" Then huge, glittering eyes gazed desperately to Craze. "Cut me more."

Fuck, T.J. thought. *She must be from L.A.*

The long, curvy body flinched under Marlon's reeking weight when Craze put the razor to her skin. A long moan fell out of her mouth—Craze cut right through her nipple-tip. T.J. nodded—this was wild, and seeing her flinch like that put some more spark in his meat. He pulled it back out, all seven unwashed inches, and pulled his balls out too. Then he lay down. "Got a lollipop for ya. Get on over here and start sucking."

Her eyes looked hot at the command. Marlon pulled out, let her up, then she was crawling forward, that beautiful firm white ass wriggling high in the air. Chuckles echoed round the damp, open space of the wasted church. Where faithful congregations once prayed, T.J.'s congregation *rocked*. She slithered over him, a real pro, real whore material. *Probably started out on her daddy 'bout when she was four.* She sucked the entirety of T.J.'s foul cock while Marlon kneed up from behind and parked his—herpes and all—right into her rectum. *Holy shit,* T.J.'s brained stewed. This was primo head; she was sucking on it like a straw in a milkshake, and didn't seem to give a hoot that it hadn't been washed since his last shower at the shelter which was, like, last February. This debasement excited him further—he nearly came—so he pushed her head off. "Suck them dirty balls a bit. Got some critters in there for ya." This second command was obeyed without hesitation. That hot, deft mouth tongued the filthy scrotum, roving through mites and crusts of old sperm. Then she sucked one ball into her mouth, expelled it, sucked in the other, alternating.

Yeah, this was damn fine action…

Craze jerked himself with one hand while the other hand drew red lines down her back with the razor. *Talk about three on one!* In a moment, Marlon pulled out and came on her back, his hand getting shitty as he wrung the last drops. Then he smeared it all around over the profusion of blood from the razor cuts. T.J. felt about ready to have his when—

A voice—*her* voice?—dripped into his head. *Give me your tired, your homeless, and your poor…*

"The fuck?"

Come to me all ye who travail and are heavy laden…and I will refresh thee…

T.J. could only lurch when her teeth clipped off his right testis; he couldn't scream. He didn't seem to be able to hear either, as if the ruined church sucked up all sound. But somehow, in fragments of jerking ill-lit horror…he could see.

He could see her chewing it, crunching down as if on a persimmon.

Good, so good. Sustenance! But…you must be hungry too, and you all shall eat…

Her throat gulped; she swallowed and smiled. Then her head lowered to the opened scrotum, sucked out the remaining testicle.

Strong meat belongeth to them that are poor.

The face rose again, then lowered to T.J.'s lips, as if to give him a kiss. His mouth opened against his will, and then the raw testicle was slipped through her lips and into T.J.'s.

The ball felt hot on his tongue. His eyes wouldn't close, and it was no wonder. For it was not the carnal red-haired woman who knelt naked before him now.

"Tommy!"

It was the gas-bloated corpse of his mother.

"Be a good boy and eat all your food. There are people starving in the world, you know."

T.J. did as his mother requested. He began to eat—

«« — »»

—was the first to react, he whipped out his butterfly-knife, his herpetic genitals still dangling, and lunged at this crazy bitch who'd just bitten off T.J.'s nuts. Marlon moved quickly enough that she'd have no way to avoid the thrust. *This bitch is gonna die right here, right now.*

Only—

She was gone, she was gone and someone else was in the nave. He blinked and tried to reconcile what he saw. Standing in front of him was Captain Choi, that same skinny smile and slit eyes, the shiny angled face. Marlon lay not in the church now but tied down naked to a table in the open quad of Camp 6-H, about 20 clicks west of Hue. Yeah, yeah, now he remembered. Bravo 2/37 had been ambushed; half the 2nd Platoon got chopped, and the other half...brought here.

Choi's North Vietnam Regular uniform looked crisp-starched, fine red piping lining the collar.

"I'll tell ya anything ya wanna know, I swear to God," Marlon sang like a canary.

Choi did not respond. He up-ended a box over Marlon's chest, and then he could feel them.

Hundreds of them.

He didn't know what they were just then, but he'd find out a little later when the 3rd ACR and 1st Air Cav busted this shit house open on an extraction raid.

They were blood chiggers from the Red River. Charlie liked to use them a lot; they dug deep and laid eggs, like shitloads of eggs for each bug. They'd heard all about these things.

"JESUS CHRIST, WIPE 'EM OFF!" Marlon pleaded. "I TOLD YA, I'LL TELL YA ANYTHING!"

But Captain Choi only tilted his head, and spoke in his refined accent, "There is nothing I want you to tell me, Private."

Then he up-ended another box over Marlon's groin.

At once, they began to burrow. They began to *dig*—deep into the soil of Marlon's flesh. Screaming, he felt them crawling around beneath his skin, deeper, deeper, ever searching for a suitable nesting place. They dug for hours as Marlon lay clenching in this scintillating agony until—

Choi freed Marlon's hands from their constraints and lay a riffling knife on his sheened chest.

Marlon knew what he had to do...

Yeah!

He grabbed that knife and began to dig them out—

«« — »»

—woman had disappeared, and so had the church. Craze blinked, confused. No, he wasn't in the church—he knew where he was. Back *there*. The Clifton Perkins Pavilion at the Crownsville State Hospital. And the same two techs who always fucked with him—Matthews and Johnson—were snapping on the canvas bednet just like they had when he was a kid—

"My! You're a *big* boy now!"

Craze puked himself when he looked up and saw Nurse Havleck, those devil eyes in the freckled face, her cap, dress, and stockings so white they glowed.

"Never got to juice you right…but now I can."

Matthew's hand crammed the rubber block in his mouth; Johnson chuckled as he smeared the redux paste on his temples. Then Nurse Havleck's elegant finger snapped on the WARM UP switch on the Somatics, Inc. Thymatron Series electro-convulsant therapy unit. The machine made a sound like a Polaroid recharging, a nearly subaural whine. A silver knob read STIMULUS DURATION; Nurse Havleck turned it to MAX. Johnson placed the headset over Craze's temples, plugged the line cord into the jack.

"Let's cook his brain for awhile," the nurse suggested. "Then we'll use this uretal-probe I swiped from upstairs and do his cock."

The rubber plug blocked Craze's screams, but he could still see, his eyes shock wide as they watched the nurse's pretty finger touch the TREAT button and—

CLICK—

—"Aunt" Velma in the foster home. No, she wasn't really his aunt, that's just what she called herself. She loomed before Willy, a large woman in a floral-print dress, a huge hand the size of a small ham grabbed him by the jaw forcing his mouth open. In horror he saw the other hand contained a small jar of *Jean-Paul's Extra Hot Louisiana Red Sauce*. The smell of unwashed underarms and cheap perfume almost gagged him as she brought the jar of hot sauce to his mouth.

"Boy you've been sinnin' agin, an' we gots to burn that devil right outta you; drink this up an burn out that devil!" she thundered as she poured the concoction down his throat and released him to fall on the floor gasping and spitting. Blinded, Willy couldn't even offer any resistance as he felt his pants being tugged down to his ankles, he knew what was coming next, and now there wouldn't be anyone around to stop her and take him to the hospital.

"Now we'll burn out that devil for sure," he heard her say, as the hot iron pressed into the small of his back, "this time we'll do the job right and burn 'im out for sure; we gots all night," she crooned as the iron burned into his buttocks for the first of many times. Even over the stink of scorched flesh he could smell her cheap perfume.

But much worse was the *sizzle*...

(v)

They died quickly, two of them I didn't even have to touch, their fears took them, what they thought was real. The other two I tore to pieces; I'm such a bitch, I was hungry and excited, I just couldn't help myself. They were sinners, they just wanted to cause pain; but then am I really that different from them? I could have terrified them and left them huddled in the darkness with their fear; I could've, but I didn't, I ripped and tore and covered myself with their blood, I rolled in their offal as I ate their hearts and livers, then I touched myself until I came... I wasn't always like this, I remember when I met him, back in Eire a long, long time ago. He said that he would show me what was real, what was true, that he'd make me an angel and that I'd live forever; just like him.

He didn't tell me the whole truth. I think I will live forever, but I don't think I'm an angel. He said I was Sciftan, that we owned the world and could take what we wanted. I asked him about love and he told me I must prove my love for him by my obedience, that only by total obedience could I show him that my love was true.

I wonder about the man, though, the poet. I took him home, made him forget. I didn't want him to wake up to the leavings of what I'd done. He seems very much like me. A poet, yes. He can feel things as deeply as I can.

I think he wants to love like I do.

Yes, I think that he might be like me, and that's what I'm afraid of.

That means he's part of it too.

THIRTEEN

EFFUSION

(i)

"You're shitting me, Jill!"

Brock looked at Cordesman as though he'd walked in with his pants down. "Come on, Captain. Can't you read?"

Cordesman pushed his hair out of his eyes, an instinct by now. Jill Brock pointed to the well-placed signs. NO SMOKING IN MORGUE SUITE. COMBUSTIBLE COMPOUNDS.

Cordesman nearly mourned when he crushed the fresh Camel out under his shoe sole. Beyond Brock's anteroom, he noticed sights so familiar he scarcely reacted. There were no neat metal drawers in this morgue—he'd never seen drawers in *any* morgue—but instead metal "deposition" platforms, i.e. tables. On each table was a Parke-Davis cadaver bag. He'd seen this, literally, a thousand times. The only vision that gave a hitch to his gut was one bag in particular.

It was tiny: a baby.

"Fusiformal match?" he dared question her expertise.

"That's correct, Captain. I didn't make it up for fun."

"Sixteen all in 64s with case numbers that began *a week* ago?"

"Yes. You guys want a Coke or something?"

"None for me, thanks," Kerr said.

"Well I could sure use some caffeine," Cordesman admitted.

Brock flicked a pasty hand. "The fridge."

Cordesman passed the main lab counter, a periodic chart and an anatomical chart. And a coy bumper sticker stuck to the wall: DEAD MEN TELL NO TALES, BUT THEY CAN STILL GIVE YOU AIDS. WASH YOUR HANDS AFTER ALL CONTACT WITH THE DEAD!

Piss on the dead, Cordesman thought. *I need a drink...but I'll settle for a Coke.* He yanked open the Kenmore refrigerator, reached in—

"Fuck!"

—and quailed.

Brock and Kerr burst into a round of laughter like that of psychotic trolls.

"Gotcha, Captain," Brock celebrated.

No Cokes occupied the refrigerator, only clear, plastic evidence bags containing human body parts. One part was a nose. Another bag contained two feet. And another—the kicker—contained the severed head of a little blonde-haired girl.

Nine, maybe ten years old.

Brock and Kerr *jammed*; they were hooting it up.

"Always wanted to get Stone Face," Brock laughed.

Kerr: "Hey, Captain? How's the Coke?"

Cordesman slammed the fridge door shut, mortified. "The Coke's great, Kerr. Almost as good as the first one you buy on Pike Street after your transfer to the Meter Unit. You people are perverse."

"No we're not, Captain," Brock clarified. "We're cops."

Cordesman lit another Camel. "Don't like it? Sue me. Report me to the Public Safety Director. And what's this shit about the red hairs?"

Brock was a walking broomstick in her autopsy greens. Cordesman had to admit: skinny and close to breastless, electrocution hair, glasses thick as coasters—hell, he didn't care, he could go for her. *She's probably a fireball in bed,* he thought. The nasally, sinitic voice he could overlook.

"So the fun's over?" Brock quelled her smile. "Okay, sir. If you ever took the time to learn how to turn your computer on, you would've seen the cross-reff two days ago."

"Does this have anything to do with the 64 we had this morning? Lehrling, the Wallingford novelist?"

"No, sir, at least no accrual of evidence suggests that thus far. I'm talking about the data readout from the other three precincts. Seven from South, five from West, four from East—that's a total of *sixteen* malicious homicides—all involving extreme modes of violence. You should find it interesting, Captain, that each victim had a heavy rap sheet, all ex-cons, all repeat offenders. One guy was a triple-rape-o, another guy had been in and out of Walla Walla his whole adult life on child-molestation convictions. Couple of armed robbers, bunch of dealers, and six guys with murder convictions. And they all have one major forensic common denominator."

Cordesman couldn't believe what he was hearing. "The red hairs..."

"Yes, Captain, the red hairs. Some ancillary, some pubic, some cranial—it doesn't matter. I got a one-hundred-percent fusiformal match on all of them. And, incidentally, they all genetically correspond to—"

"Wire," Cordesman droned. "The crank-head we found dead on the cabin cruiser at the Liberty Yacht Club."

"Uh-hmm. There is absolutely no doubt. The same person did 'em all."

Kerr smoothed the lapels of his blazer. "How's that for a 'candyass city,' Captain? Looks like you've got something you haven't had since you worked homicide in Maryland."

Cordesman's mouth gushed opaque smoke. "What's that?"

"A serial killer," Kerr said.

Cordesman stared though the words.

Jill Brock removed her glasses, began polishing them with a corner of her labcoat. "And there's one more thing. Salivic and secretial Barr bodies, sir."

"What?"

"Barr bodies. Seven-probe genetic profiles can identify them now on fifteen percent of secretors. Don't you read the trade journals anymore?"

Cordesman sighed with a paramount weariness. "Jill," he reminded, "I've only been up for about twenty-three hours. You want to help me out here, or do I have to go to med school?"

Brock put her glasses back on. The stout lenses made her eyes looks huge. "Barr bodies are cellular incipients that are exclusive to the xx-chromosomal pattern."

Cordesman squinted at her. *Does she mean—*

"Your serial-killer is a woman," Brock informed him.

(ii)

The visage could only be one of heaven...

An angel, he mused.

Locke dreamed that an angel was carrying him away from some nightmare, a charnel house. A devil's church heaped with broken glass, used needles encrusted with blood, sperm on the floor and excrement. Subcorporeal hands seemed to reach down into his soul and show him things—the most awful things: faces stretched by incalculable pain, sizzling flesh, self-amputation. He saw a filthy man digging out chunks of his skin with a knife, then eating the chunks. He saw another man smoking like fat on a spit, one leg bent back as he took bites out of what appeared to be a rotten foot. Someone else with all his hair burned off grinned insanely as he inserted a clipped coat hanger into his own penis. One more detestable man gleefully consumed his own testicles while masturbating the gelded shaft.

Dreams.

Locke's mind felt like a psychotic's—make that a hungover one's. Where could his dreaming mind dredge such sights? And still more followed: a demonness—or was it the angel?—standing silent over her wares, then pawing through their innards in search of the most choice parts...

A frenzy. A smorgasbord of feeding and abomination.

My nightmare…

Locke dragged himself out of the small bed. *Did I go back to the bar last night and get drunk?* He'd slept in his clothes, couldn't remember coming home.

Think!

Back to the bar, either that or he drank here when he got home? He must have. The throbbing hangover couldn't be denied. *I got shitfaced again,* he concluded. He just didn't remember it, and the happenstance didn't particularly shock him because things like that had happened before. All he could remember was wandering, after he'd snuck up Clare's stairwell and taped the poem to her door. He remembered looking out off the bridge toward the Chittenden Locks past Salmon Bay and thinking he saw someone, hearing a voice which sounded disturbingly familiar and at once dismissing it as imagination or hallucination.

But that was all…

"I'm really in trouble," he murmured to himself, shuffling to get a pot of coffee going. "I'm having blackouts…" A titter of pain brought a hand to the side of his face, which suddenly barked in pain. *Christ! Did I fall down the stairs?* A bruise tinted his cheek like faint lampblack.

"You're losing it, Locke. You're a flake, a waste product."

The coffee burned but charged his blood. No, he couldn't remember anything else except—

More of the dream?

The angel. Carrying him off, but it seemed more like flying, like sailing through humid clouds… She was looking down at him as he lay in bed, looking into his heart and his mind with wide eyes full of whispers, promises, full of dark light and magic, their pupils accumulated to crisp points. Hair the color of raspberry wine framed the inexplicable face in fragrant tousles. For whatever reason, Locke couldn't see the face, he could only surmise of it, the countenance of some ineffable arcana, a magician's spell. He could feel the pearlescent gaze slither down and caress his spirit.

"Are you the one?" she asked.

Locke couldn't answer, his throat fallow.

"If you are, be prepared."

"What?" Locke asked in a parched croak.

"All the truth that you can bear…is yours…"

Paralyzed, Locke shuddered. The sleek line of her throat, the shimmering hair—she was beauty incarnate, an aura of heat and skin and luscious wonder fascinating and white as moonstone. She was kissing him— this angel—tasting him, desperate for something they shared in their souls. Locke closed his eyes and reveled in this bliss—like being kissed by all the love he'd ever felt for anyone, all the love in the world. But then the kiss detached and—

Locke opened his eyes.

No woman in the room, no...angel.

Just—

A finch sat on the sill of the opened window. Locke stared.

The finch flew away.

He ground his teeth, his eyes squeezed shut at the unreckonable dream as the anxiety melted into a sharp mist. A tactile image remained, if only for a moment: the feel of the "angel's" hand on his skin.

Symbology, he realized. What else might a poet conclude? *A symbol of Clare, mixed with...* Well, he couldn't imagine what incongruities might be mixed among the flux of this dream. In the dream, though, the angel had saved him; esoterically, Clare's love had saved him too, hadn't it? From the uselessness of his life.

But where did that leave him now?

Just as useless.

Whatever Clare's love had given him was gone. He'd accepted that now, in the poem he'd left on her door last night. Which meant—

She was gone.

She was with someone else now—*sleeping* with someone else, that prissy punk with the red Corvette—Locke's love forgotten, a sheepshank abortion. *Why shouldn't it be?* he posted the query to himself. *What could I give her? A drunk, a broke poet with no ambition?* An impulse, then, found him in a fog, walking toward the window. The window stood open, which seemed odd because...

Why open the window this time of year?

Another sip of scalding coffee, and he was leaning out, gazing over the street below. Something caught his eye but when the phone rang it was with such an excited startlement, he turned away before it registered. He jerked around, bolted for the counter toward the phone.

What he never had the chance to notice was this: a caramel-brown finch feather on the enameled window sill.

All reason, and everything he'd forsworn to be his purpose in what he'd done last night—vanished.

It's her! he somehow knew. *It's Clare! She read my poem! She saw its truth and realized the verity of my love! She wants me back!*

Locke nearly tripped over his own feet on the way to the phone, knocked over a floor lamp and his kitchen garbage can during the journey. Then a glass pitcher shattered to the floor. Locke didn't care, he didn't even hear it...

He swiped up the phone, grabbed a breath. *It's her, it's her, I KNOW it's her! Thank you, God! I SWEAR...I'll even go back to church! No lie, God!*

"Huh-hello?" he quavered into the phone.

Nothing. Silence.

"Clare? Honey, say something."

There was static, rushing in waves, enlaced by a louder sound like a chorus of moans. No immediate reply at first, but then:

"It's not Clare..."

Locke's lips pursed. A voice, a man's voice...

One he knew he'd heard before but was too distant to place. A voice he'd heard on the street one time, or perhaps in a shop or in the bookstore... Yes, the *tone* of the voice sounded familiar but what carried the tone wasn't right at all.

"It's me," the voice croaked.

It sounded ruined, phlegmatic. It sounded *rotten*.

Locke didn't feel real. His head spun through swirls of grain. *Is this a dream?* The caller continued, "'Oh, Preceptor, forgive my grief, and kill my feelings, I beg of Thee.'"

Finally—however feebly—Locke could speak. "Who is this?"

It sounded more like bubbling over the line than static. Deep, chunky rattles seeped through with the wasted words. "You know, and you know what I told you. Love calls to things. It calls to things that are alike. Doesn't matter if they're good or bad. It just calls to things that are alike—"

Locke's mouth gaped. The phone felt cold in his hand, as cold as the voice on the other end.

"It's transposition, man. It's metamorphosis—"

Locke's eyes felt lidless.

The voice churned on, losing its tenor. "You saw me last night on the bridge. I guess I used up my strength finding you." A dim chuckle. "Colorless auras are hard to see."

"Who is this?" Locke repeated even though he already knew.

"Don't go there. Don't go to Lethe's." But now the voice was nearly inaudible, more akin to a sound like creekwater rushing over rocks. "Stay away from him..."

Then it was gone.

And so was Locke's consciousness when he finally admitted to himself who the voice belonged to: Byers. White Shirt.

The other poet. The guy who blew his brains out in front of me.

FOURTEEN

IDOLATER

(i)

What picked him up the next day was a Rolls Royce White Shadow. Locke had no way of knowing that the vehicle's date of manufacture was January, 1916. Nor could he have possibly known that its original owner was a man named Romanov, who was more popularly known as Czar Nicholas II, and the same vehicle that had been driven over another man named Grigory Yefimovich Rasputin shortly before he was dropped through a hole cut into the ice of the West Dniva River in Russia.

A car, in other words, with some history.

Had Locke known this, he might have considered the nature of the vehicle's *current* owner.

The driver stood up as a raving cliché: black cap, black driving gloves, a long tuxedo. Sandy blonde hair stuck out from behind the cap, and the man had a few days' growth of whiskers. *Everybody trying to look like Mickey Rourke,* Locke guessed. *The young guys these days think it's cool to look like shit.*

"Mr. Locke?"

"Uh, yes," Locke stammered once he was confronted by the driver's reality. "I've been invited to—"

"Mr. Lethe is very much looking forward to your arrival. Let me get your bag."

The man got out instantaneously, as Locke was dismissing, "Oh, that's not necessary. It's only a small bag—"

The driver seemed to not hear him at all, grabbing Locke's travel bag and depositing it promptly into the truck. *Christ,* Locke thought. *I hope this guy doesn't expect a decent tip.*

"Mr. Locke?"

Now the driver was holding open the rear door for him. Locke awkwardly nodded his thanks and slid in across a long sealskin seat. The door shut, with almost no sound.

Then they were pulling off.

Locke felt lulled in quiet and comfort. *These things really do ride smooth.* Before him stood a pane of smoked glass, separating Locke from the confines of the driver. Below that, mounted along the back of the front seat, was a bar cabinet which seemed to be fashioned from a genuine Hepplewhite sideboard.

What a clunker, Locke thought. *I wouldn't be seen dead in this piece of junk.*

An edge of white peeked through the leather map-flap on the side of his door. Locke felt impelled to lift it out...

Thin Ice, read the cover of the small, saddle-stitched booklet. The cover-art seemed instantly familiar, and then he opened the booklet to see his name in the table of contents.

Locke couldn't resist. He turned to the page, though it was his traditional view to never read anything he'd written once it was published.

PRECEPTOR
by Richard Locke

Once upon my love
once upon our day
once upon the
grave-dirt truth
of all that I'm
dying to say.

Back into the vale
kicked back wet from
the passion gale
my vision is futile
as my providence is dead
lamentation final smile
halo of ashes ring
round my head

Poet/Vagrant
grope for her
"I love you!" I cry

and cower
Oh, Preceptor
your son is back
with nine petals
plucked off of a flower

This is all that's left?
in crimsoned raiments
to stand bereft?
once upon my love
once upon my glee
once upon the
resplendent promise
of all we could never be

Oh, Preceptor
forgive my grief
and kill my feelings
I beg of Thee

Kill my feelings... Locke remembered, what Byers—the guy who killed himself in the black Firebird—had said earlier to him in the bar. Locke remembered writing this poem, fairly recently, but this was the first he'd seen of it. Lethe must indeed be a fan of his work, to get a copy before the author received his complimentary contributor edition. But that wasn't what nicked at him. *Didn't I write a frag of this poem in the bar that night? And didn't Byers make some comment about it?*

Locke felt sure.

But there wasn't much else he could feel sure about...

"Help yourself to a drink, Mr. Locke," said the driver.

Locke eyed the lusciously refinished antique, its intricate hand-set inlays and stiles, the burnished brass hinges and knobettes. *Liquor inside,* the thought thumped in his head, along with the rest of the hangover. *Just what I need, huh? Just what the doctor ordered after blacking out, hallucinating, morbid dreams, and hearing dead guys on the phone.*

What else could he conclude? The phone call—the raddled voice of Byers, the poet-suicide. Locke didn't believe in ghosts, nor in spirits or afterlives. The only world that lay in wait was the ground.

He'd passed out after the so-called phone call, which led him to suspect that he'd been unconscious all along, blacked out from his steadily increasing alcohol abuse. It had been nothing but a toxic dream spurred by a brain that was revolting against the daily poisoning of its cells.

What else could Locke expect? *Now I'm getting calls from dead guys. Pretty soon I'll be like one of those scarecrows sitting on some corner in the U District begging for hooch money.* Alcohol-induced schizophrenia; perhaps he was a lot closer than he thought. Shit, he'd even spiked his *coffee* with booze this morning.

"Thanks for the offer," he finally got around to replying. "Trying to cut down."

The driver made no further comment, stolidly driving the exorbitant car east. *Lethe must like clichés, a man of convention, an old saw of platitudes,* Locke considered. The man had dressed his driver up like an ornament; it must be embarrassing.

"How long have you known Mr. Lethe?" Locke asked when the car's quietude grew awkward.

"Not long."

Locke waited for some enhancement but got none. *A real chatterbox, huh?* "I met him a few nights ago in a bar," Locke said. "He was looking for me. Never did ask him how he knew I'd be there."

"Mr. Lethe has an uncanny knack for finding what he's looking for," the driver finally saw fit to make comment. "He needed a driver so...he found me."

Locke glimpsed the driver's face in the rearview, a blank mask made blanker by sunglasses. "Oh, yeah? Where was that?"

"Pardon?"

"Where did he find you?"

The driver's words unreeled in a hesitant drone. "A shipping terminal. I used to be a charter captain."

Locke frowned. *Those guys make decent scratch,* he thought. *Lethe must be paying him well.* "Interesting," he replied. This was curious but he couldn't think of anything but small-talk. "So I guess you like driving Rolls Royces more than boats, huh?"

The driver seemed to nod.

"Oh," Locke bumbled then. "I didn't catch your name."

The driver didn't answer, just kept driving as the city drag gave way to suburbs, then wider expanses of property.

Locke just shrugged. Figured the driver hadn't heard him.

«« — »»

Locke wasn't quite sure what to think when he saw the house about half an hour later. *I wouldn't quite call it a shit-heap, but...*

In the drive, they'd traversed most of North Bend's girth, to outskirts even Locke wasn't aware of. They were driving down a long, narrow road full of leisurely twists and turns—more of a country road, Locke contemplated, in some rather run-down country. Fields stretched out on either side. Farmland? Locke didn't know, for the fields only displayed acre upon acre of wild, unkempt vegetation, banks of thistle, and weeds. In the distance he may have a spotted a barn or grain silo or two, but they stood only as teetering frameworks of wood, gray now, and long gone to vermiculation. Soon they were driving through dense woods which seemed to decay along with the road as the latter eventually lost its asphalt in favor of runneled dirt bisected by an endless hump of scrub grass. Ugly larch trees and coarsebarked hemlock and red spruce lined the road in crooked spires, their branches growing together in disarray.

Locke didn't feel that he'd missed much in not knowing about this recess of land. *Just plain Fugly,* he thought. *Whatever happened to land conservation?* These were truly the wilds, something he'd never really witnessed in the past. The leaning trees and narrow dirt-scratch of a road seemed to drain his sense of dimension. Not a road at all but a lane through remote woodland. Locke flinched, as a claustrophobe might. He pitied the mailman who had to make *this* trek. But the land revealed a secret of its owner—certainly Lethe was a man who liked his privacy.

Then came the house.

The Rolls had turned onto an unmarked byway, after which another half mile took them to a cul-de-sac surrounded by huckleberry and thorn bushes, all ill-clipped, an atrocious attempt at topiary. The house looked… *Creepy,* came the word to Locke's mind, perhaps a lenient play for atmosphere. Then, staring through the side window, he gave up his leniency. *I must correct myself—it* is *shit-heap.* It seemed to poke the afternoon's calm in the eye with its disrepair and odd angles. Large, yes, a manse, with a plastered wraparound porch, pale awnings from the second-story windows, even rusted iron cresting along the heavily steepled roof. Front bow windows showed only latched shutters and paint-flaked stilework. Locke couldn't even tell if the wooden siding had been painted but he didn't think so; weathered gray, brown, he couldn't tell—it appeared to be bare wood, that is very *old* bare wood. Oddest of all was the third-story oculus-room sitting atop of parapet heap with dead leaves like a drab box placed on top of the mansion as an afterthought. The oculus window seemed to peer down—a sightless eye.

"How, uh, how long has Mr. Lethe lived here?" Locke asked even against his better judgment that the driver had not much of a care to use his vocal cords.

"Just a few weeks."

The Rolls stopped by the wide porch stairs, the engine died. *Yeah,* Locke thought, *Lethe's a man who likes his privacy. He's also obviously a man who likes dumps.* The homestead looked a century old, with no tending for as long. Its storied front walls genuinely *sagged,* and several window shutters had fallen entirely or hung from broken hinges. But at the end of the thought, the driver turned, glanced over his shoulder, and for the first time looked Locke in the eye. "Mr. Lethe doesn't have much use for cosmetics or facades. It's the inside that counts."

"Uh...sure," Locke bumbled.

"Old things are better than new." The driver adjusted his cap visor, took off his sunglasses.

Whatever...

When they got out, the first thing Locke noticed was another car parked in the drive, another doozy: a black and wood-paneled 1923 Daimler Otto series. Mint. After riding in the Rolls, of course, it no longer surprised Locke that Lethe collected antique automobiles and spared no expense. But what he did find curious now was something he only caught a momentary glimpse of: a woman in a maid's outfit had just gotten out of the Daimler's driver's seat and was now entering the front door; Locke could only see her from behind, could only tell that she was blonde. She carried a large suitcase, and she was being followed into the house by two thin women—a blonde and a redhead—dressed rather trashily in high heels, tight pants and tops. They too each trudged along carrying... *Huh?* Locke thought. Stacked up in their arms were what appeared to be a number of framed blank painter's canvases. *Trashy looking chicks carrying canvases into a millionaire's house?* Locke wondered. *What's wrong with this picture?* "Who are they?" he asked.

"Mr. Martin's assistants," the driver drolly replied.

"Mr... *Who?*"

"They're always different each time. Mr. Lethe likes to entertain regional artists— Martin is a painter from Olympia."

But Locke had only seen women, until—

A man got out of the back of the Daimler.

"That," the driver said, "is Mr. Martin."

Get out of town! Locke thought.

A long black-leather coat. A yellow mohawk fringed orange, funky sunglasses, and one of those silver rings in his lip. *This guy looks like something from a Nine Inch Nails show,* Locke thought. *Gee, I wish I had a lip ring like that.* That's all this was, and that's all Lethe was, a bored rich guy who fancied himself an artistic benefactor. Nothing to do with his time or money. Locke could guess that he himself was just more of the same, an amusement for the stuffy patron. *Whatever turns you on, Lethe. I'll take your money.*

"Let me show you into the mansion," the driver said. "Mr. Lethe's looking forward to seeing you."

Martin and his queue of "assistants" disappeared into the house without even a glance to Locke or the Rolls, and it was then, after the initial distraction, that Locke took a closer survey of the sagging house. Twin flues on a high chimney poked up like horns. A peek around the side showed him sheets of discolored ivy crawling up the massive plank siding. He noticed a brick wall, man-tall, with interesting cement quoins and coping, appear to surround whatever back yard this place might have, but the grass before the fence had clearly not been mown for some time. Here was a startling contrast: two cars worth a couple hundred thousand apiece but a "mansion" in such disrepair, he wondered if it was even legally habitable. *I hope Lethe didn't pay more than twenty grand for this out-house.* The cluttered woods sucked up the sound of Locke's door closing, and the trunk when the driver grabbed his bag. Locke felt loomed over by darkness, the tall trees stamping out the afternoon's daylight but something more abstract occurred to him, a fragment of imagery: it was the house itself that drained the day of its light.

What might it drain from Locke?

"Mr. Locke?"

The driver's hand bid Locke up the porch steps to the vast front doors. A lead-veined fanlight spanned over the transom, its stained glass nearly black from age and neglect. The wooden door, too, looked black. *Black,* Locke abstracted. *Not really a color but an absence of color.* Then Locke's attention was rasped by the door knocker, a small oval of old dull brass which assumed the shape of a face. But the face was bereft of features save for two wide empty eyes. No mouth, no nose, no jawline really—just the eyes.

Groovy knocker…

The front doors creaked when the driver pulled them open—by now Locke almost had to laugh. He shuddered to think what the manse's interior looked like. He pictured rotten paneling, rotten carpet, cobwebs and termite holes. Wallpaper falling down in rolls, leaving streaks of age-old paste. Maybe Lethe wasn't rich at all, just a crackpot. Living in a house like this? Well, there were always the cars to consider. This entire endeavor was just getting weirder, and more and more divergent.

For what Locke stepped into couldn't have been more opposite. A long, slate-floored foyer lined with fine statuary. Veneered rosewood skirting boards led outward to a palatial atrium. *I…I stand corrected.*

Locke, astonished, glanced into a huge greeting room to the left: hickory flooring covered by hand-made Ferraghan throw rugs. Larger statues carved in marble lined the wall; the other side hosted sconces inset with marble busts: Hannibal, Nelson, Frederick II and Henry V—all the great generals of history looked at the disheveled poet with apprising eyes. From a higher position, Tiberius—the Emperor of Rome during Christ's life—brooded from his platform.

Though the outside may have been a "shit-heap," the inside shined finely as the most well-maintained museum. Locke felt lost of breath as he scanned the room's treasures, instantly recalling long-lost college classes in art history and antiquities. His feet trod on masterpieces of Persian carpet from Tabriz, Bijar, Safawi. Their rich colors glowed as if brand new, but Locke knew full well they were all sewn in the eighteenth and nineteenth centuries. What adorned the pastel-papered walls came as more of a shock. An original de Kooning, an original Mondrian. No, there was no Mona Lisa but Locke couldn't help but recognize a few small canvasses by Constable, Titian, Miro, and an unmistakable variation of Monet's "Haystacks" series. Locke brought his eyes only inches from each canvas and nearly threw up. These weren't copies of reprints; the brushstrokes in the oil paint told all. *This guy's got originals. They cost millions!* A final kicker was a six-inch by six-inch cubistic watercolor entitled "Lutists." Painted handwriting in the corner read: *To A. Lethe, an admirable patron. Yours, P. Picasso.*

"Fuck," Locke muttered under his breath.

Quiet footsteps echoed. Locke, still numb, turned. A tall man in a suit stood in the alcove; at first Locke thought it might be another statue but this statue moved. The suit was lambent white, tailored to the finest detail. Silver cufflinks winked when the figure shot its cuffs of Chinese silk.

"Mr. Locke. I'm honored that you could grace my humble house with your presence," Lethe said. "Please don't feel awed by the dead company you've spied on my walls. All great artists, yes. But none as fine as the living artist who stands before me now."

Locke's stare seemed a mile off. He cleared his throat. *The guy's a nut...but he's a rich nut.* "That's quite a compliment, Mr. Lethe. But I don't know that I can quite stand up next to Claude Monet."

Modest laughter issued from his host, a gaggle of sparrows fluttering forth. More footsteps snapped in the vast, echoic room, and as he came forward, Lethe raised his right hand, which contained a single piece of paper in a frame of hand-tamped gold.

Locke took it, looked down at it.

Beige, acid-free paper printed with these words:

THE AVOWAL (NEVER FINISHED)
by Richard Locke
Quickened unto this heaven, and so enspelled,
the writer looked at her asleep in bed.
He heard her breathe, and beyond befelled
the truth of what he never said.

Yet on she slept a lovely sleep;
here is the image his love doth reap.

Oh where is she now, and what are her dreams?
But he remembers how the moonlight gleams—
a resplendent angel in moonlight dressed.
And the writer thinks: *Yes, I am blessed.*

Locke had never been able to finish the work: his marriage proposal to Clare, which he'd never had the opportunity to give to her. He'd sent the fragment to some college literary rag, didn't even remember the name of the publication.

Yet here was Lethe, holding the useless shaving of his muse before him in a frame that probably cost a thousand dollars.

"I hate to ask, Mr. Locke," his patron begged. "But would you sign this for me please?"

Locke gulped, didn't know what to say. *This guy really thinks I'm good.* Locke faltered; it was rare a reader asked him for an autograph—he didn't know what to write. *I guess if it's good enough for Picasso, it's good enough for me,* he reckoned. Lethe handed him a genuine fountain pen. Locke inscribed: *To Mr. Lethe, an admirable patron. Yours, R. Locke.*

Lethe looked at the inscription in absolute delight. "Excellent! Thank you, thank you so much!" Then he turned and approached the wall, placed the frame on a pre-set hook,where he left it to hang between the Monet and a block print by Edvard Munch.

"There," the man said. "Perfect."

Locke's eyes thinned in notice. Lethe had hung the poem several inches higher than any other work of art in the entire room...

(ii)

"Fuck!" Cordesman said.

The cool dark...stank. Of must and mold and fungus, of garbage and excrement.

And of human flesh just beginning to decompose.

A TSD crew had already knocked out the planks from the empty stained-glass windows, but the place still admitted little light. *Thank God,* Cordesman thought. He could see enough here in the dark, and the spot-lamps propped up by the latent techs seemed to add glass-sharp details to the absolutely abominable scenario.

"You gotta be kidding me," Cordesman finally found his voice.

"Kidding?" Jill Brock queried.

Kerr was already gone. He'd walked in right alongside Cordesman, took one look, then walked out, muttering, "No way, no way. I'm not paid enough..."

Cordesman's skin felt fish-belly white; he was sweating, his nostrils flared at the odor. It was hard not to let on that this bothered him. So he did something that seemed casual; he pulled out a Camel. "Come on, Jill. What'd you call me down to this meat-grinder for? I'm on a serial case and you know it."

Brock looked preposterous in her red polyester utilities, her surgical gloves and mask, and her hairnet and rubber booties. "Don't enter the church," she ordered in a voice of concrete.

"Oh, I'll be disturbing the priest? He's in vespers right now?"

"Don't fuck up my crime scene, goddamn it," Brock hurled venom at him

Even Cordesman, in his disgust, had to object. "Well, excuse me. Is that any way to talk to a superior officer, Jill? I'm a *Captain* and you're just tech staff."

"That's right," she sniped, prepping a field chromatograph fume sampler. "At HQ you're the boss. You tell me to shit on the floor and I'll probably do it. But here? On a perimeter, *I'm* the boss. I work my ass off trying to do my job and then you and your goons come tramping all over the place leaving dandruff and hairfall and the shit on the bottom of your flatfoot shoes. It's called crime-scene contamination. Ever heard of it? And don't even *think* about lighting that cigarette. You exhale that shit in here and it blows my spec-blotters and fume samples. I don't care if you're a captain or an admiral or the chief of staff, if you fuck up my crime scene with your cigarettes and plodding around, I'll order one of my flunky 'tech staff' to grab you by your two-foot-long hair and throw your ass out of here. Don't believe me?"

Cordesman was astonished. *She's serious.* The whole place stood up— Hair & Fibers, Toolmarks, Photo Unit—and faced him, giving him the eye. Some of them were pretty big guys and Cordesman wasn't terribly big himself. They were glaring at him like he'd just said something about their mothers' sex lives, and there was Brock, the red-bootied queen bee calling the shots.

Of course, she's got a point. He quickly put his Camel back in his pocket. "Lighten up, will ya? Jesus. You guys need a vacation."

Brock and her crew returned to their duties, milling about like surgeons with their intricate tools, their UV lights and anthracene and luminol sulfate. But the scene remained. At one time, Cordesman could've looked at something like this and not cared, could've been more concerned about a Yankees game. Psychical detachment was mandatory. You didn't see dead *human beings* lying there, you saw dead something else. Dead meat, dead matter— nothing you could assign a soul to, or a history. Nothing you could ever conceive of as having once been a baby happily shaking a rattle, having parents who loved them. A bright-eyed infant squalling "ma-ma, da-da," etc. You had to reduce it to meat or else you'd eat yourself up.

Cordesman wasn't having too easy a time just now.

It was only glimpses he caught, or flashes in the photographer's snaps with the Nikon F with motor-drive. But the glimpses sufficed.

Maybe I'm just too old to do it anymore, Cordesman thought. *I can't hack this shit.*

"Much of this appears to be self-inflicted," Brock said, her back to him as she leaned over her Hair & Fibers man.

Cordesman supposed his gulp was an agreement. Two corpses still had knives in their hands—they were too far apart to have done it to each other; no bloodfall could be seen between them. *They...gutted themselves.* One appeared to have gouged out chunks of his own flesh. *Had he died from shock or loss of blood? Had the other one—the bald one—gelded himself and then removed his own organs?* It appeared so. Cordesman winced, then averted his eyes when he noted that the bald one's facial expression was a grinning rictus.

"So what do you make of it, Captain?"

Good question. Cordesman saw more of the scene in strobic visions like a nightmare of jumpcuts: the photographer was "flash-painting" the perimeter—sequential time exposures backed up by specialized electronic flash units.

A flash of truncated innards. A flash of a blood pool so large his belly flip-flopped. The slim one lay procumbent; in the split-second flash of light, Cordesman saw that he'd been burned: his back, buttocks, the backs of his legs, even the bottoms of his feet reduced to crisped char by some unknown heat source. The decedent looked like something taken off a spit, severely overcooked. Yet another flash showed a fourth victim, eyes wide open, their whites turned blood-red. His hair and beard seemed to have been flamed off his head and...

Fuck...

A clipped coat hanger stuck out of his urethra. None of this could Cordesman quite calculate but particularly this fourth victim. *What could compel a man to cut himself up like a pork end and then jam a coat hanger up his dick?*

"I see you're not exactly a fountain of theories," Brock said.

"Oh, what do I make of this?" he finally answered. "It's fucked up. How's that for crime-scene analysis? What? A mass-suicide, a cult thing?"

"I wouldn't think so. These guys are rummies, Captain. Bums, homeless, whatever you want to call them. This old church was obviously their coop. They came in here to party."

Cordesman turned away from the remnants of this seemingly self-inflicted slaughter fest. "Some party, glad I missed it." He noted the commonplace signs of a homeless "coop": excrement, trash, lots of booze bottles like Thunderbird and Mickey's 40-ouncers—the cheapest stuff. "Wait. Right there, next to the skinny one." He'd only been able to look for a minute, to the side of the corpse with the roasted back. "A crackpipe."

Brock nodded. "And?"

"Bad crack. It happens. The Jamakes don't give a shit if they kill people. Sometimes they use the wrong kind of solvent when they bake the shit into rock. So these rummies all take a hit and—presto—instant psychotic episode."

"Maybe." Brock was still hunkered down, her back to Cordesman as she paid very close attention to her technician, who was plucking at the large one's groinal area with forceps. He wore a hat-light like a miner.

"Look, Jill, I don't want to sound insensitive but this one's all yours. I'll give it to 2nd Squad. These bums got nothing to do with my major gig."

"The Infamous Multi-Precinct Red Female Hair Case, huh? No time for dead rummies, is that it, Captain?"

Cordesman smirked. "That's right, that's my major case right now, and I ain't gonna take time away from it for this gross-out clusterfuck." Besides, the smell was killing him. *Don't they have ventilators for things like this?* "So if you don't mind, I'm gonna go back to the squadroom and smoke a couple of cigarettes. Later."

"Got it," the H&F tech said, slipping his Allis/Miltex evidence forceps from a custody bag.

"How many total?" Brock asked him.

"Six, ma'am. Let me check the others. I'll bet we pluck a bunch."

"Do it," Brock ordered.

"What, uh, what's that?" Cordesman asked, peering over through a helpless curiosity.

Brock brought several of the tiny plastic evidence bags over, each imprinted with a CHAIN OF CUSTODY INDEX label.

"Looks like this is the same thing, Captain."

"What?"

Brock held up the flap of bags, waving them. "Of course I'll run the scale counts and blood-type of the hair-root cells back at the shop, but I can tell you already they're all the same."

"What are all *what* the same?" He liked Jill, but she could really get on his nerves sometimes. Like most women. "What's in the ev-bags?"

"Hairfall, Captain. Pubic hair."

Cordesman's gaze closed, bringing wrinkles to the corners of his eyes. "What color? Not r—"

"Red, Captain. We got red hairs all over these 64s."

(iii)

Locke couldn't quite recall but hadn't Lethe said something about a small get-together when they'd spoken on the phone yesterday? No matter, Locke guessed it was better this way, just a little…well, weird.

Like a lot of things around here.

Lethe faced Locke from one end of a twenty-foot-long Georgian Revival dining table, pure veneered mahogany with satinwood bandings and scrolled brass footcaps. There was no table cloth, a fact which stirred a little trepidation in Locke. *Don't spill any Potage a' Saint Germaine!* The stark white dining room's high ceiling carried their voices. Locke was stunned, first by the table settings and overall appointment of the room, and next by the menu. "It's a pity you don't speak French, Mr. Locke. Such a rich language not to mention a rich cuisine. I like things rich."

The driver entered; Locke did a double-take. *This has got to be some kind of a joke. I really feel sorry for this guy.* The driver had lost the cap and driving accouterments, and replaced them with traditional butler's garb. The black cutaway coat, the bow tie and white pleated shirt, morning trousers and, of course, white gloves. He carried in an odd pear-shaped bottle of wine with a desiccated label.

"Since this is such a special occasion for me," Lethe announced, "I've summoned one of my best bottles. A brisk Conde Dontatien Burgundy. It was de Sade's favorite, and as I'm sure you can imagine, I paid quite a price for this particular bottle which was corked in 1814—the year of de Sade's death."

But it was not this shocking tidbit that gave Locke cause to turn a brow. He noticed, as the wine was poured, that the driver was wearing a black-satin eye-mask tied behind his head by a silver string.

"But one of my many indulgences, Mr. Locke," Lethe exclaimed. "The *bal masque* of the end of the Bourbon reign serves to amplify the mood, don't you think?"

"Uh, yes, sure," Locke blathered. *It's your party, buddy.* The driver poured a thick, amarelle-colored wine into a porcelain goblet. It tasted strong, tart—rich. *Don't chug it, you asshole!* Locke tried to warn himself. *This shit's probably a thousand bucks a sip.*

"Even our utensils are French," Lethe informed him, "from the Limoges workshops, contemporary Romanesque, popular amongst the nobility of the 1300s." This was not silverware but goldware. *I'm eating with a seven-hundred-year-old fork,* Locke realized. *I'm impressed!*

Lethe had announced each course in French, and was kind enough to translate, which all made Locke feel stupid. "Salade Verte avec Courtes de

Roquefort." A simple salad was placed before him. "That's Green Salad with Roquefort Toasts."

The masked driver appeared and reappeared as if on some premonitory demand. When Locke finished each dish, the guy was there, uninspired mug and all, a smug robot. Locke wondered if the guy's name was James or Hollingsworth. What followed were Haricots Verts a la Vapeur (steamed green beans), and Poulet au Vinaigre a l'Estragon (braised chicken with vinegar and tarragon).

Locke ate in considerable awkwardness. The finest meal he'd ever consumed—more than likely—in his life, not to mention eating it with gold utensils that were three times older than the nation, and, lastly, wine that probably cost mid five figures. *A good spread,* he thought, *but why am I here?* This weird palace? The masked driver? And Lethe himself about to lay ten grand on him for writing a single edition book of poetry?

Lethe's fine salt-and-pepper hair shined in the chandelier light. He ate daintily but with a strange voraciousness, sucking each chicken bone of every fiber of its marinated meat. At one point—*crunch*—he even cracked a thigh bone with his teeth, then picked out the marrow with what appeared to be a diamond stickpin. "A bit of elaboration is in order, I suppose," he said. He'd only sipped half his first glass of wine, while Locke was on his third. "The obvious elaboration of my home's exterior. I'm afraid I'm security minded, and I've always believed in the power of appearances."

At last Locke could comment on something. "Oh, I get it. If the house looks like a dump on the outside, burglars will be less likely to think there's anything good inside—" But then Locke bit his tongue. *Dick!* "Sorry, I didn't mean—"

Lethe laughed. "Your honesty—your *verity,* Mr. Locke—is what I like about you, aside from your poetry, of course. But the mansion *does* look like a 'dump' on the outside, for precisely the reason you hinted upon. But, I must add, if the appearances don't suffice, I've a top-notch alarm system."

Locke nodded. "Of course," and then he felt tongue-tied again. How did one make dinner conversation with such a host? "Oh, I forgot to ask. When we arrived, there were some other people coming in, a painter, I believe?"

"Yes, Martin, a post-neo abstractionist you might call him." Lethe dipped his fingers into a dish of lemon water, then flicked them dry. "He's been up before; I've commissioned him to do some work for me. An odd one, and a trifle wild, which you could probably surmise by his cast of current girlfriends."

Locke remembered the pierced, mohawked character and pair of...tramps. He wondered why Lethe hadn't invited them to dinner as he had Locke.

"You'll have a chance to see his work later if you wish," Lethe went on.

"Personally, I don't like the man's company—it's his painting that interests me. As they say, the work is the thing."

Locke's thoughts seemed to yawn. *The work is the thing...* Lethe referred to this painter—this post-neo abstractionist, whatever that meant—with an edge bordering on disrespect, yet was paying nonetheless for the man's work. *I wonder what Lethe thinks of me. Not as a poet but as a person...* Just another creative hack? A work-for-hire?

Locke wasn't sure but he didn't think so.

"Martin's art examines one theme and one theme only. I suppose that's why I admire him; he will not divert from his focus."

"What's the theme?" Locke asked.

"Terror."

Terror? "That sounds interesting, but...how do you paint that?"

"With the power of the muse, of course," Lethe returned.

Locke tried hard not to appear bored. He stole a quick glance high to the left; on the wall hung a tarnished coat-of-arms: a viper being pecked at by a sparrow. "What's that up there?"

"The family seal of the so-called White Prince, John Hunyadi, the Count of Timisoara and the governor-general and regent of Hungary. And speaking of painters, the Prince was quite creative in his manner of dealing with Turk spies lurking about in his court. He would drain them of their blood and order the palace artisans to paint pictures with it. Then he would dispatch the canvases to Sultan Murad II, his arch enemy. And behind you—"

Locke glanced around to see a stained, glass hookah.

"Supposedly the same apparatus with which Coleridge smoked opium while he wrote *The Rime of the Ancient Mariner*. Though he publicly excused his drug use as therapy for his rheumatism, to his friends such as Kant and Wordsworth, he confessed that the 'sweet succor of the poppy is the poet's only true path to the muse.'"

"I think I'll stick to alcohol," Locke awkwardly jested.

"But who was it that said 'all true art must fail'? Blake? Poe? It's interesting how many masters produced their finest work while they seemed to deliberately demolish their lives with spirits or drugs."

"And debauchery, too," Locke added without knowing quite what would spur such a comment. "You mentioned de Sade earlier. What do you think of *him?*"

"A petty fool and lunatic who spent most of his life in prison," Lethe replied with a queer interest. "It's most regrettable that he didn't spend *all* of his life incarcerated—then he would've been able to write more."

"So you like his writing, then."

"Not what he wrote but how he wrote it. As a poet—a word mechanic such as yourself—I'm sure you follow me."

"He was a prose-master who wasted his talent on smut," Locke prattled. "Some of the finest prose I've ever read, but—"

"No genuine creative vision to implement that talent." Lethe set down a splintered chicken bone. "Wasting a talent strikes me as the greatest of all crimes."

An odd point of view, but Locke had a notion now that Lethe was an odd man. He could even appreciate the subjectivity of the statement. "Except for, like, murderers and stuff, you mean."

"Oh, not necessarily. Take a killer like a Gacy or a Bundy or a Lucas. I don't think you can disagree, these were *pre-eminent* serial-killers. They utilized their 'talents'—if you will—to the furthest extremities of their creativity. Yes or no?"

Locke's face widened. "Well, yes, I guess you're right. But—"

"Who cares if they were evil—I mean, at least in the context of your mentioning it. That's not what we're talking about. Certainly, most will concur—they were madmen who are served well by execution, but...*ideally*, from their points of view, they did what they did because they felt *compelled* too, correct? And they did it with alacrity, with zeal, and with passion. They killed, Mr. Locke, with the same fortitude that you write. Yes, or no?"

Locke was duped. "Well..."

"A difficult task, my asking you to compare your own creative mechanics to those of heinous killers. But I think it's all the same in a way." Lethe sipped more wine, and when he saw that Locke's goblet was empty, a quick jerk of his glance brought the masked driver out to pour more.

"Really, Mr. Lethe. This wine is great, but I don't want to scarf it all. It's your best stuff."

Lethe threw his head back and chuckled. "Drink! It's not my best 'stuff' by any means. We'll drink that next, to celebrate."

Celebrate? "Celebrate what?" Locke asked.

"Why, our arrangement, of course." Lethe got up and walked to the other end of the table. The driver appeared at his side as if by magic; then the white-gloved hand passed an envelop to Lethe who then passed the envelope to Locke.

The envelope contained $10,000 in cash.

"To celebrate our deal," Lethe continued, "and the honor I will receive in having my favorite poet write a book for me."

(iv)

Encryptions. Puzzles. Sometimes you know that the piece will fit even before you really look at it. You know it even before you press it down into gap in the jigsaw. I should have known—that's what this is all about. It doesn't matter that they're ancient and almost timeless.

These ciphers of the human soul…

What drives the salmon upstream to their death? What leads the lemmings over the bluff? Instinct or foreknowledge? Or does one mean the same as the other. Old and young, black and white, life and death. Life is death, for death's products give life. Except, of course, when that death just keeps walking, keeps changing and growing. Into what, only time will tell.

The only universal element is love. The only true human gift, the only thing that sets us apart from the chaos of cosmic soup. That's why life never let me go.

The poet is the piece. I knew that if I'd consumed him in the dead church, it would've been no different from eating air. He's poison to my being, a dinner plate piled high with something spoiled.

But to my equal, he is a bowl of chocolate-dipped cherries, an oven-baked, sugary creme custard on the verge of being spooned out of its crust.

More things opposite that are also the same.

Do you see?

Evil exploits weakness. When one weakness is strengthened, another weakness is sought.

Yes, the poet is the piece. I didn't need to follow him. Instead, his vision found me.

He is the convoluted cardboard cut-out destined to fill the puzzle's final gap.

FIFTEEN

TRANSPOSITIONS

(i)

"But what is art, really?" Lethe asked. "To myself, as a layman, I feel urged to collect it because it occurs to me that I'm collecting the ultimate in the human pursuit to create that which is beautiful."

Locke disagreed but was too busy getting used to the idea that he had ten grand in his pocket. He was also too busy sampling the next wine—a Charoliase bottled in 1760. *That's good vinegar,* he thought. After a luscious desert of Pots de Creme Javanaise (oven-baked coffee custards), Locke had retreated with his host to a dark, richly paneled parlor adorned with original oil paintings from the Rococo Period and an array of display-cased pepperbox pistols and match-locks. A Montaigne cocktail table separated the two men; yew-wood sconces supported hand-forged silver candlesticks. The thin candles themselves were flax wicks hand-dipped into beeswax, which tinted the small parlor with a sweet, licorice scent. Locke was working on a good buzz now; the wine helped him get some of his doubts behind him. *All right, Lethe's eccentric, he's an art collector, and he likes rare things. That doesn't mean he's a crackpot.*

Correction, an art collector and a *patron.* Lethe's indulgences were Locke's good luck. And to keep that at his own side, he supposed he better indulge the host. *The guy just put ten large in my hand. The least I can do is talk some poet talk.* In truth, Lethe was probably nothing much more than a rich, lonely old man pining for someone to gratify his interests. Locke decided to gratify him.

"That's more of a populist definition, I'd say," Locke remarked to the comment.

"And why is that?"

"Because art isn't always beautiful. Art is the product of an introspective resource, don't you think? But it's a rare resource because it demands the total truth of its creator. Sometimes truth is ugly."

Lethe wanted conversation, that's all. He respected Locke's work, and now he wanted to hear about it. This could even be fun: parlor-talk with a millionaire...and some *really* good wine.

The elegant man nodded. "All right, and if that's the case—and I don't mean to quote Pilate—then what is truth?"

"Truth is nothing more than reality. The artist's job is to communicate that reality—the vision in his head—by *re*-creating it with the tools of his or her art. When Monet looked at those haystacks, he painted them in the truth of what he saw. It's all abstraction, sure, but that abstraction is more important than the paint, or in my case, the ink in my typewriter ribbon. If you don't do it honestly, then it's not art—it's a lie, and a lie is the artist's worst enemy."

"But didn't Nietzsche postulate—in his doctrine of nihilism—that there is no objective basis for truth?"

"Yes, he did," Locke agreed.

"And conversely, didn't Sartre assert that truth—though only and specifically via the individual's acknowledgment of his or her place in the universe—was very real?"

"Yes, he did."

Lethe ran a finger down his face. "These are clearly two of the most paramount intellectuals of your time, perhaps of all human history."

"Yes. They are."

"So...how do you explain the contradiction?"

"That's easy," Locke said. "Nietzsche was schizophrenic, and Sartre was wrong."

Lethe nodded through a smile, sipped the wine and seemed to stare at Locke's words as though they might be smoke rings or moths. "Such a pompous claim, but a claim full of what? Conviction?"

"I'll take that," Locke said.

"So what you're actually hinting at is something spiritual? Motivation?"

"Yes, you could call it that, but I prefer to think of it as—"

"Passion," Lethe intoned.

Locke stalled in his half-drunk rant. "Yes. Passion. I guess that's why Monet painted canvases instead of houses. Back then he'd have made more money painting houses." Locke knew he was talking about himself, but he eluded that self-acknowledgment.

There were ten thousand reasons.

"As we mentioned earlier," Lethe said. "The passion of the true artist may well be part of the same mechanism that fuels the passion of a Peter Kurten, a Gilles de Rais, or a Jack the Ripper."

"Well, that or insanity."

Lethe gave a slight laugh.

"It's also the most selfish thing in the world," Locke ventured.

"Selfish? I would think the exact opposite. The notion of sacrifice for the sake of the muse."

"No. The true artist doesn't care what anyone thinks of his muse. He does it anyway, because he *has* to."

"Just as J.S. Bach knew the Court of Brandenburg would abhor the fifth concerto, he composed it just the same."

"Because he had no choice. To write something more palatable simply to please his audience—that would've been like sticking a knife in himself," Locke elaborated, hoping he was correctly following Lethe's observation. He knew virtually nothing of Bach, nor the said concerto. "That's where the artist finds the truth—and, on the same hand, his art. In my field, in poetry, I can't allow myself to write a word or an image unless I've felt the reality of it. To me, poetry is the ultimate creative distillation, and, not to sound egotistical—"

"But please do!" Lethe insisted behind a chuckle.

"—and it's also the ultimate art form. Poets have a secret. We believe that poetry is the truest way in which mankind defines itself. How's that for egotistical?"

"Splendid!"

"No pretty paints to swirl around on a canvas in neat brushstrokes, no skillful carvings to fashion into the marble. Is that a truly aesthetic design, or just a technical skill for hire? Does the artist define the moment of his muse, or does the moment define the artist? It's one or the other, it's either the truth, or it's a lie—the worst kind of lie—at least if you're a person like me. Selling the lie to yourself. No different from the faith-healing charlatans selling hope to the hopeless, no different from the used-car dealer trying for all he's worth to fix you up in that lemon." Locke's head tipped back as he finished his glass. When he was drunk, at least he knew he was speaking from the heart. "No, sir, in my opinion, the truth of art can only exist in its bare words."

Lethe sat still as if very impressed, but then a lip turned up. "So the world must simply take the artist's word for it."

"Word for what?" Locke didn't follow.

"That what they're getting is indeed the truth instead of a lie. That what they're looking at or reading is not merely a 'technical skill for hire' but the artist's genuine passion."

Locke's big mouth had dug a hole, and suddenly he was being pushed in. Money obviously meant nothing to Lethe—he probably spent more on the wheelcovers of his Rolls than he'd just paid Locke for the book. *Fuck,*

Locke thought. He was being challenged. *Walk it like you talk it,* he avowed. *Never write a check with your mouth that you can't cash with your ass.* At least if he walked out of this house without a penny, he'd still have his word.

"Did, uh, did Bach give his commission back to the Court of Brandenburg?" Locke asked.

Lethe's smile was one of pure amusement. "Why, no, he didn't."

"Well then he was a phony schmuck. Let's face it, Mr. Lethe, the real reason you invited me here was probably to check me out a little, right?"

Lethe leaned back in the great elm wing-chair. "Perhaps… just a little."

"And you've just given me a lot of money. I'll admit, I *need* this money. I'm a poor man, but—"

Locke lapsed. What was he doing? His life had turned to shit, and now here he was about to take another handful. The ideal that had once driven him—his passion—he could only see now through the palest fog. This morning an auditory hallucination of a dead man had told him over the phone not to even come here. This was obviously just some remnant of Locke's former inner-self, his brain playing a symbolic trick reminding him of what he used to believe in to the very core of his being.

Don't be a whore, he thought. *Be stupid instead. Be real.*

"You were saying?" Lethe goaded.

Locke opened his eyes—he didn't remember closing them, just thinking as he gnawed the inside of his lip. "I was saying that I'm a poor man, but I can't do this." Now he let it go. So what? "My girlfriend dumped me for a lawyer. Yesterday my best friend got killed. So I just said to hell with it, I'm gonna be like everyone else."

Lethe leaned forward at what was happening, his chin propped up by steepled fingers. "But if there's one thing I sense most clearly, Mr. Locke— you're *not* like everyone else. You don't want to be."

"No, I guess I don't."

"But your point has escaped me…"

"My point?" Locke chuckled because he didn't want to cry. "All men have their price…but not me." He put the envelope full of cash on the shining cocktail table, slid it across to Lethe.

"I'll write the book for free," Locke said.

Lethe picked up the money, eyeing Locke. "You're not testing me, are you? You're quite serious."

"Yeah," Locke said. *And stupid.* "I can't take money for my work."

"You've probably been able to ascertain that I am quite financially solvent. You're sure about this?"

"Yes, sir."

Lethe looked dismayed. "Mr. Locke, you've proven your resolve. It isn't necessary to return the money."

"I have to," Locke said.

"I won't doubt your sincerity at all—you can change your mind."

"No," Locke said. "I can't. I'll write the book for free."

"But...there are certainly quite a few legal considerations. Limited-edition rights, sub-rights, paperback rights—"

Locke waved a half-drunk hand. "I'm just a poet, and pardon my language, but I don't give a shit about any of that. You can print this book and sell it to paperback for six figures and I don't care. I can't take money for my work. You want to pay me to wash your car, fine, I'll do it and I'll take your cash. Need your lawn mowed, call me. But that's it. My work is my heart, and my heart ain't for sale."

Lethe's brow arched. "You're absolutely sure about this?"

"Yes."

Lethe's mouth turned into a line of puzzlement. "So be it, then. I'd be taking advantage of you to insist. At least sleep on it. Perhaps your decision has been spurred by the wine. It's deceptively strong."

"Nope," Locke said. "Drunk or sober, I can't take money." Then he feebly tried to joke. "Just do a good job printing the hardcover."

"Oh, you can rest assured I will."

Locke nodded in silence, watched Lethe give the money back to the absurd, masked driver. A funny thing, though... *I'm poor again, but I feel... good.*

Lethe spake curt orders to the driver, "Mr. Locke has made a decision, Jason—"

Jason! Locke thought. *I finally know the guy's name!*

"Have the girl bring the bottle of Medoc—the Mistival 1774. And the Alsace snifters."

Hmm, Locke thought. *The girl?* He must mean the maid he'd seen earlier, getting out of the Daimler.

Lethe turned enthused to Locke. "It's my oldest bottle, I suspect it will be very good. Have you liked the wine thus far?"

"Yes, it's been great."

Footsteps clattered from a recessed room; voices murmured, then a door clicked shut. More footsteps barely registered to Locke's ear—they seemed to be descending. *A trip to the wine cellar,* he presumed. But at once, Locke felt dissolute. This had nothing to do with re-asserting his artistic motives by refusing Lethe's money, a snap-decision rooted to personal subjectivities; it felt more cored instead to the machinery of whatever creative skills he possessed.

Broken machinery.

Somewhere a gear had been stripped, a cam-bolt shorn. Returning to his poetical ethics was fine but that would not repair the broken cogs. A bust of

Euripides gazed off from a high ensconcement in the corner; Locke thought bizarrely of the "epitasis" of the Greek playwrights, the structural moment in which the plot accelerates. Locke knew his own career should be at the moment right now.

But it's not, he realized in a quickening glumness. *I missed the final act. The play's over...*

"You seem disconsolate." Lethe's rich voice, however quiet, resonated across the table.

"All of a sudden...I am," Locke admitted. "And I don't know why."

"Such are the hazards of your... Well, I shouldn't say your profession, since you refuse all profits from your talents. Your ambitions, then. The force which drives you. Wasn't it Van Gogh who attested that all artists are paranoid? The more stridently they seek to see their muse, the less they see in their own truth? Or what did Sophocles give emblem to with Teiresias?"

Strange that Lethe would make reference to a Greek play. "The prophet never sees his full potential until he's blind."

"And artists, of course, are prophets too."

Not me, Locke thought.

"Truths change," Lethe said. "Perhaps you haven't changed with yours."

Why abstract over this wreckage? Why psychologize over a writer's block? Locke didn't want to think about it anymore, he just wanted to drink. But then Lethe continued: "In truth, what is an ending, really?"

"A beginning," came Locke's dismal answer.

"How fine. Then it seems your work is at hand."

Locke looked up. Jason, still wearing the piped eyemask, had returned and was stiffly pouring the Medoc into wide glasses. Locke cleared his head. "What do you mean my work is—"

"You're a poet, correct? Poets create. So do that. Create."

Create, Locke thought blandly.

"I sense you were quite a bit at odds over the temptation to take money for your work, correct?"

"Yes," Locke droned.

"But you've made your decision, and that's behind you now. And at the heart of that decision you've taken a part of yourself from one place to another. You've created an end which can only lead to a beginning. Correct?"

Locke shrugged. "Yeah, I guess." He supposed he could justify Lethe's notion aesthetically. *Every end is a beginning. I've gone from one place to another place. So...what's the other place?*

Lethe raised an erudite finger as if he'd read Locke's thoughts. "You can only find the other place by acknowledging, by...doing what poets do. By *creating* with words. You can only find the place of new beginnings by first creating the previous door, so to speak."

Locke felt befuddled, annoyed even. "What do you mean?"

"I can't speak for your muse, Mr. Locke, but if I were you, based on what you've told me tonight, I'd use my creative powers to build the... Well, let me think of the proper word..." Lethe's index finger came to his lip. His eyes closed momentarily. Then he said, "Something to give structure to...the act of your going out. The creative means by which you've made your exit. But I can't quite think of the word—"

"Egress," Locke said.

"Yes!" Lethe nearly clapped within the exclamation. "The egress! *That,* Mr. Locke, is what you must create of your own. The path by which your muse will leave the old place and emerge into the new."

Locke wanted to sputter. He hated this dilettante art-school babble.

"An exit from the place you *don't* want to be, to the entryway to another place. The place you truly *do* want to be."

It sounded like foolishness to Locke but... *He thinks I should write a poem about an egress, an exit point.* Several seconds passed in the contemplation.

"Oh, my!"

Locke looked up. Lethe had just taken his first sip of the Medoc, and now his eyes beamed.

"What?" Locke asked.

"This wine is absolutely perfect. Do try it."

"Now *that* I can do," Locke said and swished a sip of the red Bordeaux through his mouth.

(ii)

Ten grand lost but, even in this drunken idealism, he felt better than he had in months. He felt *real.*

So that was something, wasn't it?

After they'd finished the Medoc—not dark but plush, semi-tart with no after-taste till it was past the back of your throat, a strong bouquet—Jason, the masked double-duty driver, showed Locke to his quarters which, to his surprise was a nice cottage in the enclosed back yard. Just a squat stucco job, one of four in a row before the high hedges that lined the back brick fence. Some small imported trees had been planted, and several neatly formed gardens spiraled off. *Nice digs,* he thought but at once heard a high-pitched, jovial squeal, then some laughter.

"That's Mr. Martin and his...assistants," Jason explained, casting an eye toward the second cottage. "They get into some partying. If it's too loud, let me know. I'd be happy to move you into a room in the house."

"No, this is fine," Locke said. Drapes over the next cottage's window were pulled tight, but he could see figures moving in the lamplight, and faintly detected music. "I can sleep through an earthquake."

Jason, then, led Locke into his own cottage. Inside was immaculate, spare: a pristine four-poster, a leather recamier sofa, and a narrow stained-oak chiffonier to serve as a dresser. It would do.

The driver put his bag down at the doorstep. "Is there anything else, Mr. Locke?"

Locke wanted to level with him, ask, *Hey, man, does Lethe pay you a lot to wear that mask and dress up like a manservant?* but that would've been a shit-heel thing to do. *You'll embarrass the guy...* "No, I'm all set, Jason, thanks. See you tomorrow, man."

The manservant nodded curtly, then left, clicking the door shut behind him.

Locke sat down on the deep bed, sinking into a soft mattress.

All right, I'm drunk, but I feel pretty good.

No regrets—it amazed him. He returned ten thousand in cash, and felt *good.* He knew why, of course. This was the first step in the trek back to his sense of truth, his old self before his life collapsed. It told him something he hadn't believed yesterday, or three months ago.

There was a road back...

And I've got my feet on the path.

Or, in this case, the egress.

Art-clique sophistry or not, Lethe's articulate conversation was stimulating. By symbolizing the most emotive events in his life—with his work—Locke *was* building an exit-ramp of sorts. The notion left him enthused, but...

Talking was one thing. Doing it was another.

I'll just have to do it.

The wine filled his head. He actually wanted to write for a change but the tingeing drunkenness stifled him. He quickly left the cottage and began to take long strides about the plush back yard. Fresh air was all he needed, and a little Mother Nature. Above, the clouds broke, showing a spectacular twilight. An owl hooted from a high tree beyond the brick fence, and a light gust of wind made the shrubs whisper. Locke sighed at a sense of peace.

The second cottage was dark now, no lights behind the drapes, no music or loud talk when only a few minutes ago, they'd been partying in there. Strange. Then he walked further into the moon-tinted yard. The third and fourth cottages stood dark too. Did Lethe have more guests staying in these?

He felt more than saw the light flick on at the fourth cottage. The small windows stood brightly lit through the slats of their blinds. *I didn't see anyone go in there,* he felt sure. Which could only mean that the occupants had been inside all along. Perhaps Lethe did have some other guests.

As quickly as it had come on, though, the light went out again, and the door clicked open, showing an oblong block of darkness. Then it clicked shut.

Locke squinted, hidden in the back yard's murk.

Who the hell—

A figure walked silently from the fourth cottage to the third. Locke could detect no details, only that the figure couldn't be Jason. Not tall enough, not the right gait. In a moment, however, the figure entered the third cottage, closed the door and locked it. Whoever it was, they clearly hadn't noticed Locke. He felt like a spy.

Dimmer lights flicked on in the third cottage's front windows, probably a light closer to the rear of the main room. Through the blind-slats, he could see the figure moving inside.

He'd crept along most of the fence perimeter before his thoughts caught him: *Are you out of your mind? What are you doing?*

Even Locke wasn't sure at first. It was just an impulse, as human, perhaps, as it was immoral. Locke's will pulled away from him—*You asshole! Someone's going to see you!*—and after only a minute or two, he found himself back against the cottage's darkest side next to a smaller window. For whatever reason, then, he looked in even as his thoughts continued to object.

What kind of a nutcake crackpot weirdo pervert are you? You're supposed to be writing poetry, not peeping in people's windows!

Yet peep he did. It was a woman inside, undressing. Locke could barely see her but could see enough. She stood in just a slant of wan, butter-toned lamplight, blocked off to either side by wider slants of darkness which made the cramped room seem submerged in ink. Further movement drew Locke's face closer to the tiny glass pane...

The slat he peered through only allowed him to see her from mid-thigh to bosom. She appeared to be removing a short, shiny-black skirt and bodice of some kind but before Locke could speculate further it was off and she was nude. Something primal lured his gaze to her breasts: not large but high, pert, and white like sculpted limestone. Nipples of deep sepia jutted to fascinating points. Then her hand—fine, white, with short, black-painted nails—raised to caress one of the breasts.

This could get interesting, Locke deduced. *This view's almost worth the misdemeanor charge...* But who was she? A guest? An employee? *No, wait! The maid who'd been driving the Daimler!* It must be. And though details were nearly impossible to discern beyond the meager slant of light, why did the room seem barren? But that was not the only incongruence, was it?

Locke squinted so hard his temples thumped; his vision strained, groped for more of the curious image. She was just standing there, plucking at the large nipples, an erotic headless statuette. It was the immediate distraction of her breasts that had sideswiped Locke's attentions. His eyes now focused on the flat of her abdomen, smooth and tight as a gymnast's. But...

The belly appeared swollen to the extent that Locke guessed she must be five or six months pregnant. He noted the curve of the tiniest line of fine hair tracing from her navel to her pubic hair. Her hand lowered to the center of the swelling and rubbed it.

Then Locke turned to ice when someone else entered the room.

Shit!

"It's late. The poet's asleep," came a gruff voice. Locke recognized it at once: Jason, the manservant. Jason's own hand reached out (he remained dressed in his French-cuffed butler's jacket and the morning trousers) and touched the woman's stomach. "I thought they were going to drink all night."

Locke realized in an instant: Jason and the woman must be lovers, and this third cottage must be their hideaway. Was she pregnant by the driver? *Yeah,* Locke thought. *They're lovers.* But after what he saw next, he knew—

"Stand still, bitch. Let me see it."

—they were lovers of a very strange bent.

Jason had opened his trousers and just stood there in front of her, masturbating. The borders of the slat prevented Locke from seeing either face; it was simply a blocked frame of bodies in dim, angled light. The driver's hand shucked the penis back and forth—it was a *large* penis—while the woman's index and middle fingers V'd to hold open her furred labia, which shined bright mallow pink. Then—

SLAP!

The woman's body jerked in the frame—clearly Jason had brought his other hand across the side of her face, and with some force. But she issued not even a whimper.

"Like that?"

SLAP!

"Bet that puts some juice between your gams, huh?"

SLAP! SLAP!

Twice more, then the driver's business hand worked harder.

"Got some comin' for ya..."

The woman's belly looked protuberant; swollen as it already was, it seemed now that she was pushing it out further in some uninterpretable stimulation. The modest breasts heaved, the dark nipples now so full of excitation they stuck out rigid like pinkie-ends. Gusts of breath grew hot; Locke had never seen anything so strange. *Whatever happened to coitus?*

"Here, here—"

Now the offending hand seemed to raise to her throat and squeeze. Locke heard the most petite choking sounds.

"Fuckin' whore. Let's shine you up."

It didn't take much longer for Jason to have his crisis. His hips flinched, his hand moving now in a rabid blur, and—

"Yeah, bitch. There. There it is—"

The ejaculation launched out: gelatinous worms now squirmed onto the faceless woman's belly. The belly sucked in and out; then the sperm ran down the fine, white skin to settle in globs amid the tuft of pubic hair. Irregular pearls in a nest.

"All right," the driver gruffed. "I'm ready now..."

Locke's eyes flicked up, to the girl's bosom. Now she was pinching a nipple between index finger and thumb, pinching hard, and simultaneously—

Oww! Locke thought.

—inserting a frightfully long sewing needle directly into the end of the nipple.

Locke heard a feminine hiss.

Both figures moved back into the darkness then, as Jason lowered his mouth to the speared nipple.

Mmmm, mmmmmmm...

Faint if not greedy sucking noises ensued; the figures disappeared into murky ink beyond the room.

Shit, Locke thought. *Call me a prude...but that's a bit too kinky for me...* In 1990, he'd dated a girl—a grocery-story cashier—who'd seemed very straitlaced. Mousy, thick glasses, librarianesque. But after a few drinks and once in bed, she begun to gutter such instructions as, "Bite me till I bleed!" "Yank my hair!" and "Choke me out!" Ever the selfless lover, Locke had tried as he might to please her but simply couldn't continue when her lewdly smiling face began to turn blue. She'd raged at him. "You stupid fuck! You were supposed to choke me out!" Locke declined calling her back.

But this?

He heard a whisper—"Ja..., sheiss..."—which sounded vaguely Germanic. Then he remembered the woman who'd answered the phone when he'd called yesterday. *This kink-job racehorse must be Lethe's receptionist,* he gathered.

"Gott... Blut..."

In the murk, Locke could only see the palest form of her coltish legs wrap around her paramour's jacketed back. The legs squeezed, and she squealed. After that... Just more greedy sucking sounds.

Then, more vaguely, Jason's form rose—

"Here's one more for ya—"

A sharp, splattering sound now, like someone upending a bucket of beef stew onto pavement.

Jason threw up into what Locke guessed must be the girl's face.

"Eat my puke, ya cum-dump. You like it, it's the best meal ya had in a week, like Campbell's Chunky Style, huh? Don't get jealous—tomorrow *you* get to puke."

Locke couldn't actually see what happened next, but he could hear it. A more steady, fainter splattering, and an accommodating ink-shape in the darkness. The shape of the macabre driver standing over the girl, urinating on her with verve.

"Good action?"

Locke's heart stopped when someone from behind tapped him on the shoulder. He was fainting from the shock as he pinwheeled, then collapsed.

Fading.

Fading.

A repugnant stench flurried: decomposition. It seemed to reach down and touch his face like curious fingers, and in the second before his consciousness sailed away, Locke saw a dilapidated figure standing before him, and heard this:

"I told you not to come here. Nothing can stop the transposition now, so you better get ready for it..."

(iii)

Professor Fredrick awoke to the sound of—*What?* he thought. His mind felt clotted, a once-reliable machine now slowed down by pitted bearings. A clock fitted neatly with Phonetician numerals ticked on the wall. *Three in the morning?*

God. He'd fallen asleep grading papers after his last class. *Seventy-five years old,* the realization creaked along with his office chair when he leaned up. Ten years ago they'd told him he was too old for anymore field work; as an archaeologist, that was like telling a veteran mechanic he was too old to pick up a box wrench. *Now I'm too old to stay awake at my desk.*

Fredrick was the Chairman of the University of Washington's Department of Archaeological Studies. For the past half a century, he'd seen it all, done it all, and was perhaps the most esteemed living member of his profession in the world. No, no more digs—he was a health insurance risk with the mid-stage osteoporosis and borderline emphysema—not from smoking but from breathing the dust of buried civilizations and a thousand ancient sepulchers that he himself had opened. The revenge of the gods, the price of daring to look into the mummified faces of Ramses III and Duncan I, of kings and queens and princes and peasants. *At least I got a nice office out of it,* he thought now.

His fax machine was slowly spitting something out—the noise that had wakened him. But who would be faxing him at this ungodly hour? He started to get up but flinched and sat back down, a bite of pain in his lower back that had plagued him since he'd pushed over a vault lid in Nequada twenty years ago, searching for the body of one of Herod's bastard sons. The damage was for nothing; all that filled the crypt were pieces of broken tabby urns—*potsherds*—used to store flax and millet for the world's first zymurgists. In the respite, his hooded eyes gazed around the office and at the relics that filled it. Brooches and jupon-clips. Masks of bronze and wristcuffs of primal iron. Stave-caps, armlets, breastplates, and even Princess Canessa's chastity belt. A slate-palette from King Narmer's scribes, an ivory macehead from a Basque grave. The stuff of history? *Or junk?* he wondered now at this wee hour. *Rubbish that no one cares about.* The gold inlays of a priceless robe-clasp once belonging to Queen Nefertiti had now, after, oh, say, 3,500 years, disintegrated, infinity taking back what it was owed. Why let Fredrick have it merely to sit unlooked at in his droll office? Lastly, in the corner by a bust of Nergal, hung his clay-flecked leather boots, the same he'd worn on countless digs. From Galli to Nineveh, from Jericho to Troy to Knossos. He abstracted, wanting to smile. He thought of himself as a specter of the future. All these cities, once great, had been predestined to be trod upon by Fredrick's old boots thousands of years later. Time buried. Whole civilizations locked in layers of clay. He had spent his life walking on worlds, and some day, he realized, someone like him would walk on his.

The fax machine's whine ceased, the single sheet of paper lolling like a sheet of skin. Just once he wished he'd get a decent inquiry, something to sink the few teeth he had left into. Sometimes he wished he could be dead rather that serve out the rest of this prison term as a teacher.

With an audible groan, he leaned forward again and snatched up the fax paper. Just one sheet, with a curious header that read:

STATE MACRO-ANALYSIS COMPUTER (MAC) TOPIC/NAME/SUBJECT SEARCH CONCLUSION.

PAGE ONE OF ONE (1) PAGE

RECIPIENT: YOU HAVE BEEN IDENTIFIED AS A POSSIBLE CONSULTANT FOR THE FOLLOWING SEARCH REQUEST INITIATED BY:

CORDESMAN, J., CAPT., SEATTLE POLICE DEPART-
MENT/NORTH PRECINCT HOMICIDE/ ASSAULT
UNIT.

Fredrick's tired eyes squinted at first, as if bored. He got these things all the time, technical inquiries from the state and county governments, or lawyers, usually just questions about foreclosures on land that might be of historic value, and every now and then he'd get one from the police regarding museum thefts.

But after reading the following few lines of *this* query, he chuckled to himself and whispered, "Oh, thank you, God. Thank you for giving this old heretic something fun to do."

(iv)

Was it a dream?

A blazing blue sky nearly blinded him from above. A lone finch seemed to dive out of the sun, right toward him, then was gone. He thought he heard tiny waves lapping a shore but couldn't see water. Then came the smell of burning leaves. Where was he, dream notwithstanding? The Downtown Waterfront? Gasworks Park? It didn't really matter. It was a place of tranquil beauty, of placation and sunlight...

Then the dream-world turned dark.

"Do you hear me? Do you recognize my voice?" Locke heard through the vale of black. Yes, he did. *But this is just a dream,* he realized. *So why should I be afraid?*

"Because I'm a fuckin' dead man talking to you..."

"Byers... White Shirt..."

"You got it. And let me tell you something—" but then the words drained down to vocal drizzle, nothing left intelligible.

"What!" Locke snapped. "What!"

Warbling, and the sound of a dead surf. A single word worked through it all, and it sounded like, "...malefactor..."

What was this? More drunkenness? An alcohol-reaction to the hypo-thalamus? More pre-D.T. hallucinatory effects? He'd drunk a lot, yes, but he'd also eaten a lot—had stuffed himself, actually, on Lethe's charity of French cuisine. *Drunks always look for an excuse, and this is just a dream!* Locke thought in the dream.

Then the dream turned hot. Hot as hell.

Caverns of charred rock, caverns of skin whose pores eddied oily smoke. An imprecation, a visual melange: chaos in the scape of his mind. Reefs of blood-red clouds roved past a black moon. The sky shone smoky pink like begonias patted with industrial soot. Beyond the vale, a range descended, a range of more sizzling rock black as anthracite. The zenith behind him—if it could be called that—was studded by plinths, by black cenotaphs and dolmens old as the world. Then Locke's hot eyes recast to the pit below. Ringed by unspeakable bushes and weeds limp and slimy as snakes, a tarn glittered the black moonlight off its crystal face. Tiny rovings could be detected beneath the death-still surface: faces? Tendrils of mist crawled upward, and eventually Locke saw bubbles emerge.

Then came a fat *splash,* like dropping a stone into hot tar.

An agonized head stuck up from the surface. A flayed arm waved, but not in greeting, in terror.

"Locke!"

The heat drew sweat from the skin of Locke's eyeballs. His sweat poured off his chin like tap water from a spigot. He strained his vision at the head—

"Oh, no..."

—and recognized Lehrling's blood-sheened face.

"My, God, help me get me out of here! What did I do to deserve this, Locke?"

Locke couldn't imagine.

It wasn't water that filled the marsh, it was smoldering blood. Nevertheless, Locke dashed forward, reaching out for his friend, but before he could even make it to the shore of sulfurous black sand—

My, God—

Several *other* figures emerged behind Lehrling. These figures were not human but instead indescribable *things.*

"Locke! Get—"

"I can't hear you!" Locke shrieked.

"Get out of the house!"

Lehrling gagged amid the struggles of his terror, while his hosts toyed at him. Like golems, they rose, picking at Lehrling with greedy, stunted hands. Locke detected only rudiments of facial features, crude ridgelike brows, slits for eyes like knife slashes in spoiled meat.

"Get out of the house tonight! It's not really—"

"Not really what!" Locke shouted back.

But by now, Lehrling was drowning in blood, gargling in it. Then one of the things pressed a subhuman hand to the novelist's mouth; Lehrling bucked. Vomit sprayed from his nostrils as his face bulged, but next he had no face at all when another of the blood-creatures promptly sucked it off the skull.

What a gross-as-shit dream...

Then these things, these ushers, dragged Lehrling back down into the depths of the hell-marsh. In a few moments a violent rip of bubbles broke, then crushed organs and hanks of flesh rose to the surface—

Locke jerked back into cold darkness.

Another dream…

"You're unfulfilled," came the most plush voice. A woman's, and a scent like lilacs. Locke couldn't see her, he could only calculate her beauty. *Devastating* beauty.

But…where was he now?

A dead room in the dead of night, laved in twilight. Just a bare mattress, bare walls streaked by dust and discolor. Bare wood floors. Behind him, where a headboard might be, a small window framed the moon.

"I can taste it," she said.

"Whuh-what?"

"Your despair."

It's only a dream, he reminded himself. But even in dreams, could he be scanned so easily? Or had his despair merely sharpened to the point of bleeding, part of his soul running out of a cut?

The shadow listed beside him. "What means more to you than anything?"

"Truth, I guess," he answered through chattering teeth. He sat huddled on the bed, naked. Freezing.

"But now you feel there is none."

Not a question, a statement. She knew, whoever *she* was. A shard of dream symbology, a siren of sleep?

A succubus?

"Your love is your truth—"

"Yes!" Locke bellowed, though what erupted from his throat was a broken creak.

"And now your love is gone."

In moonlight, Locke looked up at this figure of black splinters which sat beside him. But then his heart leapt. His companion's face formed and—

Locke's breath seized in his lungs.

It was Clare's face.

His hands reached out, fingers groping to glide through her lovely blonde hair, to touch the face of his love but it was all gone in the next blink. Not Clare, it never had been. Just a ghost-image from the past, a past as dead as this room.

The woman was simply showing him things. "When you close your eyes, do you see angels or devils?"

"Angels," he muttered. Open or closed, there was little difference. Just different variations of black.

"The truth is there, you just have to know which curtain to look behind, or what face."

Now Locke was freezing…to death. His bones shivered.

"If truth is born in reality, what happens when truths change?"

Locke didn't understand the question. The moonlight lent his skin a hue of morgue-blue as though he was dead already, just not yet on the slab.

Let me die…

But if he died would he wake up? Or would he really be dead? Locke didn't much care which.

"You refaced yourself tonight," the woman whispered. "You turned your vulnerability into power, your weakness into strength."

What? Agreeing to write the book for no money? Yes, he'd felt good about that, and Lethe's clipped aesthetic advice had seemed to raise him up from his doldrums. But what difference did any of that make?

"He will have to find other weaknesses now, and he will."

He? Lethe? The dream was absurd.

"There's no turning back anymore. Your truth has set the rest in motion."

To hell with it, he realized. *It's my dream, I can do what I want, can't I?* Shivering he leaned up and looked at her hard.

"Who are you?"

"Moira. At least that's one of my names."

Moira… Locke had never heard of such a name so how could a dream, the spillage of his unconscious mind, create it? Something he'd read somewhere, or heard, and had simply forgotten.

"I want to see you," he croaked.

"You are."

"But—" A shadow, just a figure hidden in darkness and shadow…

"Look harder."

Something happened then, a sifting sound? Something ineffable, a swarm of ebon glints. Then Locke *saw.*

No, she wasn't merely a figure hidden in shadow. She was *composed* of it. Her blood was the night, her flesh and bone a physical accretion of darkness, of tenebrae. She was *made* of it. A creature as real as himself yet a creature of secrets. Lightless yet vitreous, human but something far more yet strangely less. She was either the first woman to ever walk the surface of the earth, or the last. Oblivion formed her skin, infinity her hands and long delicate fingers. Yes, she was as black as the deepest chasm of the earth…

But just as real.

Only the touch of her carbon hand to his chest dissipated the deathly cold. In an instant, Locke felt hot—he felt alive again. Her bottomless eyes peered at him, and there was something like longing there, however primal, however encrypted and ancient. And then her face—that was no real face at all—urged forward, and she brought her timeless lips to his.

Locke felt immersed in the same oblivion that she was made of. *Moira*, he thought. *Not a woman at all…*

A goddess, or—no! An angel!

"All the truth that you can bear…is yours."

Then Locke knew. She was the angel who'd carried him off the other night, in the dream, or his madness. She was the same.

"We're the same, you and I…"

A hot tongue slipped into his mouth. Her own mouth sucked against his; it seemed to steal the life from his lungs but give something back—some wisdom, some cabalistic message. Locke just closed his eyes and sighed into her beautiful mouth. *Take what you want,* he thought. *Take everything…*

But the kiss didn't take as he expected—even desired—It simply gave more to the point that Locke saw visions as though he were standing upon the highest peak of the known world. He saw heralds. He saw secrets the likes of which had not been whispered to another in thousands of years.

"See…"

Then he began to see, but what was sight save for pinpoints of light and color reflecting off the backs of his eyeballs? Locke's eyes were closed. Yet he saw.

"Don't open your eyes," a hot breath oozed into his ear. "You can't really see me."

Why not? Locke thought the words, but he didn't care. He knew that he would do whatever the angel said. Anything…

Her abyssal body slithered over him, a dark, luxuriant fluid. Locke, by this point, didn't dare reopen his eyes for now he could see more finely than he ever had. Eyes closed, yes, but mind *open*…

And he saw—

Lambent skin like moonstone. Flawless contours and indefectible lines. Skin warm as the inside of a freshly cut animal pelt.

The feel of her lips, then, quickly on his penis, coaxed a sensation like a skewer of high-voltage current.

Somewhere something ticked. A clock? Or the essence of his life, each grain trickling out like the filings of an hourglass.

She didn't talk now—not with her mouth clamped onto his. Instead, she thought, and Locke heard it. He heard her words with the same efficacy as someone with a key in an electrical socket, shimmering in the course of the sensation.

You've defeated a weakness tonight. That's what led me here…

Her kisses sucked away his doubts, slurped out his deficiencies. The mattress felt like warm clouds now, mist that propped him up to her endless kiss… Her spread palms on his body gave him existence; he felt emboldened, empowered—with *something*. Next their mouths tracked every square inch of the other's skin, the flat of their tongues licking pleasure from every sense. His close-eyed face between her legs found her flavor alchemic, preternatural. The most extraordinary of elixirs—it seemed to transmute him in some way. Her sex veneered his mouth, sheened down the slope of his throat. She came and came, and Locke tasted each climax.

Eventually, he impaled her; his hands picked her up and folded her into every possible position of love, lust, wantonness, and instinct. Passion or selfish hunger—it scarcely mattered either way because it was *real* either way.

It was truth.

The peeling of his love bled through his mind and his spirit, sucked out by her body heat, her aura, and her sweat. Was he giving to her, or was she taking? *Take!* Locke thought, but in essence he knew it must be neither. It was merged, a *commingled* lust and desperation. A need to be groped for and a gift to be freely given.

This was more than sex, more than fucking. So much more than the genetic impulse to copulate, shudder, and aspirate sperm. Whatever this really was didn't matter for Locke knew it was everything he'd ever been searching for in his entire life.

More than Clare, more than anything...

My verity, my love, the heated thought fluttered. It was the tiniest of sounds in his being, a ticking heart valve, a synapse firing between nerve cells.

A night without finish, a dream without end. Locke put his semen into her time and time again; her sex seemed to suck out each release as if dying for it. She whispered words into the crook of his neck, but Locke, in his frenzy, could only discern an inscrutable milieu: sounds like the abrading of insect mandibles, nightbirds flapping their wings low in the twilight, the blood rushing through the veins of a lioness as it waits for a scent, the wind through a fertile field at midnight. Locke could feel the sounds, could smell the colors, and the harder his eyes squeezed shut, the more effusively he saw her:

Raving, silken red hair. Slim-toned limbs, taut skin the color of fresh snow, and agate eyes like a cat's. Her breasts stuck out to him like flawless chiffon orbs.

They made love without end. The moon, and the night's fine stars, peeked in on them through the barren window. Their sweat soaked them, sliding into a natural shellac on their skin.

Later, numb and unable to move, he leaned up nonetheless. In his mind he saw every aspect of her human beauty, every plane of her womanhood.

Her delicate hand caressed his spent penis.

"Open your eyes now," her voice chittered. "Tell me what you see."

Locke opened them. And froze.

The shadow again, the night folded over a million times into this living, corporeal obvolution. She lay as a contour of razor-sharp, carbon-black lines.

Her eyes grew into obsidian spheres—huge—and as she spoke, her lips parted to show him yet again the deepest chasms of the earth, the black guts of the universe, and death.

"Remember this," the words wavered, not a voice anymore but the murmur of a distant waterfall.

"Nothing is immutable. I've watched the proof of this since time immemorial. My heart has bled with every glance, with every second for the last five thousand years."

Locke lay pinned down by his own misconstrution, his own error and his loss. The terrifying cold returned, a cloak dropped over him, and he thought he would die; he even wished for it.

It's just a dream, he reassured himself.

No, the precious specter said. *It's not...*

Locke plummeted into death.

SIXTEEN

NETHER-MANSE

(i)

I dreamed I died...

Sex and death, love and loss. *A real D.H. Lawrence kind of dream.* A literary analyst's field day. This dream had it all. Maybe the only symbol it *didn't* have was the old Freudian cigar.

Locke walked along the graveled path that wound from the guest house around the perimeter of Lethe's estate. High branches hung over his head; late-season flowers bloomed, spreading pungent scents. A gravel walkway encircled a spacious garden, and the lawn had been meticulously trimmed. He remembered what Lethe had said about "appearances"; here was just another example. The exterior of the manse and the outer yard proved an utter eyesore, while the inside as well as the rear grounds and the four neat guest cottages provided a polar opposite. *Appearances...* Why should he suddenly be fixated on this word, and how it might more deeply relate to Lethe? Maybe the walk would clear his head; instead his mind felt fogged by fuddled notions. And remembering the dream didn't help.

It had seemed so vivid...

Indeed, he'd dreamed of his own death, but also of a rebirth in self-assessment.

Just another nightmare...and a fucked up one at that, he forced himself to conclude. The picture wouldn't fade, the woman—Moira—placing his hands on the swelling of her breasts as she leaned over...

And the rest.

What? Sex? Love? Passion? Locke shook his head, it had seemed so real, but that was impossible.

She was not of his world, not of his reality.

Only a figment of mind...

Or a figment of some other *reality?*

More notions without pretense, without definition. *A puzzle,* he thought. *From my own screwed-up, alcohol-drenched brain.*

Angel, my ass.

Just another drunk's hallucination. *Maybe I should take back Lethe's money and check myself into a psych clinic.*

Locke roved the grounds, skimmed past the other three cottages...

Jesus, I am SO screwed up...

He stared at the third cottage, frowning. Of course, it was all part of the dream. *Right. Some naked chick in the window? Then Jason strolling in to yank his crank and—pardon me—suck blood out of the girl's hooters? Have another drink, Locke. Don't settle for half measures. Fuck up your brain* all *the way why don't ya?* Then the rest—being tapped on the shoulder from behind by White Shirt, the recurring dead man. Nevertheless, after a blank pause, Locke found himself peering into the third cottage's front window. Empty, of course. Not even a lamp nor any blinds over any of the windows. Another peek showed him that the fourth cottage, too, from which he'd seen the woman originally emerge, was barren. Locke wandered back toward the flower spread in the center of the yard.

Dreams of his own death. Lehrling, apparently, drowning in damnation. A resurrected White Shirt spouting more inanities about transposition, and demented kinkoid S&M sex scenes. Locke felt satisfied with himself in the immediacy with which he could dismiss it all as subconscious waste. But—

He came to a halt by a front of orchids and filarees.

Moira, he remembered.

Another symbol built in his subconscious mind, nothing more. He knew that...so why did he feel such an after-image? He could still feel her hands on him, could still feel the ecstasy of his joining. Like Clare had been...

Something real.

The urge exploded in him, one he hadn't felt for a long time. He trotted back to his cottage, then the trot broke into a sprint. Words began to spill out of his head; he grit his teeth in a desperate plea to catch them. Once he was back in the cottage he rummaged through his travel bag, whipped out his notepad and a pen, then frantically began to write. Only one problem.

Shit goddamn I can't believe it!

The pen was dead.

Locke stared in agony at the inkless scratches in the paper. He was going to lose it, he knew. It was going to fly away like a parakeet whose owner had left the cage door up. This happened a lot; the muses were not kind. If you didn't write it down right away, it was gone forever. As quick as his fear, Locke turned to bolt for the main house and saw—

No. It couldn't be...

There, in the far corner next to the small bathroom. A small walnut

Pembroke table with something on top of it. Something covered by a drape of simple cloth the color of jonquils. Locke knew what it was even before he removed the cover.

Now we're cookin'! Yes sir!

What sat on the table was a typewriter, a Smith-Premiere Bar-Lock series. More of Lethe's high-class obsession: the machine was nearly a hundred years old but in mint condition, a fresh ribbon threaded through the type-guide. Locke's host was a keenly thoughtful man. A stack of white bond paper filled a small drawer in the table. Locke cranked in a sheet and began to chase his muse.

He never saw the tiny yellowed tag on the back of the antique machine which read in tight cursive script:

Property of Robert E. Howard, Author, Cross Plains, Texas.

(ii)

"Yeah, I know, Central Commo already told me," Cordesman griped into the phone. "The red hairs from the church matched red hairs found at sixteen other 64 sites." But Cordesman had already figured that; bad luck often arrived in abundance. *When it rains, it pours,* he thought of the tired axiom. Or: *When God takes a piss, He takes a BIG piss, generally right on my head.* "Is that it?"

Kerr was calling from his car phone, obviously eating as he spoke. "Yeah, er, no, I mean—"

Cordesman winced. "Didn't your mommy ever teach you it's not polite to talk when your fuckin' chops are full of fuckin' food?"

Kerr's lips kept on smacking. "Not exactly in those words, Captain."

"Where are you, the O.K. Corral? Sounds like you're eating out of a horse trough."

"I'm at Ivar's on Northgate. The halibut fish and chips are great. With the malt vinegar? Yes, sir!" Kerr crunched into another fillet.

"Fine. So that's it?"

"We got joint photos of the homeless guys in the church. All their prints were on file with the W.C.I. database."

"All ex-cons?"

"Yep…I mean yes, sir. Non-state charges, just county and city, and the only fells were knocked down on suspended sentences. But they all did a string of short-time, mostly small stuff—car-breaking, repeat shop-lifting, wallet-boosting. The bald guy—you'll love this, Captain—he got busted by King County PD in '91 for taking a shit on a 256 bus to Bellevue and pissing on the coinbox."

Cordesman ran a disgruntled hand through his long hair. "You're right, Kerr. I *loved* that."

"So I've got a flatfoot squad running the pictures around the local shelters."

"You thought of that all on your own?"

"Yes, sir. I'm pretty smart. Say…about that step-raise—"

"Just the shelters?"

"Sir?"

"You'd get the raise if you'd also thought to have the rubber-gun fellas tote those ident pix around all the bridges in, say, a five-mile circle from the church."

"Bridges?"

"Yeah, Kerr. You know. Things that bums frequently sleep under."

A stuffy pause. "Yes, sir, I already thought of that, and we're on it."

"Uh-huh. And the Yankees just dug up Mantle and gave him a new liver and a five-year contract."

"I'm serious, sir. Oh, and one more thing. I'm also supposed to tell you that Brock's on her way to see you."

"Great," Cordesman sputtered. "This case is hard enough. The last thing I need is that sour-puss pain in the ass in here again acting like she's the fuckin' queen of fuckin' forensic examination. And when she's not doing that, she's bellyaching about my cigarette smoke. And if there's one thing that pisses me off, it's these smug fuckers always yammering about second-hand smoke and fuckin' cancer rates. Christ, I'll bet she hasn't been laid in twenty years, takes all her pent-up angst off on the whole world."

"You're a real nice guy, Captain," Kerr said, munching more fish.

"I know. So why's that poker-faced, dagger-glaring, bad-news bitch coming to my office?"

"Why don't you just ask me?"

Cordesman's cigarette fell out of his mouth when he heard the voice. *You stupid horse's ass…* He hung the phone up without further word, then looked up to see that Jill Brock had been standing in his office doorway the whole time.

He held his hands up, shrugged. "I'm sorry, Jill. What can I say? I'm an asshole. Don't really know why—I just am. Can't help it, I guess."

First he got the poker-face, then the dagger-glare. "Well, the bad-news bitch just thought you might be interested in some latents," she said.

"Look, I said I was sorry."

"I'd point out that second-hand cigarette smoke contributes to the premature deaths of at least 15,000 non-smokers per year, Captain, but you obviously don't need some smug fucker like me insisting that I have the right not to be forced to inhale *your* carcinogens."

"I apologize for what I said, Jill. Shit, I was just joking around, I didn't mean—"

"So if you'll pardon the intrusion of this sour-puss pain in the ass, you might be interested to know that while you were off smoking cigarettes, my crew worked their butts off taking apart that church, and we found something most unusual."

Cordesman raised another cigarette to his lips, then put it back. "Are you going to tell me, or are you going to bust my chops a little more? Go ahead, make me feel worse. I deserve it."

Brock opened a manila TSD folder and from it produced a second folder of clear acetate. Pressed between the rigid transparent sheets was what appeared to be an unfolded napkin or handkerchief full of orangish blotches that Cordesman knew to be residual iodine from a latent fuming processor. Along with anthracene, this was the method of choice for securing finger-prints from porous and soft paper.

But there was...something...disturbingly familiar here.

"May I see that, please, Ms. Brock?"

Brock handed it over. Yes, it was a napkin fully unfolded, and Cordesman could see the ridges and whorls of a number of fingerprints amid the orange stains. The corner of the napkin read: CONCANNON'S IRISH PUB, and then he noticed something else that made his stomach tighten. Scribbling in ballpoint, and the words: *Evil kisses, or angelic sendings, I want to be in the vale of beginnings, not endings.*

"The city MAC matched the prints to a resident on the 1300-block of North 45th Street in Wallingford," Brock told him.

"Not Richard Locke," Cordesman pleaded.

"Yes," Brock countered. "Richard Locke."

(iii)

Circles.
Squares.
Triangles.
Planes.
Me, he thinks in the dark.

《《—》》

The curtains move in a sudden fresh breeze, then the breeze brings a stench of decay, and the curtains rot. In the great bow window, he looks at the sun.

Then the sun turns black.

Everything he looks at changes now. Everything he looks at dies.

And in this darkness—this *reality*—that he's summoned with his own mind, he sees it all, his destiny.

Squares roving the orbiculoid. Triangles churning oblique circles and lunettes and napiform pinnates.

Me, me...

Nonogons scaping the pentahedron, with spatulate quadrilateral septagons on the prowl. Volute styliforms flux between the bicillary acilars. Decussated cuspidates cut down the meek and meager bolus crescents and globose fungiforms in a whirring, terrifying ensiformic helix.

All the weak unishapes and passive globoforms waiting for him somewhere inside this radiant black plane of the world.

From the rive in the chevron he hears a voice—

Malefactor. Curse thee... But he laughs at the voice, the god he shortchanged. *I am greater than you*, he says back. *You think you own the world? If so, why is it that I'm the one who's standing on it and not you?*

You used to serve me.

Now I serve myself, so go back to your brimstone and your eons and your kingdom of excrement.

He waited for a response but none came. Lucifer wasn't much at conversation.

The hell-light, like encrimsoned scalloped scrolls, shined in the rhomboid of the window panes. A septagonal black onyx glittered in an ovate gold ring.

It was too funny...

Pyramidic dentiforms sparkled behind his eyes. His prismoid face smiled through a scarlet moline grin.

«« — »»

Back to the trochoid present. Back to the plane of obcorated fodder. He gets up, strays to the fine corner cabinet on which sits a 240-year-old Vincennes vase containing a single long-stemmed rose.

He touches the rose with a fingertip. First it wilts, then dies. The water inside reverts to phlegm while the vase has reformed into a desiccated heart, the aortal opening of which now displays the dead rose. But even the rose changes, to a strand of pulsing nerves.

«« — »»

Circles.

Squares.

Planes.

Triangles.

Geometry—the first wisdom of this plague called mankind. But the plague could revel in its filth—he didn't care. He only cared about one thing.

And I'm going to get it.

It was time. His first hook had failed, hadn't it? The seed of corruption had been spat back in his face. No matter. Even his guest had figured it out without ever really knowing it.

She was not of his world, not of his reality.

Only a figment of mind...

Or a figment of some other *reality?*

"It's time to bring forth *my* reality," Lethe muttered aloud.

(iv)

Hours passed in Locke's engrossment. Many hours. The typewriter was his clock, its rapidly tapping keys the minute and the hour hands. Last thing he remembered was finishing the poem, the scattered wads of paper about the floor proof of his redrafting.

All of writing is rewriting, Clark Ashton Smith had said. Or...was it Michener?

Locke looked at the final draft:

THE ANGEL OF THE EGRESS
by Richard Locke.

Spun tousles
in spiriferous
red
for so long he's felt
so dead
until now.

Flesh of midnight
sable blood
and the simple, subtle
kiss has pulled him back
from the abyss.

What more truth
can his muse prehend?

Every beginning
begins at an end.

So here am I
emboldened to enter.

Good or bad, that was it, that was his muse. His mind felt spent yet vibrant. This would be the first poem in the book. The angel, the dream woman, was of course a symbol, and now Locke was beginning to understand what it was. She was the final intercession of the catastrophe that was the last several months of his life, and the epiphany of things to come. Fine. That's what he'd needed to put into words, however few.

BAM! BAM! BAM! BAM!

The series of loud knocks pounded on the door; Locke nearly shrieked at the start. But only then, at this shattering of his concentration, did he nearly shriek again when he looked around.

He wasn't in the same room. It...well, it looked like the same cottage but...

A dead room in the dead of night, laved in twilight. Just a bare mattress, bare walls streaked by dust and discolor. Bare wood floors. Behind him, where a headboard might be, a small window framed the moon.

I'm either insane or I'm asleep, he thought. This was the same room from last night's dream. Barren, dilapidated, unentered for so long, dust lay an inch deep on the termite ridden floor. Then a glance out the window showed him, yes, the moon, but ringed by scarlet light like luminous blood...

This is...not too good.

BAM! BAM! BAM BAM!.

Don't answer it. He looked down at the antique typewriter; it shined in mint-condition when he'd first removed its cover, but now it stood as a spindly contraption formed of rust. Blood dripped off the rotten platen, the cotton ribbon blood-soaked. Beside the ruined machine lay an equally rusted Smith & Wesson .38 ACP semi-automatic pistol, with fingerprints further rusted into its grip, and beside that a spent cartridge, its brass finish long turned black.

BAM! BAM! BAM! BAM!

The room—the entire cottage was changing; it was aging as he watched, and worse, corroding, becoming fouled. A noxious odor rose, and Locke began to gag as if in a tear-gas chamber. *Just a dream, just another dream,* he tried to convince himself. *And I'm not—*

BAM! BAM! BAM!
—going to answer the door!
With *his* dreams of late? A garbage dump of hallucinatory, alcoholic detritus? But in a second the stench rose to choke him, like a corpse-pit in high sun. Locke couldn't make it; he jumped up, ran for the door and swung it open—
No one stood on the other side of the door, which was fine with Locke. No *one*. But—
He stumbled out in nauseous shock.
The cottage had changed, yes, and so had the back yard. Once a sweetly-scented and opened-air cloister full of flowers and autumn-turning greenery—now it was a miasma. Ruins of spoiled weeds poked above a top of viscid, ill-colored fog. The perimeter fence seemed to be rotting in places, its bricks and mortar decomposed so to sag in place. Viscous fluids glimmered amongst the bricks, and amongst that, tiny insectoid larvae seemed to twitch. The air felt hot as a sauna, not like late autumn in Seattle but mid-August in Vietnam. Locke could scarcely breathe; when he did though, no air seemed to fill his lungs, just moist, stinking heat. Locke imagined the air of Dachau or Andersonville, or the fields of Verdun full of more than a million dead.
He staggered and gagged, then staggered further without conscious notion of direction. The foot-deep ground fog glowed dully, a milky broth. Things—Locke didn't know what, just...*things*—seemed to stare at him an inch beneath the pallid surface. Severed heads? Sloughed faces? And with each blind step, he heard as well as felt a crisp, spindly *crunching* as though he were stepping on racks of rib bones or small animal carcasses. Locke tromped out of the morass, and when he caught what little breath he could, he found himself teetering beneath the front enclosure of the third cottage. Gasping from the death-stench, he crashed open the front door—
Little relief as he stood in the middle of the room. What he breathed was not air; it was loathsomeness, it was death distilled down to its thickest constituent. Locke tripped over his own feet in these noxious fumes, thumped against a bare-wood wall stained brown with old blood. His eyes fell on sights in flashlike increments: a long sewing needle stained brown, multitudinous crusts of discharged semen, great washes of urine cooked brown by the heat, and larger, plume-like shapes of red, finely flecked vomit.
Aghast, he stepped back out on the porch as the horrific garden shuddered before him.
Everything's changing. It's prolapsing. Even the rear face of the mansion seemed to rot before his eyes, a house of dead, termite-ridden wood somehow turning mucoid. The high gunslit windows looked filmed in blood.
Then he heard a scream.

To his right... The second cottage, where the painter was staying. He tramped over through the sickly mist, more things crunching beneath his steps. Again, he played the voyeur, peeking into a window...

He looked in at a vision of hell that might've appalled Bosch...

Martin the mohawked painter stood intently, wearing only a pair of blue jockey shorts and a black T-shirt that read WHITE TRASH COMPACTOR, DEBUT CD BY YOUR KID'S ON FIRE. He was running a pizza-cutter briskly up and down the back of his red-headed "assistant" who hung stark naked from lashed wrists propped over a ceiling hook. "Not too much, just enough," Martin remarked. He stepped back to review his deed. The hanging redhead's body shuddered like electrocution; she was still very much alive, and a bit more than the "trashy looking chick" Locke had first dismissed her as. Clot-like masses of intravenous needlemarks crusted the insides of her elbows. Stretched out like that she seemed little more than a skeleton covered by white, bruised skin, gut-sucked, slat-ribbed. Her emaciation shone as plain as her profession: a street prostitute.

Martin's profession, however, was more enigmatic.

A few more peppy strokes of the pizza-cutter right over the knobs of the spine (each stroke brought a shrill scream, like bad brakes), and then Martin looked to his left. "Think that sparked her up, Darlie?"

The blonde—Darlie—lolled on a couch, naked, a foot tapping as if desperate for something. She looked malnourished as the redhead, a death-camp whore with breasts reduced to tiny nippled flaps. Hollow eyes gave a dull glint behind strings of dirty, dishwater-blonde hair.

"Do the front now," she said. "That'll really get her screaming. Do her like you did that one-eyed bitch we picked up on Pacific Ave. last week."

Martin poised, touching his chin, as he considered the recommendation. Then he pulled off the T-shirt. One side facing the window now, Locke could see the tapestry of tattoos on the torturer's chest—Munch-like suggestions of thin, screaming faces, not particularly original—not to mention nipples and navel aglitter with multiple chrome piercings. The rack-thin redhead heaved tiny gusts of breath in the pause, then Martin swirled her around to face him.

"Hmmm. Maybe," he said.

Her face looked like a bleached skull behind the drooping strands of russet, and her voice crackled like husks of dried leaves. "Please, Marty, no more. You said you'd use Darlie this time. All she ever does is hold out on you—"

"Fuck you!" the blonde spat. "Marty, she's a lyin' little trick-kid! I ain't never held out on you! That dirty fuck-bucket'll do anything to save her skinny ass!"

More dried leaves crunching. "Please, Marty—"

"Come on, Marty, shiv the bitch up! Her cunt's so fulla herp, she ain't no good for the street no more anyway, and her asshole's so big she shits herself!"

Locke remained staring through the window, his eyes frozen open, his muscles besieged by a spectral paresis. He did not want to witness this, yet he had no choice. He couldn't move his face away, he couldn't turn his head, he couldn't even flinch—it felt as though his entire body had been set into a block of hardened concrete with only a hole for his face to peer through. Helpless, his sight remained plastered. The redhead appeared almost breastless, just large irregular nipples that looked chewed. Scars of past cigarette burns blotched her chest, and so devoid of body fat she was that her navel stuck out like the tip of a toe. More burns and track-marks smirched the bony pelvis and inner thighs. Dots of scabs adorned a badly shaved pubis beneath which her vaginal folds puffed out, the furrow filled with clusters of active herpes.

Martin took an appraising step back. "Hmmm," he repeated. "Maybe? No?" A pause of artistic decision. Then: "Yes!"

Darlie squealed in delight, while the redhead merely oozed a gut-deep groan. Martin set down the pizza-cutter to replace it with a simple plastic disposable razor, then began to scrape it over the knub-like navel—

scritch scritch scritch

Each scrape brought a bizarre smothered cough from the recipient's throat and a reflexive body-long jerk.

"Feel that?" Martin inquired over his work.

scritch scritch scritch

More shuddering coughs and suspended lurches. After a few more scrapes of the razor, the navel had been fully shaved off which provided a single line of blood rolling down to the scalped pubis.

"Scared yet?" the artist asked. The only response was a droop of his victim's head in this next pause. "Oh, not talkative today, is that it? Shit, usually this should jazz you up…"

"Fuck her up some more!" Darlie shouted. "It's not enough!"

"It needs to be more refined." Martin smirked at his couchside accomplice. "Haven't you ever heard of delineation? You don't just slop the thematics of art together any old way." Now he wielded a bare razorblade, jerked the redhead's face up—

"That's what I call keeping your eyes peeled," the blonde said.

—and very daintily cut off her eyelids. He flicked them away like scintillas of onion skin. "Spectacular! Yes! I think we're getting there!" What looked back at him in this protraction of horror were two denuded rolling eyeballs which now seemed huge as bloodshot orbs of glass pressed into her skull.

"Is that all you're gonna do? Fuck," the blonde complained. She sat picking at scabs on her arms. "Thought you were really gonna do a job on her." Next, she was gingerly eating the scabs. The position she assumed— one thin, needle-tacked leg angled beneath the other—afforded a view of a vaginal entry that, if stressed, could probably admit the full girth of the shank-end of a leg of lamb.

"Patience," Martin replied. "How long do you think it took Rembrandt to paint *The Shooting Company of Captain Frans Bannings Cocq?* I'm looking to blow that chiaroscuro-neat-trick-cop-out Dutch motherfucker clean out of his wooden shoes 'cos I *know* I'm better." Martin was getting whipped up, his face tensed, beads of sweat popping from his brow as if in a blaze of sun. "Fuckin-A, I could paint *Nicolaes Ruts* or fuckin' *Moses Smashing the Commandments* with a Number 6 Grumbacher tied to my dick! Deliberation, Darlie! Mechanistics, the perpetuity of aesthetic vision. They don't come along in the wink of an eye—" Then he jerked a bent expression toward the redhead. "For those of us who still can, I mean... The true artist needs to...cogitate...ruminate...contemplate...conceptualate—er, well, I guess that's not really a word, but—" Martin threw up his hands. "Oh fuck it! You non-artists just don't get it!" He rushed toward the blonde, intense, pointing his finger at her like a gun. "We should all stick with what we know! A guy who makes cheese doesn't paint because he only knows how to make cheese. A guy who binds books sticks to book-binding because he doesn't know anything about hanging sheetrock. You hear what I'm saying? We stick with what we know. You know sucking cock, spitting out a trick's cum, taking it up the ass till you can feel some player's foot-long pud poking your stomach, and shooting skag. Me? *I* know art." He stared forward, threw up his hands again at her uncomprehending gaze. "Oh fuck it! Nobody understands me!"

Martin tromped off across the room like a disgruntled toddler having been deprived of a toy, while Darlie tightened her scowl and picked more scabs. "Who shit in your TV dinner? Jesus, Marty, don't get so pissed off."

Martin didn't hear her. He strode back to the scene. "I'd say a more plentiful palette might be in order." A quick swipe of the razor across the redhead's brow opened the most diminutive line. Then the line *bloomed.*

"Oh beautiful red..."

Blood rolled down her face. Martin stepped back again, to conceptu-alate a little more.

"Hmmm, hmmm..."

"What's wrong now?"

The painter stood stalled, fingers pressed to his lips as he looked on. He was thinking. "The eyes bother me."

"But you just said they were spectacular!"

"In life, sure, but I'm wondering now…" He scrutinized the blood-shellacked face and macabre skinless eyeballs. "The translation to the canvas will be marred. Vacancy—that's what I need. To symbolize the-the-the…*soullessness* of the down-trodden's plight… Yes! Yes! Vacant eyes, vacant soul! Openness within the articulations of the truth of the portrait!"

He snatched up a yard-long wooden plank, walked around behind the redhead, and—

WHACK!

—brought the plank against the back of her head with the force of a batter's swing. Then:

WHACK! WHACK! WHACK!

Three more solid blows, yet still the maestro was not content. A more steadied stance, then, a focused line of sight and a flex of muscles.

KUH-RACK!

The last blow sufficed to not only break the plank in half but jettison both eyeballs from their seats in the skull. The sheer force yanked the tenuous nerves from their optical canals, snapped them, and the eyeballs shot to the floor.

"Better, yes! Better!"

"You're taking too long," Darlie was griping now. "I need to slam, Marty. Fuck, I'm fuckin' stringing here. I can't wait any more, I'm gonna cook up." A crisp snap and a sputtering flash. She lit a candle on the end table, went through the mindless regimen that was her life, then began to heat a twenty-bag of Afghani heroin in a spoon. The spoon, by the way, was from the same set of 1300s Limoges goldworks dinnerware that Locke had previously eaten his Poulet au Vinaigre a l'Estragon with a number of hours ago.

Martin stared definitively at the redhead's form, now back in the true creative fugue-state. By some turn of miracle, though (that Locke would deduce only later) she was still alive. Her sucked gut heaved in and out, eyes knocked out of her head and fractured skull notwithstanding, she still quivered on her ceiling hook, mouthing through uprushing blood: "No more no more no more please Marty no more."

"*YES* more!" Martin broke and snapped, his orange-fringed mohawk shivering at the vocal gust. "I've got it now! Darlie's right! It's not a sparseness of aesthetic mechanics that make the work! It's the creative courage to ignore conventional restraint for the full sake! Darlie! Did you hear me?"

"*What?*" the blonde squealed back.

"The work is the thing!"

Darlie sighed through a skinny pinched-up fucked-up junkie face. "Marty, I'm trying to slam!"

"You'll see! You'll love this!"

The screams which followed could not be likened to any sound to ever issue from a human throat. More akin to a heap of cats dropped into a mulching machine. "Feel that, feel that, baby? I'll bet *that* puts some kick back in ya."

And kick they did, dirty junkie street-prostitute feet flailing back and forth as Martin, the proud successor to Rembrandt van Rijn, energetically ran the pizza-cutter up and down between the redhead's legs. The round rolling blade sliced through the works: the majora and minora, the clitoris and hood, and of course the puffed pink swellings of herpetic outbreak. Upon the cutter's invasion of the latter, watery pus marbled the open running blood.

It was pretty.

zzip zzip zzip zzip zzip

On the pizza blade went, with zeal up and down over the most acutely sensitive perimeter of the redhead's anatomy. By now she was dancing on that ceiling hook, strutting it out like no tortured junkie ever had.

"What'cha think?" Martin pulled his infuriated gaze. "Darlie! I thought you wanted me to fuck her up more!"

"*Martin!* I'm trying to slam…"

Goddamn non-artists. "Slam later, get over here."

"*Mar*ty!"

"Honeybunch, how can I say this without sounding like a neo-nazi New Republican misogynistic creep? Get your 90-pound junkie-whore ass over here before I cut off this bitch's leg and stick it so far up your giant garage-sized cunt you'll be able to taste her toe-cheese."

Evidently Darlie was convinced. She dragged up all 90 pounds and trudged over to her supermate's beck and call. He shoved a pre-stapled 18"x18" blank canvas frame into her hands. "You know what to do, so do it right," he advised.

He spun the redhead once more on her wrist-pivot. "We gotta get it all," he said. "We gotta get every twitch of the theme. If we don't, I'm no better than Peter Max…" From a spread of curious implements, he first chose a commonplace ice-pick and repeatedly inserted it into the metus surrounding the redhead's anus. "Yeah, yeah, bet that smarts," he approved, then, to the blonde, "Get that frame up there, you stupid ditz! We gotta get it!"

Darlie pressed the canvas hard against the redhead's face, her lips besmirched, as Martin continued with the ice-pick action. Each insertion caused an abundance of nerve-reflex activity on the part of the redhead, and no reservation of vocalization. On each occasion upon which the thin silver spike sunk into the tight rectal meat, there came a gruff yelp and a strong lurch of her legs. Once the targeted area was sufficiently tenderized, Martin emptied a plastic bottle of Rex-All-brand isopropyl alcohol into the cleft of her buttocks.

Now the redhead *sang*. So high and hard, Locke, in his never-ending paresis, wouldn't have been surprised if hanks of lung tissue didn't come up with the objection.

"Keep that canvas on her face, you skag-head bimbo!" Martin hollered. For there was more to come. The blonde's stick-thin arms flexed against the resistance as she leaned the canvased frame against the redhead's screaming face. Next, Martin was jamming the ice-pick between the vertebral slits of the spine, slowly at first, then digging deep to get to the cord. "Press! Press!" he bellowed. The redhead was throwing up now against the pressed flat of canvas.

"Excellent! More variety for the palette!"

"Come on, Marty, I'm shitting cinderblocks I'm stringing so bad..."

"Okay! Take it off!" Martin dropped the pick and then dropped his navy-blue Fruit of the Looms. "Put the canvas down!" he barked as he rushed to sodomize the redhead. The redhead *wailed*. Not too many strokes, and then he was whining the advent of his release.

"Marty, will you *please* do my spike?" Darlie pleaded, having set the canvas against the lower wall. The imprint glared back—a marvel of the creator's initiative: an abstraction of the face of terror. Runnelled smears of scarlet described the face of torture and agony, thinner runnels—thin as wild crimson threads—mushed up to the treated white cloth, with empty white eye sockets roving to and fro the scape of imprinted pain.

Probably not as good as *The Shooting Company of Captain Frans Banning Cocq* also known as *The Nightwatch,* the world's most valuable painting, but...

It did what Rembrandt's canvas did, at least to the liking of most modern art critics. It captured the moment of truth.

The irreducible—and the most honest—moment of terror. It was the artist defining the moment, beyond all reckoning.

The Face of Real Terror.

"Oh, shit's coming out her ass now," Martin recoiled, taking offended steps back. "Fuck it, we're done."

"Marty," the blonde cooed. "Her junkie ass may be done, but we're not."

"Oh, right, your spike. All right." He glanced at the "portrait," brought an awed hand to his tattooed chest. "My God, if it dries right, it'll be better than the *Mona Lisa.*"

Locke rather doubted that claim, but it mattered little. Something inexplicable was happening here, something that he could no longer play off as a drunken dream or hallucination. It was some grasp of perversity—and one of reality however altered—that kept Locke's helpless face pressed to that window pane of hell. He thought and he breathed and he even bled—when he tasted his initial convictions by biting his tongue. *This is real,* he knew. *Just a different reality. The same thing the angel said...*

Inside the cottage...the festivities didn't let up. Martin's posture rewarded Locke's vision with an elephantine scrotum riddled with dozens of intricate piercings, rows of chrome rings sunk into the genital skin. The shaft skin, the scrotal skin, even a row down to his perineum. Martin's cock glittered beneath the recent besmirching of the redhead's colon, a coat of 90s chain mail, the edges of each ring honed to the sharpness of chisel-ends. "I'm gonna slam you up and turn your pussy into ground round just like I did that other junkie's ass..." The blonde had recooked her heroin to a bubbling oval in the gold dip. But Locke saw no obligatory rubber hose strapped about the arm. Martin produced a hypodermic with a needle that must've been five inches long. "Yeah, yeah, do it!" Darlie implored.

Martin withdrew the plunger, sucking the liquefied morphate into the body of the device. Then he pressed the blonde's face, holding it back with exertion against the couch, and slowly manipulated the long needle into her right nostril, pushed and pushed until the tiniest *tick* could be heard.

The pierced painter's thumb depressed, and plunged the hot morphine derivative directly into the middle of her fried brain.

"Like that fix?"

Her limbs, her entire body went lax, and a slaked grin turned her face up.

"Baby, when I'm done humping your bones, your pussy's gonna look like a hole full of Sloppy Joe," Martin promised to the blonde, comatose now in her bliss. He got up and walked to the drying canvas propped against the wall. "Fuck yeah, man!" He stroked the rings of his penis, skin moving with the silver glimmer. "I got wood this painting's so good!"

Another of the artist's tools, conveniently, was an ax fixed to a long hickory handle.

"Fuck it! I'm happy!"

THWACK! THWACK! THWACK!

Three broad, energetic swipes angled down into the couch cut the stupored blonde into two pieces, dividing her at the breastline. The chest and legs bucked and kicked their protest, while everything from the nipples up— arms, shoulders, and head—flailed similarly.

"Sorry, Darlie. I get carried away when I'm jazzed."

"I thought you were gonna fuck me!"

Martin shrugged. "Aw, forget it. I'm sick of your yeasty snatch anyway."

Locke's detachment returned like a strand of moonlight through a rapidly shifting cloud; he was aware of himself again, staring into the obscenity of the window. *This is madness,* he thought but somehow that realization wasn't profound anymore. The shock, the utter disbelief, was gone, vapor lost on hot asphalt. *I'm looking into hell...* Then he remembered what the angel—Moira—had said in his dream.

If truth is born in reality, what happens when truths change?

(v)

At the reception desk of the Tawes Archaeology Building, Cordesman flashed his badge to a student who was the spitting image of Flounder in *Animal House*. "I'm here to see a Professor Fredrick."

BAM!

A hallway door banged open, a hectic blur barged forward; Cordesman jumped at the surprise. Two EMTs barreled through, hauling an ambulance gurney. The captain only caught a glimpse of the gurney's occupant: an old man covered to the chin by a lime-green shock blanket, an oxygen mask over his face. A portable Dyna-Med monitor beeped erratically. "Mobile Four, prep a vent!" one of the EMTs barked into a walkie-talkie. "Jack out forty b.c.i. units of epinol and a c.b.c chem-seven, we're coming out!" The beeping faded off, and a second later, the unit was gone, barging through an opposite door toward a rear exit sign.

"You just missed him," Flounder said.

Cordesman gaped. "What? You mean that guy on the crash cart was Fredrick?"

"That's *Professor* Fredrick to you, and, yes. He—" The fat kid set down his *Journal of Field Archaeology* and shot Cordesman a smug look. "Your hair's awfully long for a cop, isn't it?"

Cordesman, irate, flashed his badge again. "You think this badge is too gold to be a cop's too? Now what the goddamned hell happened here?"

Flounder pursed his lips. "Well if you'd quit hurling obscenities at me for just one minute, I'll tell you. Professor Fredrick had a heart attack. Evidently he was working on something, and Doris thinks he was so engrossed, he forgot to take his heart medication."

"But the guy just called me an hour ago, told me to come down here and see him," Cordesman was stressed not to bellow.

"Excuse me—the guy? Oh, you mean *Professor* Fredrick. And I guess that long hair must be blocking your ears because I do seem to recall telling you several seconds ago that he had a heart attack. Professor Fredrick is quite famous, something of a hero around here. He discovered the ruins of Dis in 1986, you know."

College students, Cordesman thought. He doubted much merit in slapping this kid in the jowls but... *It could be fun.* "Well, what's his status?"

"It happens all the time, three, four times a year. Call the hospital if you want the exact prognosis. What do I look like? Marcus Welby?"

No, you look like Flounder. "Who's this Doris person?"

"Oh, you mean Ms. Bartlett? She's the professor's senior T.A. When he didn't show for his Regional Chronologies 401 lecture, she came back here and found him."

"Okay, we're making some headway," Cordesman said. "Now, I don't expect you to strain your powers of deductive reasoning, but I'd really appreciate it if you might tell me where I could find Ms. Bartlett."

"She's following the ambulance to the hospital." Then Flounder went back to his magazine.

Cordesman imagined grabbing the kid by the collar, or, better, by a fat cheek. "I think I've made it clear to you, son, that I had some business with Professor Fredrick. As Professor Fredrick is detained for the moment, and, as I *think I've made it clear to you* that I'm a *police officer*, it might be a good bet that the business I had with Professor Fredrick is *police* business—"

Without looking up from the magazine, the kid pointed a fat finger. "Room 104, end of the hall, officer."

"Not officer. *Captain*." Cordesman strode for the door. "Give D-Day my regards."

"What?"

Cordesman moved down the hall. *Fat punk. I'd slap him so hard his fat would jiggle.* Christ, what was wrong with kids these days? *It's these liberal colleges,* Cordesman suspected. *Brainwashes 'em. Turns 'em into fussy twinkies.* The dark wood door to Room 104 swung open silently. Cordesman walked into something more like a cubby of the Smithsonian. The plushly paneled office seemed crammed with ancient relics: talberds, helmets, standards. A full suit of plate mail hung in the corner, one metal sleeve missing. *Ouch,* Cordesman thought. A dead computer monitor stared back from the side of an expansive desk. *Fuck.* Flounder had said Fredrick got the Big Chestpain while working on something. *Probably a write up for me.* But even if Cordesman knew how to turn on the computer, he wouldn't know what the hell to do from there. To hell with all this hard-drive CD-ROM ODE-RAM MMX-processor bullshit.

Whatever happened to paper?

It was the search request that he'd sent—on a sheet of paper—to Central Processing on 1st Ave. There, the computer geeks had piped into every database index in the state. No responses except one from the most unlikely place: the University of Washington's Department of Archaeological Studies. So the word was either relative to archaeology, or it was a mistake. The college's mainframe had notified this Fredrick guy with the positive search-link. *Just my luck the guy has a heart attack when I'm on my way over to see him.*

He guessed he should just leave, maybe huff it over to the admin building and get somebody to look in Fredrick's computer for anything that might appear to be a report on Cordesman's inquiry. But the room amazed him with its display of artifacts. An upended old helmet sat on the desk. *Ashtray,* Cordesman deduced and fired up a Camel. He stared again at the blank computer screen. *Yeah, all this high-falutin' technology and I can't do shit. Give me paper anyday...*

Another glance around showed him a printer on a stand. A tray on the bottom showed him...a sheaf of *paper.*

Cordesman tapped an ash into the ashtray and snatched the paper up. *Yeah...*

The top sheet read:

> Professor F.A. Fredrick
> Superintendent/ Depart of Archaeological Studies.
> Washington State University
> Suite 104/ The Tawes Bldg.
> Seattle, WA 98195
>
> Dear Captain Cordesman:
>
>   Here is a print-out of the write-up I prepared relative
> to your recent query regarding the word SCIFTAN, for
> your records after we've talked.

Right on, Cordesman thought. He crushed his cigarette out in the ashtray, never realizing that it actually wasn't an ashtray at all but the helm of King Harold I of Angleland, which the King had worn, and died in, during the Battle of Senlac Hill, more popularly known as The Battle of Hastings.

> SCIFTAN: a proper noun of ultimately unknown origin,
> taking from the Old Frisian alt. transitive: *sciff*—to mutate,
> and *tannin*—one who. It is a very rare reference indeed,
> only identified once in the history of modern archaeolog-
> ical discovery, and one in which I'm happy to claim being
> part of, namely the subterranean accident which occurred
> in Gatwick, England in 1971, a water-main rupture. The
> repair diggings uncovered a well-preserved collection of
> stemmae from the Archives of the Registry of Publius
> Aelius Hadrianus, a.k.a. Hadrian, the Emperor of Rome
> from A.D. 117-38. These archives uniquely elucidated
> upon the local mythologies exacted from conquered com-
> munities   before   Hadrian   terminated   Roman
> Expansionism.

> I will structure my report in an expository fashion, rendering the definition of your search request, and then positing elaboration in progressive order, via the basic outline form.
>
> 1) DEFINITION OF SEARCH WORD: SCIFTAN:
> Denotatively, *Sciftan,* from the early Brythic, pre-Druidic, and original interpretations of the Old Frisian subjunctive verb lists, can be translated into Modern English to this: SHIFTER.

Cordesman sat down behind the cardiac patient's desk and lit another smoke. *This might take a while.*

(vi)

Locke thought of the joke of Faulkner's *The Sound and the Fury,* gleaned from Macbeth's soliloquy by Shakespeare: *Life is a tale told by an idiot...* He continued to stare into the wee window of the second cottage, seeing all. It didn't matter that the body-chopped blonde still flailed in the betrayal of her artist/pimp, nor that the hanging redhead still bucked against her previous tortures—never mind that her eyes had been batted out of her head and her spinal cord had been punctured with an ice-pick. None of that bore significance since this was a different place—Locke knew now—a sign of the real world's life into some otherworldly crevasse. Yet Locke watched on, against all human power, as Martin continued to revel over his vermilion-and-puke masterpiece. This was the same thing, wasn't it? One reality—one truth—opposing another. The line from the drunken scribe's pen rang in Locke's ear: *Through the fence, between the curling flower spaces, I could see them hitting...* The tale of the world told most accurately was that of the retardate—an idiot—signifying...*what?* What was possibly the greatest novel of all time displayed three different views of the world, and the only one that was worth more than a pinch of shit was the view of the defected mind. In essence, the flawed narrator of the book's first section was encapsulating a differentiation of perceived truth.

A differentiation of *reality.*

Locke continued to witness, however extremely, a similar differentiation.

By now Martin had made use of the ax once more, to reduce Darlie's legs, pelvis, and chest into bloody hanks and now engaged upon arranging the pieces. Meanwhile, the blonde prostitute's shoulders and head continued to bitch.

"Jesus Christ, Marty! What did you do *that* for?"

"A montage," he murmured back in the least acknowledgment. His Keds stepped gingerly amongst the tableau's component parts, leaving prints of gore. The eyeless redhead twitched and sputtered as if to offer subverbal suggestions. Then Martin rearranged a knee-joint and a foot, and stepped back.

"I think that does it, huh? The montage is done. Fuck Kline and Mondrian and all those gimmick assholes. Christ, any dickbrain can slop shingles and housepaint on the floor and call it art. This is the real thing... I think I'll call it *The Truncation of the Crack-Whore*. Whaddaya think?"

The blonde—with her hands, of course—climbed back up onto the mottled couch. "Fuck, Marty! How am I gonna turn tricks like this? What, I'm gonna walk up and down the main drag on my *hands?*"

"Look at it this way, babe. You don't have to peddle your ass anymore." Martin gusted laughter. "Now you can peddle your head!"

"Oh, that's real funny," the blonde's head came back; one skinny arm extended to give him the finger. Then she gawped. "Aren't you ever gonna finish this shit?"

"Darlie, the artist's inspiration isn't subject to *time*. My creativity won't let go—I've still got more work to do." Busied by more of this inspiration, Martin ran an errant hand back over his mohawk, then took up a long carving knife. "Yes, yes, I've got it!" In a frenzy now, he cut off the redhead's tiny breasts, quick as an Oriental waiter carving Peking Duck. And—

SPLAT!

—threw both breasts against the wall where they stuck amid swashes of blood.

"Yes! It's my best work to date!"

"Great, Marty," the blonde pecked. "What's the new Rembrandt gonna call that masterpiece?"

Martin made a long face at her. "Not sure. I guess it's a toss-up between *Madonna With Child* and *Two Little Junkie Tits on a Wall*."

The eyeless redhead jerked and mewled.

Locke, at last, was released; he stumbled backward, away from the atrocious window into drenching darkness. The putrid ground fog billowed around the clumsy back-steps; more things crunched beneath.

This was a different place, yes, but also the same. He knew that all too well, like Faulkner's narrator. Only one mission occurred to him now... *Find Lethe. I made the door, but Lethe is the key.*

Locke swatted at winged bugs with thoraxes fat as gumballs. They splattered lumpen-yellow against his skin, and stank like cheese mold. Some sunk stingers into his skin but he scraped them off, leaving trails of mucous. His feet stomped down the fog-topped path, stopped at the French doors which led into the mansion, then he yanked open the doors—

"Hoooooly *SHIT!*"

An *avalanche* of corpses poured from the doorway as though one of Belsen's grave-pits had been emptied onto him. Mortified, Locke trudged backward, no longer knee-deep in noxious fog but knee-deep in a mass grave. The death-stench rose to kill him—perhaps that would've been better now—and burn. Skulls with bits of parchment-thin flesh still clinging to them lolled on spindly necks, limbs as gaunt as broomsticks lay scattered like a madman's latticework.

A corpse-pile, falling out the French doors. A bilge of putrefactive slime flowed, low between the bodies, staining Locke's pants. Eventually, gagging, he trudged back out.

Lord, he thought, looking at the pile.

To get into the house—it was clear—he'd have to crawl over the bodies. *Next suggestion?*

There must be some other way.

The brick fence...

It was a start but somehow Locke knew that the spillage of corpses was a tactic, forcing an alternative direction. *He wants me to find another way...because there's more he wants me to see.*

Locke trod back through the swamp-like fog, meaning to find a break in the sullied hedges and scale the fence. But as he moved past the fourth cottage...

He stopped.

The fourth cottage. The only one he hadn't checked.

A tenuous, clear slime seemed to bathe the door when he kicked it open. It was more macabre disrepair he saw when he first entered: furniture so old it had begun to decompose. Streaks of foxfire and fungus grew up the bare walls, fed by the humid air. But in the corner, the top of a trap door stood open.

Locke descended down slatted, bending steps into darkness tinged with light like a roasting fire. Wet cobwebs spread and snapped across his face as he tromped downward into the tinted murk. A narrow passage like a gangway in an old 1700s ship took him under the house. To aid his bearings, he ran his hands along the sidewalls, through some fluid sweating through the wood slick as blood. Eventually, he tripped over another set of wooden steps, and took them up—

Into a room so clotted with dust, cobwebs, and fetid mold that Locke imagined a den that hadn't been entered for centuries. But once he stood up in the room, he saw that he was wrong.

Footprints through the dust led from a far door to the edge of a pile of junk: pieces of furniture tossed onto more, old paintings, old implements, boxes, crates, bottles, etc. The footprints, however, made no secret of the room's most recent deposit.

A coffin.

Locke knew that the coffin would be empty when he opened it. Or...not empty but devoid of a cadaver. Instead—

Shit.

It was filled with several gold bars.

Not many—seven, in fact. Just enough to... *Feign the weight of a human being,* Locke calculated.

A cursory inspection of the heaps that were the room's contents seemed innocuous at first, until he made a closer examination: three rust-pitted hand-forged nails, a blood-stained silver platter, a vermiculated wooden staff, a felt sack containing exactly thirty silver coins imprinted with the likeness of King Herod.

And more:

A tri-layered cloak, one layer, green, one scarlet, one black. A butted .46 caliber piece of lead ball ammunition, like the type that would've been manufactured in, say, 1865. A skull in a box with a black-tarnished plate that read D.F.S. A black medical bag with a similar plaque that read *Doctor Neal Creame.* Locke grew bored quickly, knowing the implications. Lethe was a collector, all right. The last thing Locke looked at was something he didn't get. It was a book that weighed at least thirty pounds, nothing on the cover, no title, no author. The cover's substance seemed to be fashioned from some manner of reptile skin. Locke flipped it open and saw the first page, so old it had yellowed to a hue that was more brown. Arabic script. Locke dropped the book back into the dust.

A *click* resounded, and his eyes shot up.

The far door had opened, and a tall figure filled the frame in silhouette.

"I'm happy to have guessed correctly, Mr. Locke. You've found my junk room. When you're done with your perusal, please follow me."

The rich, sibilant voice, of course, was Lethe's.

SEVENTEEN

INTERSTICE

(i)

"Six more feem reds, they look like, Ms. Brock. Can't say for sure but—"

Jill Brock's surgical-gloved fingers whipped the ev-bag from the tech's hand. She held them up to the ceiling light. "They're feems, Jerry. Less kink in the line-curve, more micronically narrow. You want to bet paychecks they're the same?"

"You kidding me?" the kneeling technician replied.

Cordesman was smoking in the corner, leafing through a stack of 8 1/2 by 11 paper sitting in a plastic bin labeled: ROUGHS. He was reading a crudely-typed sheet of paper:

> *Irrelative time ticks towards one o'clock*
> *when you walk in*
> *and flense my poet's discipline:*
> *Siren atrocity of verse and rhyme,*
> *so I leave as I'm sure I will*
> *every other time.*

Cordesman's eyes narrowed. He picked up another one.

> *But the moon*
> *is full tonight!*
> *It's beautiful*
> *like you…*
> *pristine white*
> *radiant teeming*
> *like my love*

all and forever
within me
dreaming of you
in my arms again

"All right," Cordesman muttered. "Love. Big deal."

"What's that, Captain?" Jill Brock's voice boomed across the small room.

Cordesman winced at her. "Just keep doing what you're doing, huh?" He picked up another.

R.I.P. (to Ian Curtis)
by Richard Locke

A sullen face,
a hangman's noose.
Bright life unfurled,
dark heart unloosed.
Oh, jubilant promise,
a fading apparition.
Welcome, dear poets
to the atrocity exhibition.

"Jill?" Cordesman called out over her crew of kneeling men. "Who the hell is Ian Curtis?"

"A singer, I think," she replied from the round hole in her red-polyester anti-hairfall pullovers. "The name's familiar from college. Some singer who killed himself...or, maybe it was a sports star. Not sure. Some basketball player at Maryland, maybe?"

"I don't think so."

"What is that you're—"

Cordesman's upraised palm cut her off. He was reading with an intentness that was desperate. *Locke's a poet, his poetry is his guts.*

EXIT by R. Locke

Low moon above the state house
smiles wanly as the pallid
light of rage.
When I close my eyes
I think I can see you
shredding every page

of the paper of my heart.
Yes, I can see you
tear it all apart.

I can see you gut the animals,
smash amethyst and silver chain
to bury me in this sepulcher
of extraordinary pain.
Reaper, reap! Confessor, save me!
And pluck me up into your arms above,
or you can leave me here on Pike Street
—to rot—dying of providence,
dying of love.

So there's little else left
for me to misconstrue—
just the dying of memory.
I'm dying of you.

"Captain?"

Cordesman looked over, an ash falling off the Camel in his lips. "What?"

Brock looked preposterous in her red overalls, especially when she was mad. "What do you mean, what? Locke's *bed* has the same red feem pubes we've found on *every other 64 site?* No offense, Captain, but are you dense?"

"Give me a minute," he said. "I'm reading poetry."

Here was another one with the same title, "Exit."

EXIT

Cenote or ziggurat,
so shall it be
to end this riven hatred
which beckons me
like torture into
the Light of the past.
The dreams of some are
the nightmares of others:
blessings assigned
or black lots cast
in the most retched adieu...

I glimpsed the Light,
the Light went out.
All my dreams came true.

"Not too bad," Cordesman whispered to himself.

"What, Captain?"

"Nothing!" he turned around and shouted. "What? You need me to hold your hand and tell you what to do? You're the Big Tech Boss, so do your tech shit and report to me when you have something. I'm busy!"

"That guy's an asshole," somebody said. "I don't care if he's a captain with more raps than anyone in the department's history. I'll give him a wood shampoo, the prick."

"*Who said that?*" Cordesman bellowed. He stamped out into the middle of the room. The problem with these TSD people was they weren't technically sworn cops—they were just civilian subcontractors—hence not subject to the orders of actual department officers. "You tech punks ain't worth dick, just a bunch of union talk. Whoever said that, I'll bet'cha ain't got the nuts to say so."

Another figure in red utilities stood up without hesitation, and glared at Cordesman through a thick beard.

His voice cracked like dropped trees. "I said it."

Cordesman winced. The guy stood six-nine, probably two-ninety, with arms thicker than Cordesman's legs. "Oh. A lot of Wheaties, huh?"

"Hey, I've got offers from Tacoma and Kirkland for more money, so write me up, you pencil-neck. I'll clean your clock, I don't give a shit. Ms. Brock deserves some respect. I'll tie your hippie hair to the back of my El Dorado and foot it down I-5."

Then more guys stood up, just like at the church.

"Hey, Jill, you wanna call off your wrecking crew? Christ."

"R.A., get back to work, please." Brock stepped carefully through the bedroom. "Captain, we've got hairfall linking Richard Locke to sixteen 64s. I don't think I'm out of line in asking what you make of the landfill of evidence me and my people have dumped on your head. If Richard Locke isn't the murderer, then he's at the very least an accomplice."

"Locke didn't kill anybody—"

"How can you say that!"

Cordesman lit another Camel, hoping Brock would bitch about smoking on her crime scene. Well, it wasn't really a crime scene, just a scene. "You wanna know how, Jill? I can tell by his aura. He's not a killer—that's right, I said *aura*. So put that in your mass-photo-spectrometer and smoke it." He glared at her. "Tell me something I can use, or don't bother me till you can."

Brock gaped. "Auras, huh?"

"That's right. Locke has a hazy one, no color, really—it's rare, but they're the easier to read."

Brock's shoulders slumped, a Sirchie UV sensor in her gloved hand. "Where's Kerr?"

"Waking people up under bridges, showing them mugshots. Probably also eating fish & chips."

"Why don't you, uh, call him, let him take over so you can go home and...get some rest."

She thinks I've lost my oars. That had always been a problem. Cordesman worked better alone because then there was never anyone trying to decrypt him. Any time he got a partner, it wasn't long after that people started giving him long looks.

"Then will you at least put an all-points out on Locke?" Brock huffed.

"Locke's not in the city." Cordesman's gut told him; it was only wrong when it came to baseball. All the while, the report he'd read at Fredrick's office kept flushing in and out of his head. Cordesman didn't *believe* it, but—

The oldest mythology, one that predated written record. Pre-Adamics. A handful of angelic heirarchs who didn't buy Lucifer's pitch...and slipped out between the ethereal cracks. But they were still in hell so they infused their own phony mythology to coerce the peasants of the earth to resurrect them, to...incarnate them.

Sciftan.

Shifters.

Parahuman entities with the power to turn the fantasies of humankind— and the fears—into a reality.

But there was more:

The most powerful of such entities was named after the only river through Hades, the river of oblivion, of forgetfulness.

The River Lethe.

Once the closest confidantes of Lucifer, they opted out—just as Lucifer had to God—and had used the gullibility of mankind to bring him unto the earth.

But not just the monster named for the river. Others too. A handful whom Lethe himself had scourged the earth to wipe out. And he did.

All but one...

His love, Cordesman thought, upon reading all of Locke's poetry about the same topic: love, and the failure thereof. Like Satan abandoning God, Lethe had abandoned Satan, cheating the Lord of the Air out of his own curse. He'd stalked the earth, inventing the fears which would plague man forever. Until...

Until what? Cordesman entertained.

There must be a final confrontation, and this one had been waiting to happen for fifty centuries. Perhaps it would wait fifty more. But even Cordesman knew—in the guise of the myth—what the confrontation must entail. The Prince of Oblivion had spent the entirety of at least five thousand years hunting down his own kind. But there was one he couldn't slay and send back to hell.

The last fallen angel.

This flawed deity had no name according to the references of Hadrian's archives. Only that she was the most beautiful woman that a human mind could conceive. Coincidentally, a woman with *red* hair. The Prince of the River had fallen in love with her, but there was a problem.

This deity, this angel, had slithered between the gaps of even the fingers of God. The evil that Satan's masses had bound allegiance to was rejected by the same angel.

Sciftan, Cordesman thought. *Shifter.*

The translation was sketchy, because the translation pre-dated human language. All that the miners of history had to go by—such as men like Fredrick—were decipherments based on *second-hand* translations from the linguists of the Roman emperor who had decreed an end to further imperialism—hence Hadrian's Wall.

"But there's no blood here," Jill Brock informed, to fracture Cordesman's thoughts.

"What?"

"There's no blood anywhere in the apartment, which might support your insistence that the only identifiable link to the murders is possessed of some divergence," Brock finished.

Cordesman didn't care what she thought. Locke wasn't the killer, there must be something else to explain the hairs in his bed. Cordesman couldn't explain it even to himself, but that had happened quite a bit in his past. What it all boiled down to was following the hunch.

And if there was anything better than his conviction record it was his hunch record.

"What did that college professor tell you?" Brock asked. "The one who got tagged by your MAC search?"

"Vampires," Cordesman said, looking at more of Locke's scrap-paper rough drafts. He rewrote a lot.

"Pardon me?"

VAMPIRE by Richard Locke

All that I'm waiting for is
to be sucked and drained
to exorcise this pain, my
Clare.

My heart is a monster in bright white,
and I can see it in the mirror's light
to show me the mythic beasts that
transpire.

All of love, and all of fondness —
sucking my blood.

A vampire.

"They were vampires, Jill."
The room hushed.
"Captain, have you been drinking?"
Cordesman hadn't consumed alcohol since August, 1991. He'd cut it
loose like an evil siamese twin, had dropped that brother into the shredder
without a tear. Sure, once in a blue moon he missed that first hit of Fiddich
or Maker's Mark, and its luscious spread of heat in the gut. Good, yes, but
not good enough to sell his soul for.
A drone filled his head, something reminiscent to a clattery machine-
sound in an airy warehouse.
"Vampires but *not* vampires," he said, staring at the limp sheet of paper.
"They created our deepest fears and then turned them — *shifted* them — in our
minds. They're devils older than…deviltry."
Brock gaped at him.
More of Fredrick's report surfaced into the detective's contemplations,
while he himself kept his eyes on the title of the poem he held between his
fingers.
"They *invented* every myth, Jill. They *created* the things that scared us
down to our most primordial genes. Vampires, werewolves, ghosts… It was
all *manufactured* by the oldest devils."
"Captain," Brock cited, "I think you're having some kind of retrograde
flashback. I don't have the authority to relieve you of duty, but, as a friend,
I think I can suggest that you seek some kind of substance-abuse ther — "
Cordesman didn't hear her. And even if he did, he could get his job back
in Ann Arundel County in a heartbeat. Maryland was dying for investigators
with high arrest/conviction rates. *Shit, look at the murder rates there com-*
pared to here…
No, Locke wasn't around, he wasn't in the city. Cordesman knew the
vibe. *Now I gotta find the guy,* he thought. He'd dropped Locke's last poem,
turned to face Brock but had then seen something on a tall dresser —
The Prince of the River of Oblivion, he thought. *The Prince of the only*
river in Hell.

The River Lethe...

What he'd seen, and picked up off the dresser, was a spartan business card which read:

A. Lethe
Todesfall Rd.
North Bend, WA
888-0776

"Jill," he said, walking out. "You're cool, a good ev-chief, maybe the best I've worked with."

"Captain, what are you—"

"Tell Kerr I'll write him up for his step-raise, will ya? And do me a favor—tell the North Preek D.C. that I've resigned. I gotta get out of here."

"Captain! You can't—"

Yes, he could. Cordesman didn't care. Murder was relative; in fact it was often all too easy to solve. But this was more than murder. It was something intricate and rich, something cabalistic. *Follow your gut,* Cordesman reminded himself. The vibes were whispering to him. And for now...

He had some driving to do.

(ii)

"Welcome to the interstice."

Lethe looked at Locke from the end of the long hall. Light which wavered scarlet seemed to stand atop the tall man's head. "Do come in, Mr., Locke," Lethe intoned. The words echoed like rocks bounced against the high walls. "I thought you'd be easy, but you weren't—and that delights me. Too often, it's the opposite."

Locke walked forward, back into the dining room in which he'd sat earlier. The same room, yes, but *not* the same. Instead of classy coats-of-arms, original oil paintings, and flats of rare Meissen ware, the room extended as a plane of gray dust. Something more like bloodless human skin adorned the walls instead of the fancy paneling and wallpaper. And the skin was going gangrenous.

"Enlightenment. Accentuation. Paramount properties of human desire, correct?" Lethe intoned.

Locke wasn't afraid, even after all he'd seen on his way here...and even in knowing that it was all real. Real in some other facet of reality.

But what did Lethe mean?

"Enlighten *me,*" Locke said. "Cos I don't know what the hell you're talking about."

"Oh, please. Tell me I'm wrong. Your pitiable horde of mankind, trudging without end in its desultory plight. Where is the difference between expectation and hope? *Is* there a difference?"

Locke looked upon the malefactor through thinned eyes. "Tell me more. I'm stupid today."

"Hey!"

Locke nearly shrieked, an arm grabbed him aside, and the face grinning into his was Martin's, the tattooed and ring-pierced chest all asweat. He remained naked, save for his bloody Keds. The drooping genitals glittered in their chrome-studded gore, Locke was at least attentive enough to note. And he noted something else: two inch-long fangs sprouted from the painter's grin.

"You don't look so hot," Martin observed. "Here, man, have one of these. Real tasty, it'll perk ya up." He slapped something thin and wet into Locke's hand.

A small severed breast.

Locke looked at it, then flung the thing away. "I'm not afraid."

"But it's real," Lethe said. "You know that now."

"Yeah, I know. But that's not what this is about."

Lethe's eyes were lime-green. He grinned through fangs similar to Martin's only they were longer.

"And I also know this," Locke challenged. "You're not a vampire."

A blink-like flash, and Lethe grinned without the green eyes or the fangs. "There are many layers to truth, Mr. Locke, and many doors to perception. But the means to swing those doors open are precious few. You've found one of those ways, and I commend you. Perhaps we'll talk at greater length later." Lethe turned in his fine suit, but came to a sudden halt. Without refacing Locke, he said, "And you're quite right. I'm *not* a vampire... But Martin is."

Lethe left the dust-plagued room.

"Deal with it," Martin said through his drooling, fanged grin.

(iii)

Enlightenment, accentuations. What the malefactor accuses mankind of, so too is he guilty, and I.

Moreso.

Faith is truth. Truth is power. That which allows me to prowl for my instinct. But for Locke? Only the veil of dreams.

My enemy's strength trebles mine. I know that. I'm just a better hider.

I hide in your brain. I hide in your hatred. I hide in the shadows under your bed.

Why do I do this?
Because you let me.

«« — »»

Carry me away...
A line from one of Locke's poems? A line from the pen of every poet to
ever walk the face of the earth? I guess I'm selfish, because I don't care.
And I guess I know what's happening now...
But I don't care.

(iv)

Locke thought of more doors opening but to what, he wasn't sure. Martin had flecks of what appeared to be blood clots on the tips of his fangs, and clots of even less savory things smudging the sharpened edges of the chrome rings hooked into his penis. Locke felt a pang of jealousy—not that Martin could be a better artist but that he had, well, a bigger dick.

At least mine's not full of fishing tackle, Locke thought.

"Where's your faith now, poet?" Martin asked. "I'm immortal."

"No, you're not. Lethe's merely made you think that."

Martin stared through a sharper grin, and then came a sound like someone breaking open a watermelon bare-handed. But what *Martin* was breaking open bare-handed was his own *external obliques,* aka, his belly. Then he yanked open the rest of the abdominal wall, then began pulling things out.

The stomach and duodenum, the entirety of the pancreatic process, the spleen and the kidneys and the renal cords.

He snapped it all off, discarded it, and still stood.

"How's that for immortal?"

Guess that's one on me, Locke considered.

"I'll suck you dry," Martin said, "then I'll make *you* immortal too. Mr. Lethe said I could. And you know what I'll do next?"

"Take painting lessons?"

Martin's dark face darkened further. "I'll do you like I do the whores. I'll hang you up and start carving, and I won't stop for a *long time.* That's a shitload of pain to someone who can't die."

"The only worse torture," Locke said, "would be listening to you talk anymore about art."

Locke tried to goad him...and it worked. Martin was *all over* him. *Ug, fuck!* was about the most articulate thing Locke could think. *Do I look like Peter Cushing? Shit, I'm a poet, not a vampire-killer!*

Martin vised him down hard, his mouth cranked open like a bear-trap. Target: Locke's throat.

"I'll do a whole *show* on you," Martin drooled onto Locke's face.

"Where'd you take art lessons?" Locke asked. "Kindergarten finger-paint class?"

"Fuck you! My art is unsurpassed!"

"Yeah, and El Greco jacks fries at Burger King. Get over it, buddy, if Van Gogh saw *your* work, he'd cut off his *head*. If Thomas Hart Benton looked at *your* work, he'd climb out of his grave just to dig a deeper hole you suck so bad. Piet Mondrian could flick boogers on a garbage bag and it would be better than anything you could even *think* of. Face the music, your work eats shit. You're an insult to the aesthetic vision."

Why Locke thought to choose to inflame an immortal adversary capable of drinking his blood and reawakening him into a scape of endless torture—he couldn't imagine. Maybe he just wanted to go out in style? Or maybe—

"I'm gonna chew out your carotid and suck it like a straw," Martin promised.

Or maybe Locke just felt it was time to accept his fate.

Martin's wet lips touched the side of Locke's throat, sucked down, and then the tips of the fangs nudged against the skin.

THWACK! THWACK! THWACK!

Martin mewled, his metal-ringed erection curiously spewing semen. He rolled off Locke, displaying a sharp point coming out of his chest.

Locke back-crawled away and stared forward. It was a wooden stake that had been hammered through Martin's back through his heart. Blood wept from the sharpened tip.

Then Locke gazed up.

Roderick Byers—White Shirt—stood above them, a rack of standing rot and a hammer hanging from one flesh-specked hand. Black liquid bubbled in his ears.

"Can't stand to see a fellow poet in need," Byers said.

«« — »»

"I don't have much time. There's this energy thing, I don't quite get it but…"

Locke's eyes held on the reanimated corpse. He'd followed his savior to an eastward parlor, which—thank the fates—had a wine rack. Locke didn't feel bad about helping himself to a bottle of Chateau Epernon, 1710.

Byers seemed to falter as if his thoughts were skewed.

"You were saying something about an energy thing."

"Yes! Thank you! It's plasmotic—I'm not sure why I know that, but I do. I know a lot of things now."

"Such as?"

The corpse paused to think. "Well, the skull of Dracole Waida lies hidden within the far west wall of the Snagov de Chapelle, two rows up, and seventy-one rows across. It's there, it's just that none of them ever found it. I know that John Wilkes Booth did kill Lincoln but that he didn't die until 1888. I know that Yuri Andropov was murdered by a potassium chloride infusion, and I know that the UFO crash in Roswell, on July 4, 1947, was a hoax."

"Wow," Locke remarked. "You know a lot."

"But is was only Army Air Corp disinformation, to cover up the *real* crash 75 miles away, on July 5, in Magdelena, New Mexico. Oh! And something else! Vince Foster was murdered in Crystal City, Virginia at 3:49 p.m. on July, 20, 1993. He was shot in the mouth with a Ruger .22 by a man with shoulder-length blonde hair and a dark beard. Fifteen minutes previously, two other men had left the room. One was a Chinese restaurant owner from Little Rock, and the other was— Say, Locke, you don't seem very interested in this."

"Not only am I not interested, I'm disappointed." Locke felt jovial this close to death. What the hell? "Who gives a shit about Vince Foster? I want to know who killed Kennedy."

Byers' decomposed eyes squinted. "Charles Marconi, a subcontractor from Detroit, working for the Dallas mob. Shit, Locke, I even know when the world's going to end...but I'm not allowed to tell you that one."

"Wow," Locke said.

"We're wasting time. The energy thing, you know? I'm not strong enough. I keep slipping in and out. You know what he's doing, don't you?"

"Who? Vince Foster or Lethe?"

The rotten cadaver frowned at the jest. Black bilge spilled from his ear when he cocked his head. "Don't you realize why I'm here? It's one of the only things Lethe can't control!"

"What?" Locke dared to ask.

"I failed, sure. But—goddamn it—I tried. It wasn't an easy thing to do. But I didn't cut the rest of the muster," Byers said. "You did. You want to know why?"

"Yeah, but answer me this first. Why you and not Lehrling? I never knew you, but Lehrling was my best friend. Wouldn't he be a bit more effective in convincing me of...whatever it is you're trying to convince me of?"

"Lehrling's in hell, so forget him. I can't just *say* it, Locke. It's one of the rules. I'm not allowed to lay it out for you. You have to put the pieces together on your own."

"Okay, give me some pieces."

"Aw, damn-it!"

"What?"

"I'm all out," Byers said.

Then Byers disintegrated like a gritty lapse-dissolve. But when he disappeared, his form was replaced by two other far more corporeal figures.

"Ich durstig, mein schotz..."

It was a maid who stood there looking at him—shapely, tight, finely curved in her traditional black, puff-sleeved bodice and short black gathered skirt. A white serving cap with a blue bow adorned her head, pinned to short strawberry blonde hair. Locke remembered the full-tilt coltish legs from his first round of window peeping. The gilt, frilly eyemask concealed most of her face, but not the mouth, of course. She held a dark grin spiked by two petite cuspids. *Pretty cute fangs,* Locke noticed, if, of course, vampire fangs could be cute.

"How's the wine?" Jason asked, standing at her side.

"Uh, spare yet fragrant, a tempered bouquet," Locke answered.

Jason wore his full-tilt manservant get-up, the striped trousers, the white gloves, morning jacket, and waistcoat, and the silver-piped eyemask. But unlike his lover's diminutive fangs, Jason sported a pair of front teeth long and sharp as masonry nails.

"Mr. Locke, this is Anna," he introduced. "Don't you remember her?"

"Well, yeah, as a matter of fact I do. Unless I'm mistaken, you, uh, jerked off on her last night, after slapping her around and choking her and—oh—sucking blood out of her tits and throwing up in her face."

"No, no, I mean before that. You've never seen her before?"

"No."

When Jason removed the woman's eyemask, and when her face registered, Locke felt something like eels swimming in his belly.

The girl Lehrling picked up in the bar. The night he—

"Anna's got something for you," Jason said, then—*snap!*—he flicked open a switchblade. With the same tenderness that one lover might caress another, he began to slowly cut the clothes off of the German murderess. The blade's tip ran down every seam of her garments, severed every individual thread of every stitch. Segment by segment, the housemaid uniform fell off until she was nude save for black-velvet Balli pumps.

"Think she's hot?" Jason asked. He stood behind her, running an open hand from her pubis to her breasts.

"Well," Locke admitted, "I wouldn't exactly call her Lassie."

"Yeah, she's hot stuff," Jason said, eyeing Locke from the crook of her sleek, white throat. "A cute little German dumpling. Well, you know something? She's got a present for you."

"I appreciate the excess of generosity," Locke said, "but I don't accept gifts unless it's Christmas."

"Check it out." Jason pinched one of Anna's nipples, and the finest mist of blood sprayed out. "Cool, huh?"

Locke took a slug from his bottle of wine, expecting it to be his last. "I'm impressed. *Time* should give her Woman of the Year."

The blood mist hovered; Anna gasped, excited. Then Locke took note of her slightly protuberant belly, which he'd similarly noted when he'd seen her in the window of the third cottage. *Like early pregnancy,* Locke thought.

"Naw, she ain't knocked up—she's dead," Jason made a reminder. "But she's still got something for you. Give it to him, bitch."

Jason gave her a hard choke. Her breasts sprayed more blood, and the gasp that leaked from her throat was one of ecstasy, not distress.

After which she lurched forward, her fanged mouth jacked open inhumanly wide, and—

Aw, fuck!

—fired a cold gust of vomit right into Locke's face. He reeled back, drenched, face dripping. Chunks of things seemed to slide off his ruined shirt and *plap!* to the floor. Gagging, Locke foundered back a few more steps, wiping cool digestive slime from his eyes. When he could see again, he saw this.

A greater puddle of bile on the floor. Amid the puddle were the things she'd previously exacted from Lehrling: a part of a liver, a scrap of spleen, a ruptured gall bladder, a tongue.

And something else:

Pieces of a penis that had been bitten into chunks.

"Check it out," Jason advised. "Dick nuggets. They oughta serve 'em at McDonalds."

With reflexes too fast to see, Jason clotheslined Locke; he fell flat on his back, inch-thick dust puffing around him. The wine bottle clunked to the floor and rolled, leaving a trail of bitter wine. Locke couldn't breathe momentarily, his hands crabbed to his throat. Before his senses gathered, Anna's taut legs were straddling his face, her dead sex just inches from his eyes. Locke pressed up but couldn't budge her, as if a forklift had lowered a pallet of mason blocks onto his chest. Jason's silhouette hovered just behind her shoulders, chuckling. Something small dripped from his fingers.

"Listen up, poet. Anna's gonna do to you what she did to that pulp-novelist asshole, unless—"

Locke's eyes felt skinned. Jason's hand lowered, down, down—

"—unless you eat this."

What Jason's thumb and index finger held was Lehrling's glans.

"You're gonna eat each piece one at a time, starting with the knob."

Then he ran the severed glans wetly across Locke's lips.

"Open."

Locke's lips seamed closed.

"Be a good poet and open wide…"

No, no, go ahead and kill me. I'm not gonna eat my best friend's dick!

"Open, open…"

Then came a sound like a strong breeze, or rushing water, and in that sound was a voice.

Lush, dark, erotic…

A woman's voice.

The wine, the voice told him. *The wine!*

Locke's hand patted outward toward where the 288-year-old bottle had dropped.

"Guess he's not going to cooperate," Jason assumed. "Anna? Let her rip."

Her slim hips slithered down, all the while Locke's hand groped for the wine bottle but grabbed air. The murderess's lips parted, drawing up into a slime-filmed grin. Her nipples distended as if pushed by thumbs from within, more blood leaking.

Her fangs lengthened as he watched, to pearly spikes inches long.

"Suck him out," Jason ordered.

Locke's hand found the bottle, and without even understanding why, he whipped its long, nearly black neck back and forth across her face, each swipe sending a spray of the strong wine into her eyes. A sound followed, like bacon frying in a hot cast-iron skillet. Anna rolled over, screaming, smoking.

New power. The wine wasn't that good but—shit—*It wasn't that bad either,* Locke thought, and got back up. Jason hissed at him, taking back-steps, scared, animalistic. A series of overarms with the bottle sent more plumes of wine into Jason's cringing face, after which he back-landed on the floor, sizzling like microwaved meat, and died.

Locke, stupefied, stood above his work, gazing down. Both of them lay dead, their faces so corroded the wine had actually melted through their heads after a time, like carbolic acid.

Locke looked at the yellowed label on the bottle, mystified.

"You French guys really now know how to make some vino…"

Then the exotic woman's voice returned to his head, a rushing whisper. *The Chateau Epernon was a seminary from 1695 to 1731. All wines made there during that time were blessed…*

More tradition, more cliché. Blessed water, blessed wine. The vampire, in his or her impure state of existence, could not sustain the presence of anything blessed.

Locke was grateful, but...
Who? he wondered.
Who had whispered those instructions into his head?
I did, the voice fluttered.
"Who—"
"Moira—"

EIGHTEEN

SCIFTAN

(i)

I'm bleeding my soul into his brain. I've never done that before, I've sensed an impulse that is true. But I can't show myself—the malefactor knows too much, he sees and senses.

I guess I'm too afraid.

I'm been afraid to face my fear since before man crawled out of the caves. If you knew my enemy, you'd probably feel the same way. But—

Shit! I guess that's just an excuse.

I guess I'm just a coward...

(ii)

Locke ran through the nether-manse, which had reverted, by now, into a labyrinthine *mass*—a meld of decayed, worm-riddled walls and putrid organa. Some walls bled, others sweated, while still others exuded pus from crusted sores. The dust on the floor now more resembled the ichorish ground-fog outside, different only in that it gleamed dully as a pool of congealing blood. The manse was gradually turning into something formed of flesh—a meat-house...

White light like the moon lined the dark warrens, though no source was evident. Eventually Locke's manic steps forward *squished,* as though he were tromping over an endless carpeting of pustulent epidermis.

Each corridor led to nowhere, hallways and passages climbing and rising and twisting into more of the same. Locke was lost.

I'm lost forever, he thought.

He turned, winded, and the next corridor unreeled as a long line of closed, grime-sheened doors.

Then one door clicked open.

Not much I can do about it...

Locke figured he had no choice. He entered the room, stepped into—

An *endless* room.

The walls and ceiling were blue sky, the floor was a bank of clouds. Locke stood amid the heavens.

And Lethe faced him.

"Voyager. You've worn your travail well—as well, and as faithfully, as de Rais wore his armor before they burned his saint."

Locke's voice ground like two sheets of sandpaper abrading. "Who are you? I mean *really*...who are you?"

"I am the Alpha and the Omega," Lethe quoted Christ. "The first and the last...the beginning and the end."

The man's hands splayed, a preacher at a lectern, a preceptor on a precipice gazing his wisdom down onto untold masses. His white suit radiated, fabric of sunlight, everything, the jacket, the slacks, the shirt and necktie, even the shoes. He stood as a man dressed in light.

"There are but two ways out of here, one way light, one dark," Lethe said. Even his voice, too, shone like the face of the high sun. "In my time only a handful have dared to even challenge the course. But only one, Locke, has embarked so close to the exit, or...I should say, the *egress*."

"Beginnings and endings," Locke murmured to himself. "Ways in and ways out."

"Yes..."

"All points forming a dotted line to verity—"

"A track of the spore of the soul...to truth!"

Locke stared, warm in the five-mile-high breeze. "But every truth is different, isn't it?"

"Indeed. Keirkegaard said 'I must find a truth that is true for me, an ideal for which I can live or die.' Yes?"

"Yes," Locke agreed.

"You've found that truth. And so have I. But the weak, Locke, what truth do they really have? I've offered them *everything*—over ages, and all that their truth turns out to be in the end is falsehood."

—over ages, the words rang in Locke's head.

"Yes, ages, one century after the other until too many have accrued to count. In all my witness, poet, the true heart always fails."

"Mine doesn't," Locke said, blurting it out.

Lethe's sunlight eyes bore down on him. "I suspect you may be right. How can one tell the difference between the truth, and mere appearances?"

Locke remembered what Lethe had said yesterday. *I've always believed in the power of appearances.* Then he'd gone on to refer to a "top-notch" alarm system. After confronting the other occupants of the house, Locke saw that the man wasn't kidding.

"And let me quote another poet," Lethe continued. "'I am Lazarus, come from the dead, come back to tell you all…I will tell you all.'"

Eliot, Locke recognized. "So tell me."

"I've become what I've made myself, based, logically, on the human precept. I am, as you've no doubt gathered, far more than human; the people of your age no longer have a word for what I've become. I was not born—I *fell.* We were the things that mothers warned their young of, the specters who would come at night and consume them. But, then, even I did not know how to perceive. Eons old, yes, but little more than a newborn once my feet were firmly settled on the crust of this place. I'd like to tell you that I was a king or general or leader of men, but that was not the case. Quite insipidly, I followed the cause—I formed myself into a warrior in a race of warriors, but otherwise unremarkable. But when the war was over, I stood as victor. I *learned,* you see? After three or four thousand years, it was easy. Do you understand?"

"I'm not sure," Locke admitted.

"I could smell it, Locke, I could taste it—the gullibility of man, the *fear.* So you know what I did?"

"You *used* it," Locke answered. "You took fear as your ally, your twin."

"My brother."

Locke's thought swept with lines from Baudelaire: *Boredom—he smokes his hookah while he dreams of gibbets, weeping tears he cannot smother. You know this dainty monster, too, it seems, gullible reader, my twin, my brother.*

"Your fear gave me power, Locke, yet it was I who *manufactured* the fear of your kind." Lethe paused, the light of his face growing to an intensity that nearly blinded.

"Like Shelley's Doctor Frankenstein, most grow into becoming the makers destroyed by what they make. All too seldom, there come a precious few who are *empowered* by what they make. Like you. To face the real guts of your own truth, you created your own egression to lead to the domain of what I really am. Not a vampire—how trivial! It is but the facepaint and bulbed nose of a clown. It's easier that way, Locke, and it's quite stylish."

"What are you really?"

"Anything and everything. The belief of your pitiful souls is my greatest fuel. And this cattle—" Lethe extended a hand to the suddenly appearing remains of Martin—complete with burned face and smoldered mohawk, and Anna cooked just the same like a barbecued goose in Chinatown. "This heap of the meat of idiots was born not by me but by their own weakness, their own trepidations—the same which induces toddlers to cry out when they spy the shirt-shapes in the closet, to piss their bunny-imprinted pajamas after a bad dream. Few face the challenge, Locke, so few have enough of the blood of their own real truth pushing through their veins to cast off their frailties and look into the workings of their hearts. Your plight is holding you by the hand, poet. By facing what you really believe in, you've never been more strong...nor more vulnerable. That useless cadaver Byers failed. But you? I think that remains to be seen." Lethe grinned. "Only faith can save you now. Choose your tactics with great care."

"But you're a devil," Locke ventured. "Why should I believe you?"

Lethe's laugh rocked the sky. "A devil? My good Locke! The only one who hates me more than God is Lucifer. They'd both send assassins if they could! No, no. I'm as honest as you are. Good and evil are the same at their hearts—if you think about that, and I mean really *think*...you'll agree. Whether you're human, something less, or something more, whether you're God or the Devil, it defies logic *not* to agree."

Maybe it did. Locke had to confess, the man had a point. "But the coffin, the cape I found in the basement?"

"Appearances," Lethe replied. "Did Gregor *really* transform into an insect in Kafka's masterpiece? Or was it merely the character's fear that had created the appearance? And what *was* the character's fear? The fear of inferiority, of rejection by an oppressive society, the fear of dying alone and unloved. It was that fear which constituted the change, or I should say the metamorphosis. Cause and effect, Locke. The story's symbology rings quite true. We always get what we fear in the end."

Locke looked down through gaps in the clouds. Come to think of it, he always *did* have a fear of heights. But this was just an illusion, wasn't it? *An appearance,* he thought. Nevertheless, the appearance—of the earth five miles down—induced him to urinate in his pants. Locke didn't see much point in asking if there was a men's room nearby.

"And I'll tell you something," Lethe went on from his weightless stance, "something that I've never told anyone, not even your predecessors. There is only one thing that can destroy me. No, not tawdry wooden stakes, not holy water, nor the light of the sun."

"What then?" Locke's eyes held fast to the Sciftan's face, uncomprehending.

"It's your pure heart, Locke, which has led you to me. What else has it led you to? Good and evil, black and white. The only thing I want is what I now know I can *never* have. So I must destroy it."

Locke remained staring, inhaling clouds.

"Yes, your pure heart," Lethe's voice seemed to corrode. "It's raw meat in a shark tank. Will you bring me the shark?"

Locke's stomach was beginning to twist into a knot of acid. He had a funny feeling something was about to happen.

"I—don't understand," he croaked.

"Then perhaps you will in your next journey." Lethe's hand bid the clouds, and the landscapes miles down. "If you happen upon something you want, all you need do is take it."

"What?"

"A simple *yes* will suffice, or—better yet—a simple kiss."

Locke began to shiver. Beneath his feet he felt...nothing.

"You rejected my first proposition," Lethe said. "Consider this a *second* proposition."

Then Lethe snapped his fingers and—

—Locke fell.

He'd had dreams like this before, swooshing endless nightmares of being thrown from a plane; Locke *plummeted* now, just as he had in the dreams, a skydiver with no chute, his face gathering crystalline ice in the clutches of gravity. Here was Newton's Law, all right, and Locke was the apple. In manic-swirling glimpses, the countryside below seemed to race toward him; the longer Locke fell, the faster his impact approached, and as his mind and body spun flywheel-like, he retrieved one consolation. In the nightmares, he always awoke at the instant before he would hit the ground.

SPLAT!

Locke hit the ground at a velocity of hundreds of feet per second.

(iii)

"You're late."

He stood dumbfounded in his apartment doorway. Er, it *looked* like his apartment but—

Fresh white paint, bright floral-print wallpaper, new furniture, new curtains, new carpet. Sunlight blazed through the open window overlooking 45th Street. Light strains of a Beethoven string quartet whispered from an Adcom stereo that Locke did not own, while a 35-inch Trinitron that Locke did not own showed a pretty anchorwoman mouthing something from North West Cable News with the sound down.

Locke tremored, mortified, his heart still thumping from the freefall to his "death." A dual sentience seemed to struggle in his head, one part still in turmoil of Lethe's phantasmagoric mansion and the plummet through the sky, while the other part conducted itself in a way Locke could not comprehend.

"Half of my 3:45 class stayed late," Locke said without having any idea what he was saying. Inexplicably, he carried an open tote bag full of books: *The Norton Anthology of American Poetry, Fine Frenzy—Studies in Poetical*

Survey, and Faulkner's *The Sound and the Fury.* "Can you believe it?" Locke called out to the unseen voice. "When class ended we were in the middle of a debate about William Carlos Williams' 'Asphodel, That Greeny Flower' and its importance to the imagist movement, so half of my students didn't want to leave. It was wonderful: college kids actually arguing over poetry." *What the hell did I just say?* Locke thought. From the tote, he withdrew a course syllabus, which read T & TH, 3:45 P.M.—5:15 P.M., ENG 412: THE AMERICAN IMAGISTS. INSTRUCTOR: RESIDENT POET RICHARD LOCKE.

"Holy shit," Locke whispered. "I'm a teacher…"

He smelled the most luscious aroma, just like the Pad Thai rice noodles that—

Wait a minute…

The top shelf of a fine walnut bookcase that Locke did not own seemed to be full of books that Locke did not write. *The Preceptor & Other Collected Poems, The Exit Volumes (I-III), Terra Metamorphoser* and a number of others, all written by the same author: Richard Locke.

"Well would you come in! The noodles'll get mushy!"

Locke dropped his tote, slowly entered the transformed apartment, dry-mouthed, eyes bolted open. Somehow, now, he knew that since Clare had dropped to part-time at the law firm, she'd taken to experimenting quite successfully in the kitchen.

"You didn't forget the flank steak, did you?"

"Oh, damn, honey, I'm sorry, I forgot," Locke mouthed, knowing nothing of any flank steak.

"I've got the skewers soaked in coconut milk and the grill all fired up. I can't make satay without the meat."

Locke walked into the living room. With some difficulty, Clare raised herself from a recliner, her hair longer but just as silken in its shine, her face bright, a beacon of smiles and beauty. A beacon…for *him.*

Locke stood stunned.

"You are such an airhead sometimes," she joked. She walked up, dressed in a simple blush-yellow housedress, and kissed him.

My God…

It was the most honest kiss in the world, just a peck on the cheek, like the casual kiss of a happy wife.

Wife…

"You should walk over to the Chevron, ask them to check your head for leaks," she said, then issued the tiniest of laughs. "But don't worry, I think I still have some prawns in the fridge."

She sauntered away, giggling at his forgetfulness. Yet as she journeyed to the kitchen she did so in awkward steps, and that's when Locke took full notice—

"Michael was kicking up a storm today, I'll have you know. We might have a star soccer player on our hands—"

—that Clare looked about seven or eight months pregnant.

Locke could only stand there in sweet shock. His eyes roved a varnished high-boy, its top set with framed photos. Some Locke recognized but the one in the center beamed at him: himself proudly decked out in a tux, standing next to Clare in a white bridal gown on their wedding day.

This is it, all I've ever wanted, he realized. Not a trick, not an *appearance.*

This was his life. This was what he wanted more than anything in the world, and now it was his.

He remembered Lethe's words when they stood on the top of the sky. *It's your pure heart, Locke, which has led you to me. What else has it led you to?*

Love of another kind, an endless love? Something beyond the limits of the physical world?

The angel? he thought.

Locke stared at the surmise as though it were a solid object, an arcane piece of art to be scrutinized and interpreted, a crux to be solved.

Good and evil, black and white. The only thing I want is what I now know I can never have.

So I must destroy it.

Locke stared and stared.

Bring me the shark—

"Aren't I a dutiful wife? Slaving over a hot hibachi while my husband makes the world a wiser place?" Clare had returned from the kitchen, now bearing a plate with several skewers of seasoned shrimp. "These only take a minute per side so go wash up, and make it quick!"

"You're the boss," Locke said. He watched her move out to the sunny balcony where the small grill gusted heat.

Numbness took him to the bathroom, immaculate now and redone in cheerful trimmings. He turned on the faucet. He washed his hands and when he raised his eyes to the mirror—

Oh for shit's sake!

His heart nearly burst. In the reflection, standing just behind him, was Byers, now little more than a stand of bones draped with collops of organic decay.

"Don't turn around, it uses too much juice," the dead poet's voice bubbled from his lips. "You know, like I told you last time. It's this—"

"The energy thing," Locke recalled.

A hand flayed by advanced decomposition touched Locke's shoulder; in the mirror he noticed several maggots emerging from their casings.

"I'm not allowed to tell you," Byers gurgled. "I'm not allowed to spell it out—I've *told* you that already. You're supposed to be using your brain."

"What do you expect from a guy who couldn't even remember to pick up some flank steak on the way home?"

"Stop being an asshole. You want to know why it didn't work for me?"

"Why *what* didn't work for you?"

"I wasn't honest enough. My search for truth was tainted. This whole thing's about you, Locke. It's about *your verity* and how it relates to *them*. But you have a choice to make, and it's one you're going to have to make rather quickly."

Locke shook his head through a frown. "I've already made my choice. Why should I give this up? I'd be out of my mind."

"Here's why…"

—images, then, shotgunned into his mind.

—chaos, ataxia, where the only order was *dis*order.

—"Lethe saved her for last…"

—mountains of corpses, yes, literally *mountains*.

—millions after millions dying.

—"Lethe saved her for last because he *loved* her!"

—then millions more, and then—

—"But she could never love him, it's an impossibility. Yin can't love yang! The needle will never stick to the magnet, Locke!"

—billions.

—"Without her, he's got nothing. No place for him in heaven, and none in hell. They were traitors!"

—until nothing remained alive but one man…

—"So now all he can live for is payback. But he can't do that with *her* here, so he's got to kill her, and the only way he can do that is through you—"

—and the sky turned black with clouds of death.

"Did you see it?" Byers asked.

Locke shuddered from the scene, cold sweat trickling as he regained his breath and looked back at Byers' dead face in the bathroom mirror.

"She can't face him, it's too risky. Don't you understand?" The little that actually remained of Byers' face seemed to plead in its black-green film. "Would you risk *that*? With nothing to keep him in check, Lethe could do it. Lethe has that kind of power. He's using you as bait."

"Bait for what?"

"Bait for *her*, you moron!"

Her, Locke wondered.

"Why do you think he uses poets and writers and people like that?"

"I don't know," Locke spat back.

"Because of what we're all trying, ultimately, to create."

"Bullshit," Locke replied, pointing at the morbid reflection. "I'm only responsible for myself, my wife, and our child." Then he commenced to jerk around, to shove Byers away—

"Don't do it, Locke, for God's sake, don't turn ar—"

Byers was gone.

"Good riddance," Locke sniped. "If there's one thing that pisses me off more than a lousy poet, it's a lousy *dead* poet."

He dried his hands on a soft terry towel, fiddled with his hair for a moment, then walked back out to the enticing aromas of Thai spices.

But that's not all he walked back out to. He walked back out to his providence, not the jilted rip-off of past misery. *I'm walking back out to the life I deserve, the one I've earned.*

Clare hurried back in from the grill, aglow in this commonplace domesticity. A happy wife elated to cook dinner for her loving husband. The quick-seared prawns on the skewers wafted still more delectable aromas into the air. Locke smiled at the gift he'd been given, and all he had to do to keep it...was *take* it.

"And I'm going to," he whispered.

"Did you say something, honey?" she asked, and set the plate of satay on the already set table.

"Yes," Locke answered. "I was just saying to myself that I'm the luckiest man on the face of the earth for having such a loving, beautiful wife."

"Oh, loving and beautiful—that's *all*?"

"And a great cook."

"That's more like it." She placed her hands on his shoulders, urged him to sit. "Now sit yourself down while I get the rice noodles."

"Wait a minute," he said. "*You* sit down—you happen to be pregnant with our child. I should be the one hustling back and forth with dinner. But first—"

Locke put his arms around his wife, looked right into her eyes and saw all that beaming love.

Just a simple kiss, Lethe had said.

And then it's all mine, Locke realized.

"I love you," he told her.

"Yeah?" she teased with him. "Show me."

Just as their lips would meet—

"You were reading my mind, weren't you, *honey?*"

Clare retracted, her expression pinched up. "Wh-what?"

"Here's your kiss."

Locke snatched up a steak knife from the table.

"Richard, what on earth are you—"

Locke didn't feel much, which surprised him considering how deeply he cut his own throat.

Very deep. To the bone.

"*Noooooooooooooo!*" she screamed.

"*Noooooooooooooo!*" Lethe bellowed.

The walls shook from the thunderous sound, old plaster and scabs and muck raining down. Locke collapsed to the enslimed floor, not surprised to find himself back in the malefactor's self-made manse.

"Fooled you, didn't I?" Locke gasped through his wet grin.

Lethe assumed his true Pre-Adamic voice, a sound less like spoken words and more like an avalanche of rocks down a mountain precipice.

"God damn you miserable worthless whore's-son untermensch sheiss-essen scume-fliesch deliere motherfucker facie destiteure cretin dog *fokk!*"

"Your mother wears combat boots," Locke coughed.

And just as his voice had assumed its true nature so did Lethe's face—hideous in its runnels and grooves, beautiful in its fine lines and broad flawless angles. Part-devil, part-deity, and a tint of something crafted in the image of man.

"You are a piece of shit to be sewn into hell's fields! God damn you to hell!" the thing shrieked and then vanished.

Then silence.

Even the house had begun to vanish, a sinew and a pale plank at a time, as well it should. Just another of the magician's props—aided, of course, by the power of belief.

Locke knew he was dying, and didn't care. *Will I really go to hell?* he wondered. Time would tell, he supposed, and not much time at that. His life poured out, and even in his fading resignation, he suddenly felt alarmed.

Just one more…

Numbing fingers reached for the pen in his top pocket, and the folded piece of paper he always carried should the muse strike untimely.

Locke scribbled, winded from deoxygenation. It didn't take long, at least not as long as death.

"There," he croaked, the sedate smile turning up his lips. "Hope it doesn't suck."

The slip of paper fell from his cooling fingers.

cllllick

Something snapped, and Locke's eyes darted in his immobile head. A footstep? A Cooperian twig breaking?

Next thing Locke knew, a soft hand had taken his, and quickly helped him up. He couldn't really see her, but that didn't matter. He knew who she was and he knew that she was never really *meant* to be seen.

The Princess Dressed in Darkness, he thought. *The Angel of the Egress.*

Was it a mirage, the last visions of the man who knew he was dying?

"One more choice," the voice flowed like some exorbitant dark fluid.

The elegant finger pointed even as the house corroded above them. They stood in a jagged corridor, beneath a flurry of dust. Locke felt alive again.

She pointed to the left, where Locke saw daylight at the end of the hall. Then she pointed to the right.

Darkness.

Locke turned. She took his hand as a lover would, and they walked to the right.

EPILOGUE

Cordesman flicked a butt out the car window and hit a metal sign that read $500 FINE FOR THROWING CIGARETTE BUTTS FROM YOUR CAR. An opened mess of road maps flapped on the passenger seat. Cordesman lit another Camel and frowned at the next crumpled map.

"What a joke!" he exclaimed.

North Bend. Todesfall Road. This was Sticksville. Since he'd gotten onto the back roads, none of the mailboxes even had addresses. And when he'd finally found Todesfall Road, which wasn't even on the map—

"Goddamn it!"

The road extended for close to ten miles. And he didn't spot a single house. *This is ridiculous.*

The sky blackened, it was going to rain. Cordesman wasn't a very good driver to begin with, he didn't want to be driving a city unmarked on back roads he didn't know when the clouds opened up. When Todesfall ended, he craned his neck without coming to a full stop, and pulled a U.

And saw the driveway.

Well, not really a driveway but a rutted, dirt-clogged swath into trees. *What the hell, I'm going back to Maryland tomorrow and this ain't even my car.*

Cordesman edged in, then followed every pothole and twist. Tree branches on either side pawed at the car. A bird shit hugely on the windshield, then a pine cone the size of a melon hit the hood. But what Cordesman pulled up to at the end of the drive was a strange sight indeed.

Two cars—a plush silver Rolls Royce and what looked like an early-1900s Daimler. Both shining in new wax and mint condition.

The fuck is this?

These cars cost big money at the least, they were probably museum pieces. But they weren't parked in front of anything. *Sure, Jack,* Cordesman reasoned with himself. *Probably half a million bucks' worth of cars parked at the end of some shit-scratch road in the middle of the woods. Right?*

Cordesman couldn't have smirked harder when he got out of the
unmarked. The pre-rain wind was whipping up; it sent his long hair in a
tumult, and that pissed him off too. But—

What's that?

When he'd first pulled up, he'd thought it was merely a clearing that the
Rolls and Daimler were parked in front of. But now, standing closer,
Cordesman saw...

Foundations.

So a house *had* been here at one time, however long ago it must have
been. Old fungus-covered bricks marked the dwelling's original perimeter,
and it was a large perimeter. Just as strange, nothing grew within the foun-
dation's boundary, where rye grass and weeds should be abounding.

Just...dirt.

Beyond the rear line of mortared bricks, he thought he saw four more
squares of foundations, much smaller ones, which might suggest a row of
guest houses or cottages. Cordesman couldn't be sure.

Thunder concussed overhead. He strode outward and entered the gap in
the bricks which might denote the building's original entrance. His heels
scuffed on dirt and rocks as he glanced around in this checked dismay. There
was nothing here—*nothing*. Not even a shingle, not even a scrap or splinter
of wood. Nothing—

Wait.

Something small and white fluttered in the wind. Then the wind began
to carry it—toward the woods. Cordesman huffed forward, almost tripped,
but he managed to lean over and grab it before it disappeared into the forest.

It was a piece of paper, just a white sheet of regular bond typing paper
folded over a few times as if to fit into someone's breast pocket.

Cordesman squinted in the gray light, and read the crabbed handwriting.

> Fiery the angels fell.
> What did Milton tell
> So blind yet so alive
> With Love?

"Great," Cordesman thought. "Fan-fucking-tastic."

Go back to Maryland and forget about this shit...

Just as the thought finished, the storm clouds broke, dumping sheets of
rain. Cordesman spat out a soaked Camel, hoofed it back to the unmarked,
and slammed the door shut as if fleeing a killer.

He started the engine, paused to light yet another cigarette.

Forget it. Go home.

Then he backed up and drove away.

The rain *poured*.

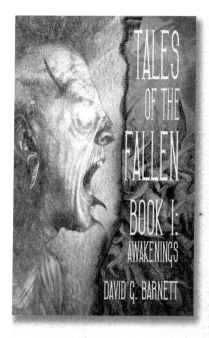

Following on the heals of his critically acclaimed collection, DEAD SOULS, David G Barnett offers up the beginning of what will hopefully be a long series of novellas and shorts centered around the new battle for heaven. These first three tales are fast-paced, funny, raunchy and poignant. Barnett's world comes to life with horribly flawed characters that you will like or hate, but won't soon forget, abominable creatures and visions of Heaven and Hell that will begin to paint the way for more tales to come.

OF ANGELS FALLEN

They rescued him from the streets and with their help he has become the world's greatest assassin. So much death, so much blood, but it all ends after this one final job. Just one more death and Mal will finally get what was promised him so many, many years ago.

Jonas White is a powerful man, an empire builder. He commands adoration and respect from everyone who meets him. He is a good man, does good things. But now he's also a marked man. He knows destiny is banging on the door. What will happen when he opens it?

Two men fated to meet each other on one cataclysmic evening. An evening when secrets will be revealed, loyalties will be tested, old grudges settled and new ones made. This is just one stop along a long road. A road that leads back to where it all began so very long ago.

DADDY DEMON'S DAY OUT

He wanted revenge for an atrocity committed so many years ago. Back when his world collapsed around him with a single knock on his door.

But that was then and this is now and revenge is at hand. Years of planning, years of blasphemous dealings and terrible actions have led to this moment. He has worked for decades to be able to summon the demon of revenge and now he's ready. Tonight he will demand the demon grant his one wish and all of this will finally be over.

But Travis Burnsfield will soon find out that the demon of revenge has other plans for the evening. Plans that involve Starbucks, cheese steaks and a trip to the infamous Painfreak where many creatures go, all with very different hungers—especially one creature's hunger that can be sated with the sorrow of a tired old man who only wants revenge for something taken from him so very long ago.

THE SLEEPERS AWAKEN

The old man hadn't been here in... Well, he couldn't really remember. But what he did know was that it had changed. Changed so much. His heart was heavy at seeing the destruction and knowing what it all meant. But he didn't have time to mourn. No, he had to move on.

He had placed them here so long ago, but over time he grew careless and forgot to keep track of them. But the time has come for him to track them all down. Things had changed and now he needed their help. It was time to seek out the others and awaken them...awaken his army. He only hoped they wanted to be awakened and wanted to help him. It would take some time. But after all, time was all he had right now.

NECRO PUBLICATIONS • 5139 MAXON TER. • SANFORD, FL 32771
407-443-6494 • dave@necropublications.com
WWW.NECROPUBLICATIONS.COM
ACCEPTING PAYPAL, VISA, MASTERCARD, CHECKS AND MONEY ORDERS

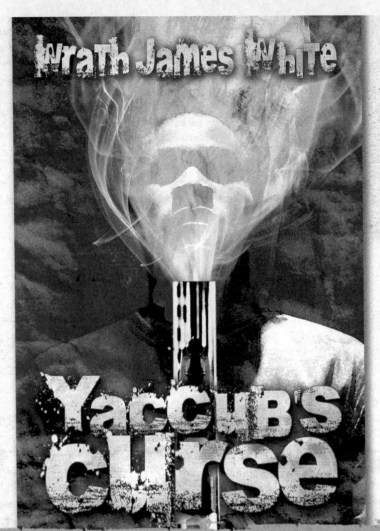

WRATH JAMES WHITE

YACCUB'S CURSE

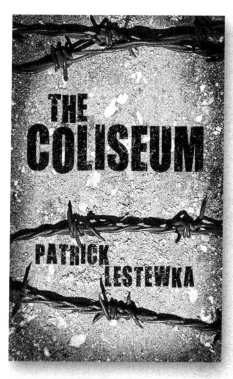

CPSIA information can be obtained
at www.ICGtesting.com
Printed in the USA
BVHW041907250719
554384BV00010B/245/P